LET IT ROLL

KC FLETCHER

KCB

ONE

"HMM. FIVE DRINKS."

"Matty! He's like sixty!"

"Yeah. But he has nice eyes. Like Andrew's."

I snorted into my champagne, dusting my face with the tiny popping bubbles. I hoped Matty was just trying to distract me from my dad's antics on the dance floor and not actually considering hitting on my aunt's husband. We hadn't had five drinks yet, but we were close.

Matty leaned in. He would keep going until he really made me laugh. I wouldn't give it to him easily. "Blue like my soul after being separated from my boyfriend for three days."

I rolled my eyes. While we weren't at five, he'd had too many drinks to be clever. That alone almost had me laughing.

"Or like a pool I'd like to drown in."

I didn't give him a reaction.

"Those two-inch-thick lenses just enhance them *so* well…"

Alright, my snort was a bit closer to a giggle. I blame the champagne and Uncle Phil's owl eyes landing on us at just the right moment. Matty sat back, a satisfied smirk bringing out the dimple in his right cheek. He'd dressed well, a suit and pink tie that nearly matched my dress and popped against his light brown skin. The matching pink hadn't been intentional. We'd laughed for about five minutes when we saw eachother and then took selfies as if we were a couple going to prom in front of the hotel mirror before heading to the wedding ceremony.

That photoshoot was the highlight of my day.

My grandmother heard my laugh from the table next to us and decided it was a surprising enough occurrence for her to get involved in the conversation. I tensed as her white fold-out chair creaked and she turned to face me. "Does your father know you're drinking, Cheryl?"

I tensed at the words and the use of my full name. She wore a sky-blue pantsuit she'd probably owned for thirty years and yet remained the peak of fashion for her age group.

"Yes, Grandma," I said through my gritted teeth and forced smile. "I *am* almost twenty-two."

Matty had been terrified of my grandmother since we were children. He remained silent beside me as we watched my grandmother take in my flushed cheeks, bright eyes, and pink dress. Just a step above pastel pink, I had needed it the moment I saw it.

My grandmother didn't mention the color, how I shouldn't wear it with my strawberry blond hair, or how when I sat it didn't suck in the roll of my stomach. Maybe she knew her eyes said it all plain enough. "I've been checking the mail," she said instead. "When should I expect your graduation announcement?"

I shifted and wished she would have brought up my dress. "I switched majors, so it won't be very soon."

"Didn't you *just* switch majors?"

If she knew that, did she just ask me if I was graduating soon to remind me I was behind schedule? "I did last semester, but I didn't love the classes."

"No one loves class. It's only an investment and you're already in your third year. You have to stick with things." I didn't respond. Grandma glanced toward the dance floor. "And how is your mother holding up?"

Drunkenly. In Italy. I could only dream of such an escape from this event. "She's enjoying her trip."

"She *has* always been good at running from her problems. I hope you've learned to cope with hardship better, Cheryl."

Matty sucked in a breath. My grip tightened dangerously on the stem of my champagne flute. I wanted to stand up for my mom. To tell my grandmother she was being unfair. Tell her that the divorce had been mutual, not a hardship for only my mom. I wanted to back the conversation up and tell my grandma I wasn't a quitter. I wanted to be brave enough and badass enough to be the woman that could talk back.

I began to draw in air, searching for a way to articulate it all. To force the words out despite my heavy tongue.

Amanda touched my grandmother's arm. "Your great-granddaughter is asking for you." My beautiful, kind, and anti-conflict cousin turned my grandmother neatly away. Relief washed over me, and my tongue returned to normal.

I sighed. Next time. I'd speak up next time.

I mouthed my thanks to Amanda and she winked at me over her shoulder. I sat back in my chair with a huff and Matty gave an exaggerated shudder.

He pulled himself together in little time and leaned close to whisper, "One drink for Cousin Mandy."

I nodded. "Eleven drinks for me to go there, but only because we're related."

"Fair, but I think those rules should be less strict for same-sex relations."

Matty basked in the true laughter that drew from me. He raised his glass. "Seven more to go!"

I joined him in downing the fizzy champagne, focusing on that instead of the break in the crowd of wedding guests that gave me a clear view of my dad dancing with his new wife. He was smiling bigger than I could remember seeing him smile before. The sensation of my heart lifting and breaking at the sight was growing familiar.

I didn't have a problem with Stacy as a person. My parents' divorce two years ago was a *long* time coming. They waited until I was out of the house, though they insisted that wasn't the case.

My dad had been a mess but faring better than when he was struggling to keep things going with my mom. After a year, he decided to try dating online at his sister's encouragement. A couple of months later, Stacy swept in.

Stacy was my mom's opposite. Nurturing and patient. She was willing to give to my dad far more than my mom had been. Under Stacy's encouragement and attention, Dad gained weight and energy. Stacy added decorative touches to his apartment and convinced him that gray didn't go with every color and that yes, cream was a color. She'd inspired him to do his woodworking again, something he hadn't touched since I was five. She appreciated every romantic gesture my mom had been spurning for years. The surprise trips Mom would have been angry not to have been consulted about first. The bouquets of flowers that were shockingly ugly. The sweaters that were two sizes too big that Stacy knotted and tucked in to look adorable in every Facebook post while my mom would have been angry he hadn't bothered to check her size from the clothes in her closet.

I'd seen early on that my parents didn't work together. My dad was amazed how dating Stacy was the furthest thing from work. Stacy and my dad took dance classes together; not that anyone could tell from the way they were acting on the dance floor right now. They went on a walk around the park every morning with the dog they adopted. My dad would die for Rudy, and I tried not to resent my pet-free childhood due to my mother's allergies because I found myself loving Rudy too when the two of us were at my dad's apartment together.

Stacy made my dad open up. She got him into therapy. Sometimes I resented that too. I couldn't get through a phone conversation with my dad these days without him saying something that made my eyes well up. My relationship with my dad had never been better, but the work we were putting in was exhausting. I had Stacy to thank for his effort and for this reason alone, I could never hate her. I had to be happy for her. Her cheeks had to be aching from her constant smiles today. At forty-two, this was her first wedding. She'd explained to me yesterday she had gotten pregnant with her son, Nate, when she was twenty-three and had thrown herself into work and raising him. She'd cried during her vows when she admitted she didn't think she'd ever get her big romance until my dad came along.

So I didn't hate her, but every smile they shared made me think of my mom and how much I missed her. She'd left for Italy four months ago, right after the engagement was announced, with indefinite plans to return.

Glasses empty, Matty and I exchanged a look and rose to return to the open bar. We passed Amanda's daughter, Lizzy, entertaining my grandmother with her latest tap routine in her white flower girl dress. I hoped she was too young to realize how she was being used to ease tension and didn't end up suffering the trauma of being a buffer. My other cousin's wife was beginning to show her bump. I silently encouraged Lizzy to keep going, the baton would pass to that little bundle of joy soon enough.

Matty smiled at the bartender, a tall man with dark brown skin, perfect teeth, and slightly bushy eyebrows. I felt my own grin turn flirtatious as Matty and I leaned against the bar as one. Usually, our taste in men differed enough we never felt like we were competing, but this man fit perfectly in the center of our Venn diagram.

"Two vodka cranberries," Matty said.

I shot him a look. *We're switching to the hard stuff now?*

He shot me a look. *Hell yes.*

We turned to smile at the bartender again.

"Alright, but I've been asked to inform you this was your last round," he said, casting a nervous look toward my dad and Stacy. The bride had paused in her dancing long enough to give me a nervous smile. My jaw clenched.

"Oh really?" I asked sweetly. I didn't know where I would

have gone from there, but Matty bumped my small bag with his hip, reminding me of the shooters we'd packed and that I'd promised to keep the peace.

"In that case, make them doubles," he said.

The bartender nodded and took to the task.

I couldn't let it go that easily. "Can I ask, has anyone else been cut off?"

"Not yet," the bartender said carefully.

"Hmm." I glared across the outdoor space to where my new stepbrother and his best friend were truly going at it to the latest pop song. My stepbrother was smiling and dancing in place while his friend jumped in circles around him. I could hear his dress shoes striking the temporary wooden dance floor even from here. There was no way they were any less drunk than Matty and me.

As we stepped away from the bar with our drinks, Matty bent slightly to speak in my ear. "First, to uphold my own promise to your dad, I want to remind you of the promises you made regarding this beautiful ceremony and your behavior." He took a long pull of his drink, wincing at the taste even as his hand slipped into my bag. I drank enough of mine to keep up, then lowered my drink and took Matty's so his hands were free. He dumped a shooter into both our cups while discretely using the skirt of my dress to hide his actions. "That being said, are you going to say something?"

I nearly gagged at the taste of my doctored drink. In his hurry, Matty had dumped in tequila instead of vodka. Still, it was worth the almost instant numbing in my cheeks. "Sober, I probably wouldn't but… I'm still fired up from my sweet grandma." I took another drink. "I'm thinking about it. It just doesn't seem fair that I have to go to this thing, pretend to be having fun, and not be rewarded for it all by spending my night sleeping curled around the toilet."

"Here, here." We drank to that. Then drank to drinking to that.

My cup was half empty and my head was light and brave. I licked my numb lips and nodded to Matty. It was go time.

Did I need access to the bar at this point? No. Did I want to get much drunker than I already was? Also no. Was the reception only scheduled to last another hour? Yes. Was this about Stacy trying to parent me when I was already twenty-one and had basically been parenting myself for years and didn't need or want her help? Maybe.

Would I regret approaching Stacy and my dad on the dance floor during the most important night of their lives together? Absolutely.

When Matty and I were thirteen, we snuck a bottle of vodka out of my mom's stash under my parents' bed. I remember when we stood up, I'd looked at the bed for a long moment, dimly remembering how we all used to end up there. It might not even be a real memory, just something my parents talked about. Almost nightly, my brother and I would fake a nightmare and crawl into bed between our parents. We probably would have kept at it until we were far too old.

Now I couldn't get into the bed. I hadn't since I was four. It didn't smell the same as it did when I was a kid. It smelled like my mom and in the mornings, the couch smelled like my dad. I didn't know when they'd last slept together, but I heard them making plans to convert the office into a bedroom. I had tightened my grip on the bottle, fighting tears and fear of the unknown. My family just kept breaking.

Matty had grabbed my hand. "One time I had a sex dream about your mom," he said. "I think I should go to therapy."

My laugh wasn't quite right, but I was back in the present with Matty just like that.

"Disgusting." I pulled him away from the bed and we snuck to the basement, hiding the bottle between us and giggling uncontrollably. My dad would have known exactly what was happening if he'd looked up from the TV. My mom would have known in a heartbeat if she hadn't been out cheating on him.

Matty and I each took one sip from that bottle and decided

adults were insane and tastebuds must die with age. We mourned the loss prematurely as we ate candy and watched TV. Neither of us said anything when I heard my mom pull into the driveway and I turned down the volume. We were silent as we listened to my dad greet my mom and ask if she'd gotten everything done at work. She didn't say anything. Just shut the door to their room.

Her room.

I turned the volume back up when my dad started sniffling. I sat in silence, flooded with the pain that was so heavy. Spiraling between the desire to go comfort him and the guilt that I hadn't confronted my mom. I was addicted to the pain of reading her texts with Brad. I wanted to pretend I was too young to under-stand any of it so I could tell myself none of it was my fault.

Matty took my hand. I made a joke about the show we were watching. He threw a handful of skittles at me. One hit my tooth with an audible and painful click. We laughed so hard that the spiral pain in my chest released.

Now, as I came to a halt, somewhat unsteadily, in front of my dad and Stacy, Matty's hand in mine grounded me yet again.

"Roly-Poly!" My dad's cheeks were smiling and red. We both turned red when we drank. I probably matched my dress at this point. I barely managed to keep my drink from spilling when my dad hugged me.

I tightened my grip on Matty's hand. It hurt that my dad's hugs were so frequent now after they'd been absent when I most craved them.

If my dad noticed how I stiffened, he didn't comment. "It's been an amazing day, right? You're having fun?"

And just like that, the fight flew out of me. I couldn't ruin everything with an hour to spare, but I was also too drunk to keep that resolve. Better to leave now before I spoiled everything. "Yeah, Dad. It's been great. But I'm kind of tired. Matty and I might go back to the hotel."

My dad's face fell. Stacy's eyes went from my drink to the bar to my dad's expression. She stepped closer and dropped her voice as one of my dad's college friends captured his attention. "Come on, Roly. Stay."

Usually, I loved my nickname. When I was little and chubby, I fell in love with gymnastics. My dad started calling me Roly-Poly because I somersaulted everywhere from the age of two to four. Cheryl was an old lady's name. Everyone called me Roly. But it was *my* nickname, given to me in a time when things were happy and Stacy wasn't a thought. I didn't like the name on her lips.

The fight started to churn again in my stomach. My smile turned forced. I took another drink before answering and ignored the slightly drunk slur of my words. "I'm just tired, Stacy."

"I wanted to make sure you had a good time. I know when I was your age, all I wanted to do was party and there are some memories I missed out on because I had too much to drink."

I let my face show Stacy just how little I appreciated her advice. How much I wished to forget this day.

Her smile faltered. She stepped even closer. "Roly, I love your dad and I've been so looking forward to this weekend and getting to know you. Why don't we just dance it out?" I was mildly impressed by the smile she was able to muster again. It was almost convincing.

"I'd rather n—" As I spoke, Stacy reached for my arm. I pulled it out of her reach. Unfortunately, that meant my elbow hit the person behind me in the stomach. They grunted and I was so surprised that I tried to overcorrect the situation. This meant yanking my arm forward again. This meant my cranberry vodka tequila sloshed forward.

This meant red splashed down the front of Stacy's white wedding dress. The dress she waited forty years to wear.

Matty gasped. The surrounding area went silent. Stacy blinked down at the spreading stain. When our eyes met, hers were welling with tears. She tried a shaky smile and opened her mouth, but the person behind me that I bumped spoke first.

"What the fuck is your problem?" The voice belonged to Stacy's son's best friend. John? Jake? Some J name. I'd only met my new stepbrother, Nate, at the rehearsal dinner last night, but Matty had pointed out his friend at the ceremony declaring it would only take him half a sip to make a move on him. I had to agree there was something about Nate's friend that made it hard to look away. Maybe it was the pouty lips and how his face transformed when he pulled them up into a half-smile. His short, light brown hair was still styled in a perfect upward sweep even after his riotous dancing.

Nate stood beside his friend, his eyes wide. Half-sip pulled me a step away from Stacy and I was so shocked, that I went willingly. Then kept going in a stumble as alcohol affected my feet in their heels. Matty tried to right me, but Half-sip was already holding my arm and caught my weight, pulling me so close I noticed a hint of green at the center of his brown eyes. Those eyes rolled in annoyance as he righted me.

By now a flock of bridesmaids had surrounded Stacy. Everyone was trying to help with the inevitable stain. Nate and his friend rounded on me. In my heels, I was as tall as Nate. His friend was just a bit shorter, but the expression on his face made me feel ten inches tall.

"It was an accident," I said, far too defensive.

"Can't you just try to be happy for them, Cheryl? We're all adults here," Nate said, but his voice was soft. He was watching his mom, looking so sad for her that I felt even worse.

"I didn't m—"

"Stacy didn't deserve that at all," Half-sip's tone was the opposite of Nate's. Harsh and angry. "I can't believe anyone would stoop so low." The disgust on his face turned my stomach.

I squared my shoulders. My face was burning. The stares I was getting felt like punishment enough. Somehow, this guy's expression and words touched my nerves just enough. Maybe it was the alcohol, but for the first time this weekend, I was able to speak up for myself. "I *said* it was an accident."

"And did you accidentally get drunk? What did you think would happen?"

"I didn't think I'd spill. That's what I mean by accident."

We were glaring at each other. "You should apologize to Stacy and go sober up."

"Excuse me, but I don't even know you. Maybe you should at least marry my dad before you try to parent me too."

Stacy's startled noise behind me made me aware of how quiet the dance floor had become. Matty looked impressed, but everyone else's face echoed Stacy's shocked hurt. None more so than my dad's.

"I'm sorry, I..." There was no salvaging this situation. I had hurt my dad. Broken all my promises. Ruined his wedding. Shame curdled and churned in my gut.

Matty smiled at my dad and stepped back to my side, linking our arms. "I think we can all agree it's been a long weekend."

With him having eased the silence, I was able to speak again. "I'm sorry. I didn't mean that, and I didn't mean to spill."

Stacy's smile was still shaking. My dad latched onto my words, willing to believe me if it meant his wedding night could be saved. "I know you didn't, Roly."

Matty said something about the sunset to the woman next to him and the tension broke. People stepped away to talk and return to their dancing. Stacy went with her sister to try to fix the stain in the bathroom. I made to go to my dad, but a hand on my arm stopped me.

It was Half-sip. "Listen, Stacy has been like a mom to me for years. You should give her a chance. I know she'll forgive you when you apologize."

My glare was back full force. "I *just* apologized."

"You didn't mean it."

I stuck a finger in his face, sucking in a breath to retort, but my stepbrother pushed my hand cautiously down. I probably enjoyed the fear on his face more than I should. Nate's eyes went to his friend, pleading. "Jack, let's just let it go."

"You said yourself she's not even trying," Jack said.

"I think Nate has the right idea," Matty said, turning me with hands on my shoulders. "Have a nice night you two."

Before I knew it, Matty had escorted me off the dance floor, down a winding path through the grass between the tables, and up to the street. As our rideshare pulled up in front of us, enough time had passed for me to process and let go of most of my anger.

"Half a sip, did I say?" Matty asked in the quiet. "No way. After that broody show? No drinks. No drinks at all for that one. Jack, was it? No-drinks-Jack. God, he was gorgeous."

"You're drunk."

"*Goooorgeous.*"

"I'm walking to the hotel."

Matty laughed and threw his arms around me. "No chance. I can't talk about this stuff with Andrew anymore, so you have to listen to me gush about those lips until we get to the hotel and then I won't slip when we call him."

I rolled my eyes and got into the car. "I don't want to hear about Jack or his lips again."

"Too bad!"

TWO

"DO you remember getting hit by a truck last night?" Matty asked the next morning over our coffees. "I don't *think* we blacked out, but my body is telling me that's what happened at some point."

"It wasn't a truck, it was a train," I said.

Matty grimaced in agreement. We'd taken turns puking in the toilet last night. I'd woken up on the hotel bathroom floor while Matty's snores echoed from the tub. There was still a line on my forehead from where I'd tied Matty's tie around my head in the hotel bar before we went up to our room. I rubbed at it and the ache in my brain.

"All I know is I'm never drinking again. Your dad and Stacy better last, I won't survive another wedding."

"My mom could always get married next."

"True. Remember how hard we worked to be happy for your dad and all encouraging when he and Stacy started dating? Let's not do that with your mom so we can avoid the hangover."

"And confrontations with stepsiblings and their rude friends."

"Cheers to that." We clicked our water glasses.

I'd worked at a restaurant long enough to see the concealed annoyance in our server's eyes as they came back to refill our glasses again, leaving the pitcher behind this time. They were getting a fat tip. Brunch was in full swing around us. Matty had made a weak joke about trying hair of the dog, looking pale as he eyed the rounds of mimosas the women next to us were consuming. I think they were ahead of us on their number of refills. The server probably wished they could just drop off a mimosa pitcher.

"I thought we were too young for hangovers," I complained.

"It's only because we started drinking so young," Matty said, making me laugh. After that first sip of vodka, neither of us drank again until college.

"We really can't tell Andrew about this."

"Oh god, of course not."

For years, it had just been me and Matty. We met in gymnastics when we were kids. I had trouble making friends, but he was insistent. He practically forced me to hang out, asking my parents if I could come over behind my back and always partnering up with me when he could. I was distrustful of other kids, but Matty wore down my walls. He moved to town when we were ten and once we started hanging out, I'd shamelessly used him and his house to escape the tension building between my parents. Before I'd known it, Matty was my best and only friend.

Matty never commented on my weight. Matty also loved Taylor Swift. Matty didn't look at me like I was the girl whose brother died. The girl who barely remembered her dead brother, which might be even sadder. His parents didn't ask how my parents were doing with forced sympathy or the desire for gossip. Matty didn't watch his words around me or tiptoe. He made fun of my middle school outfit choices and cried with me when we watched sad movies. Nothing was too dark for Matty. No subject couldn't be eased with a joke one of us made.

When I came out as bisexual to Matty, he'd done the same, telling me it bothered him how often people just assumed he was gay. The years were filled with mutual crushes on women and judgment of the other's taste in men. We applied to the same colleges and did speech and debate together. I was convinced there would never be another person I could spend so much time with. There was no person in the world whom I could be as honest with. Matty was my person. As the years passed, I'd accepted he would be my only person. I was let down too often by my parents and the people around me to risk letting anyone else in.

Then we moved to Fort Collins for college and I met Andrew in English 101. I'd been surprised by his insistence to talk to me, the rainbow pin on my backpack his first icebreaker. Whatever I said made him laugh and he sat next to me the next day. Then the next. When we had our first exam, I agreed to study together. He always showed up first, often bringing me a coffee. Never once did he pry, never once did he flake. The maturity in which he approached building a friendship was nothing I'd ever experienced in high school or in the suburb Matty and I had grown up in. Before I knew what was happening, I had a second friend. Then one day, I was having coffee in the library with Matty and Andrew showed up. I think it was love at first sight between them, though they insist it was their mutual love for me that drew them to each other.

They took a long time to start dating. The three of us were inseparable throughout freshman year. I knew it was a matter of time, but they were afraid of testing the friendship we'd built. It took one insufferable frat party left early and a case of stolen beers for them to make out in Matty's dorm room during finals week of our sophomore spring semester. There was no denying their love after that. And I loved that they were in love. They made such a point to ensure I wasn't excluded that a rumor spread we were a thruple. While that wasn't the case, I knew more than I wanted to about their relationship and sex life.

Andrew never failed to tease Matty and me about our inability to hold our alcohol. We agreed it was his greatest flaw. The events of last night could not be mentioned.

"Shit," Matty said.

"What?"

"I snapped him at two in the morning last night," Matty

confessed, looking up from his phone. I vaguely remembered smiling for a picture with Matty's tie around my head. As we looked, the triangle went from a solid color to just an outline. Andrew had just seen whatever picture we'd sent. I let my head fall into my palm. We would never live it down.

My phone began vibrating. Matty sighed. "Let it begin."

I answered the FaceTime to Andrew's laughter. "You're alive!"

"Barely," I said.

"How'd it go?" The laughter in Andrew's eyes dimmed with concern.

I shrugged. "Most of the weekend was fine. We still have to send off my dad and Stacy in an hour for their honeymoon."

Andrew put his camera up to his face. "What kind of answer is that?"

I winced. Matty scooted his chair closer and leaned in. "She spilled a vodka cranberry on Stacy's wedding dress."

Silence. Call ended. Andrew called again. I answered. Call ended. Matty's phone started to ring. Matty answered.

"Babe, you're joking."

"Babe, I'm not."

"That's…"

"Bad," I said before he could. I rubbed my temples and sighed. "You think I should just go home? I don't think they'd want to see me today anyway."

They thought about it. I saw them trying to do one of their not-subtle conversations with their eyes. They both ended up looking confused. Matty put a hand on my arm. "Roly, I think you have to go. I think you need to apologize again and say goodbye before your dad leaves."

The thought of my dad leaving the country too made my stomach sink. My mom left shortly after they announced the engagement and I hated not knowing when she'd come home. My dad couldn't stay away like she was. His and Stacy's jobs wouldn't allow it. Even telling myself that, a part of me protested. Despite how much independence my upbringing had fostered within me, it was still reassuring knowing a parent was always an hour's drive away. Stacy and my dad would be in Spain for two weeks.

What if something happened while he was gone?

Matty squeezed my arm. "But if you want to just head home, you know I support every bad decision."

I stabbed at my omelet. I'd barely been able to eat half. For some reason, I kept thinking about Jack's face last night and not Stacy's. He'd been disgusted by my treatment of her and my drunkenness. I had never felt so judged in my life. I dreaded facing him and Nate again. "I just hope Jack isn't there."

"Who's Jack?" Andrew pulled his phone too close to his face again in interest.

"Just this guy who yelled at Roly for spilling," Matty said.

"Was it hot?" Andrew asked.

"It was hot," Matty answered without hesitation.

"Did Roly think it was hot?" Andrew asked.

"No!" I protested too loud and too fast.

Matty leaned with his phone so I was out of the frame and stage whispered. "She wouldn't shut up about him last night."

The two of them laughed and I rolled my eyes. Matty and Andrew continued talking in soft tones, Matty telling him more about our time here while I considered my options. In the end, there wasn't much choice. I'd rather face Jack and his judgment than my dad's disappointment if I didn't show. He and I had made too much progress in the last few months for me to jeopardize it over some boy.

"I think we should go," I said.

"I think that's a good choice," Andrew said. "Just maybe try to sound at least a little happier about it when you get there."

Thankfully, the send-off wasn't a huge affair. The plan was to meet in the hotel lobby to exchange hugs and well wishes. Matty and I got his car all packed and were ready to leave as soon as my dad and Stacy did.

Besides my dad and Stacy, we were the last to arrive at the small gathering. My grandmother, my dad's siblings, their spouses, Nate and Jack, and an older woman who might have been Stacy's relation. That was it. All my cousins had left the night before with their kids. Most people who traveled had already gotten on their morning flights or hit the road.

My grandmother immediately pounced. "Cheryl!"

I forced a smile. Her eyes narrowed as she drew near and took me in. She tsked. "Dear, your skin shouldn't already be looking like this at your age. Next time think about drinking less."

"Grandma, I barely ever drink as much as I did last night. Matty and I just stayed up too late."

She flicked her gaze over Matty. She knew better than to say anything about our close friendship, but her frown said enough about her suspicions over what we'd been up to last night. "Well, I dare say I wouldn't be able to sleep much either if I'd ruined someone's wedding dress."

My grandmother was never easy to be around, but she wasn't usually this disproving. I dropped my eyes. Matty shifted, likely struggling with the urge to come to my defense and his decade-long fear.

The moment broke when Stacy came up from behind me and put an arm around my shoulder. I stiffened but didn't duck away like I wanted. "Now, Katherine, we all know it was an accident. She just bumped into Jack."

"Now, Stacy." Oh, Grandma was on one. "If she hadn't been drinking, it wouldn't have happened."

"I agree if she hadn't been holding a drink she couldn't have spilled, but otherwise the situation was quite out of her control," Stacy said, speaking more firmly with my grandmother than anyone else dared. My respect for her heightened just a bit at the tone.

"Mom!" Sweet, oblivious Dad arrived. He swept my grandmother into a huge hug, drawing one of the smiles only he invoked from her. She fussed over him, worried about his first trip out of the country while he reassured her all would be well with Stacy in charge.

He looked so happy. I focused on that as I turned to Stacy. "I really am sorry about your dress."

"It's alright, Roly." She smiled at my dad. "Hopefully, I never have to wear it again."

As happy as their happiness made me, I really shouldn't ever have to see someone stare at my dad like that. She was still flushed from her wedding night. She smelled like my dad. Gross. When she turned to look at him, I saw her hair was a mess in the back. I caught Matty's eyes. He mouthed the words *sex hair.* Gross. Gross. Gross.

"Let's get some pictures!" One of my aunts came forward with a camera and Stacy's sex hair and I were immortalized together.

Matty waited patiently as I was shuffled in and out of pictures. Why we needed so many after spending hours yesterday with cameras flashing, I couldn't tell you. I was on autopilot for most of them until Stacy gleefully suggested getting one with "just the kids."

The next second I was pushed into a tight group with Matty, Nate, and Jack. I tried to go on the outside, next to Matty, but Stacy insisted Nate and I stand in the middle. He was tense but complied with his mother's wishes and put an arm around me. Jack threw an arm around Nate's shoulders and his fingers brushed my shoulder, making me stiffen even further.

We forced smiles until the adults decided that was enough pictures for one morning and Stacy and my dad needed to get going. Matty stumbled away from our cluster, feigning blindness from all the camera flashes. I laughed and was surprised when Nate and Jack joined in. I met Jack's eyes and our smiles died quickly.

Dad stepped forward and drew me off to the side, breaking my stare down with Jack. He hugged me tightly. "I'll be back soon, Roly-Poly. Before you know it. Send me an email every day about the start of school and how your classes are going."

I nodded. I couldn't help the tears that welled up even though I would bet Matty's car the emails were Stacy's suggestion. My dad stepped back. Holding my arms, he looked at me closely. "I know your mother and I weren't the best parents for a long time there. We tried to make things work, but I hope you can see from us learning that you have to be willing to let things go to make yourself happy. Look at your mom! She's always wanted to go to Italy. And I loved her, I really did, but we got pregnant so young and we… it was hard to grow together. My only regret is that I wasn't there for you enough. I should have been a parent and not… well. I've been talking a lot with my therapist about how I shut down and I promise it's something I'm working on, but we also think you might have developed a habit of shutting people out and it's making rebuilding our relationship harder. I can only do better moving forward, and I hope you'll give me a chance."

The sound that left me wasn't very pretty, but my dad muffled it by wrapping me in another hug. I knew I shut people out and I didn't know if I trusted his promise. It was a hard one to believe after all those years when my mom and I fought and he stood off to the side, terrified of making things worse. He wasn't there, not like he is now after Stacy and therapy and a job change. All things that had nothing to do with me. All a life I didn't know and wasn't part of. How was that supposed to make our relationship better?

But this felt like the closest I've gotten to an invite into his new, adult world. He was talking about me with his therapist, noticing me enough to try to figure out what I was thinking.

And he was leaving just when it felt like it was working.

I sighed. "Travel safe, okay?"

"Okay. I love you."

I stepped back and wiped at my tears. "Love you too."

We walked back to where Matty was standing awkwardly

with Jack while Stacy said goodbye to Nate. Dad clapped Matty on the shoulder. "You know the drill, Matthew."

"I sure do, Tom. Drugs, parties, leave no time for homework, set her up on dates with anyone who wants to get in her pants and—"

My dad laughed and jumped forward, catching Matty in a headlock and ruffling his hair. Sometimes it felt like the two of them were closer than I'd ever been with my dad. Still, I had to laugh. Jack watched them with a surprised smile that died yet again as soon as we made eye contact. I glared. He rolled his eyes and looked away, clearly relieved when Nate and Stacy returned.

"Well, we're off! You kids get home safe and email every day," Stacy said.

"Even me?" Matty asked, fixing his hair.

"Sure, Matty, even you. Jack, let me know how things turn out with that roommate situation. Hopefully my advice helps."

"I'm sure it will, Stace."

Stacy gave all of us one last hug and before I knew it, my dad was remarried and driving off into the afternoon sun with my new stepmom.

Nate stopped me before I could make my own getaway with Matty. "Hey, Cheryl, can I talk to you?"

"It's Roly."

"Roly?" Jack asked in the way people always did. That tone that clearly said, *you sure you want to be called that?*

"It was that or Cher and there is only one Cher," Matty said.

Jack laughed, sounding nicer than I was expecting. Matty's charm was working on him. Mine was not. Who cared? I turned away with Nate.

"Listen," he started, "we're family now. I feel like we got off on the wrong foot and would like to try and remedy that if we could?" Shy uncertainty turned Nate's words into a question.

I didn't know how to handle Nate's entrance into my life. It pressed on a bruise deep in my soul and yet I couldn't say no to him when he offered his phone. I put in my contact information. He smiled with relief.

"I go to school in Denver, but I go up to Fort Collins a lot. Maybe we can hang out sometime? I know it would make our parents happy and I hope we can be friends."

It would make one of my parents happy. "Sure. Just text me. Matty and I have to go."

Nate and I looked at each other, both of us wondering if a hug had to happen. In the end, Nate lifted a fist and I bumped it. I walked back to Matty, ignoring Jack completely. Matty waved a cheerful goodbye, only dropping his smile when he made eye contact with Grandma, and we left the hotel.

The sunlight hit my eyes painfully, reminding me of my hangover. Even so, I breathed deeply for the first time all weekend. It was finally over. I survived.

THREE

I WOKE on Monday and smiled up at my ceiling. Back to normal life. Class, coffee, homework, work. Structure and independence. Parents an entire phone call and email away. Grandma not even a thought. When I was with family, I sometimes forgot how happy I was. I reverted to the angsty teenager who just wished her parents would look at each other.

Here at school, I was another face in the crowd. I was Matty and Andrew's best friend. Priya's best work friend. Head server at the Study Room Restaurant and Brewery where I could stand in for anyone front of house or back after two years of working there. I could get anywhere I needed on my bike, an adorable blue cruiser we named Trevor. I was a regular at Moonbean Café and occasionally went on dates in which I'd mastered keeping things light and fun.

Here, on my own, I had it all figured out. When it came to my parents, I was a mess, but it was surprisingly easy to separate myself from that life when I was just another college student.

Matty was an early riser and preferred going to the gym first thing. I was home alone as I got ready in my robe, making my favorite ham and cheese omelet and coffee. I dressed in overall shorts, a green Colorado State t-shirt, and my white converse. I put my hair half up in a bun then switched my nose ring to the black one. Matty and I had gotten our noses pierced on our eighteenth birthdays and kept a collection of rings and studs on our bathroom shelf. We religiously cleaned them but would never tell anyone we shared nose jewelry. Andrew was catching on, but we denied his suspicions with our every breath. He learned to let it go.

A hint of eyeliner and I was ready for the day. I blew a kiss to our Taylor Swift shrine and pulled on my backpack. In minutes, I was peddling down the flower-lined paths of CSU. I loved campus. It was a hot day and people walked everywhere with their dogs. Couples held hands and the sun lit the world. I smiled at the people who smiled at me. The difficult weekend was nothing but a memory.

My first two classes were a blur. I stuffed syllabuses in my bag with the first stirrings of dread. Class was a necessary evil of my life here and the path toward the future I needed. The one where I had plenty of money to move far, far away from my family. I didn't let any of the sure to be boring courses ahead ruin my mood. Instead, I texted in the group chat to Matty and Andrew that I was heading toward our favorite coffee shop. Matty was on his way to his next class, but Andrew said he'd be able to meet in ten. Matty sent back a picture of him pouting for going without him. I sent back a video of me blowing him a kiss before unlocking Trevor and taking off down the bike lane.

As I walked into Moonbean Café, I got in line with a thrill low in my gut. Last semester I had just about the same schedule and Emily was always working behind the counter on Mondays when I came here. Even over the summer, we'd kept up a steady banter anytime I happened to come in while she was on shift. Sometimes, I woke up early just to get a coffee and see her. Matty had done some light internet stalking, and what do you know? She had a pride flag in her bio.

This semester I was going to ask her out. I was working on my Andrew-diagnosed Fear of Commitment and recently Daddiagnosed Habit of Shutting People Out. I wanted to be better, I really did. Maybe therapy was the smarter option, but I was used to doing things on my own. I could at least try to figure these things out first. I planned to go into this semester of seeing Emily with the intention of looking for more than a fun hookup.

I was three people away from the counter. I pulled my headphones out of my ears and double-checked my pocket for cash. I could do this. I ran through the lines in my head. Maybe I'd start by saying something about Mondays, which we both loved, or ask her about the start of the semester.

No, that last one wasn't good. I wasn't excited to be starting classes and she might be able to tell. I couldn't go in with negative energy. I was feeling good about everything else, just had to stay away from school and family. Easy.

Two people away. I pretended to text so I could come up to the counter all casual, happy, and surprised to see her. I would just ask how she's been. Make it about her, then swoop in to ask her to… drinks? Not coffee. The thought of a dinner date made my skin crawl. Maybe I should do that then and work on my issues. Or I could…

One person between me and the counter. Andrew texted in the group chat *Thank god Matty can't come. I feel like he won't leave me alone.* Then another message right away, *oh no, that was just for Roly.*

Matty's all-caps response had me laughing, so when it was my turn to look up and order, my smile was natural and ready for Emily.

But I didn't look up to see Emily. My smile fell away as I came face to face with none other than Jack.

"What the hell?"

Jack smiled nervously, glancing at the manager standing a couple of feet away. "Good morning to you too, Cheryl."

"What are you doing here? Where is—" I cut myself off before I asked about my crush.

Jack gestured to his apron. "Just trying to work. What can I get for you?"

"Do you live here?" I demanded. My brain was struggling to catch up with the situation.

"No, I don't live here. I work here, I just told you that." Jack spoke slowly and with a teasing glint in his eyes. That was enough to snap me out of my surprise.

I narrowed my eyes at him. "Do you go to CSU?"

"Yes. It's my second year."

"But… I've never seen you."

"Maybe you did, but we wouldn't have known each other considering we just met last weekend." Jack looked again toward his manager before leaning forward. "But seriously, I'm new here and don't want to be *that* guy. Can I just get your order and talk later?"

"No need for the second part. I'll take an iced vanilla latte and we can leave it at that."

Jack raised his eyebrows and put my order in. I paid and left a begrudging tip. I might not like the guy, but I'd worked food industry too long not to.

"See you around, Cheryl!"

I rolled my eyes, took the number he offered without letting myself notice how warm his fingers were where they brushed mine and found a table as far from the register as I could. Which wasn't far. It was a small but crowded coffee shop done in light blues and dark orange with a subtle astronomy theme. I loved it. I hated that Jack might ruin it.

I pulled out my laptop and perused used textbooks sites, refusing to watch Jack behind the counter. I almost wished I already had homework to do so I could seem busy. A girl dropped off my coffee, not Jack. Then Andrew slid into the chair across from me and captured all my attention.

"So, register guy keeps checking you out."

"He isn't checking me out. Stop looking at him."

Andrew raised an eyebrow. "Do you know him?"

Last night, Andrew came over and Matty and I caught him up fully on all the wedding drama. "That's fucking Jack. Apparently, he lives here. Well, not in the café, but he goes to CSU."

Andrew's blue eyes grew huge. "He *does* look familiar. I think we had biology together last semester."

"Really?"

Andrew pulled out his phone. Seconds later, he showed me Jack Matthew's Instagram feed. Lots of pictures with Nate, Jack playing soccer, and a few with a little girl in high pigtails and what looked like his dad and his soccer coach. I reached for Andrew's phone to look closer.

"One dirty chai!" We jumped when Jack appeared holding Andrew's drink. Andrew's phone fell when I jerked my hand away. The world slowed as it does when the horror of embarrassment floods through you. Jack bent to pick the phone up for us. I lunged for it a second too late. Jack smirked when he saw his profile open on the screen.

"Oh, that's really embarrassing," he said, handing the phone back to me.

"Mine!" Andrew tried to save the situation and grabbed it out of my hand. The damage was done. Jack's shoulders were shaking with laughter as he walked away.

"I think I hate him."

"Please. You might be prickly, but you hate very few people."

I rolled my eyes. "Just let me have this one, Andrew."

He waited just long enough to give me a look to say he wasn't buying it before he changed the subject. "I've had a thought."

"Have you?"

"Yes."

"Are you going to tell me?"

"It depends. I don't want you to get sad, but I'm hoping it's a good thing."

I was instantly on edge. "What is it?"

"How long do you think your mom will be in Italy?"

"I'm not sure. She said she'd be back for Thanksgiving, but last

I checked she'd signed for another month on her lease." I said the words stiffly. Andrew was right to be cautious. This was a touchy subject.

"Okay, so what if, hypothetically, she seemed ready to stay until winter break and the three of us went to see her?"

"You're hoping my mom stays estranged long enough for us to have a place to stay in Italy over winter break?" I couldn't help but laugh, though the thought of my mom staying away that long hurt. It hurt because it seemed so likely. My mom was in no rush to come back. She even forgot to call me last night and hadn't answered when I tried her.

"I'm not hoping it happens, but if it's a possibility, we should plan a trip. Maybe get passports and stuff just in case. We could also just plan it either way. I've always wanted to go to Italy. Not to guilt you into it, I just think it could be fun and nice to see your mom if she is still there. Just think about it, okay?"

I couldn't look at Andrew as I considered promising even that. For some reason, my eyes went to Jack. He was smiling at an older woman, pointing to something on the menu for her. He winked and made her laugh. I dragged my eyes away. "I'll think about it and try to get answers from my mom."

Andrew smiled brilliantly. I checked my phone again as he got his laptop out. Still no calls from Mom, though an email had come in from my dad. Surprisingly, another one came from Stacy. I clicked through the photos she attached. I glanced over at Jack again, resenting his presence.

Fort Collins was supposed to be my escape from family and everything to do with them.

***

Matty was sitting on the couch in the living room when I got home from work Tuesday night. It was a busy week at our brewery restaurant called the Study Room with the students back and homework not yet an issue. I usually get off around ten-thirty, but it was approaching midnight when I unlocked our apartment door. There was a wad of cash in my pocket, I smelled like beer and fried food, and I just wanted to take off my shoes and fall into bed.

It took me a moment to notice Andrew sleeping with his head on Matty's lap, body almost completely covered with blankets. A movie was playing and our holy-looking Taylor Swift candle flickered as it filled the room with the artificial smell of the woods.

"Busy night?" Matty asked softly, careful not to stir Andrew.

"Yes. And barely worth it. Shockingly, college kids still tip like shit."

Matty made a sound of sympathy and paused the movie. "You didn't meet us at Moonbean today."

I shrugged. I didn't have an excuse. I just hadn't wanted to see—

"Jack wasn't even there."

I sagged into our circle chair. "I can't believe he goes to school here. Why didn't anyone mention that when they were introducing us all?"

"No idea. I guess I just assumed he went to school in Denver with Nate. Have you talked to Nate at all?"

"No. We just exchanged numbers. I don't know how I would even start if I wanted to."

"Do you not want to?" Matty was speaking carefully, watching my face intently in the blue light of the TV. I usually loved how well he read me, but right now I didn't want to know the expression on my face. I didn't know how I felt about all this.

I shrugged again. Nate had followed me on Instagram yesterday and I followed him back. Then, in a moment of weakness as Priya cheered me on at work earlier tonight so we could stalk Jack, I requested to follow him too. Avoiding Matty's eyes, I checked now to see if he accepted. No dice. I went to my own profile and got stuck scrolling through my posts, trying to imagine how it looked to Jack. Mostly pictures of Matty, Andrew, and me. I didn't post often. The only picture not from college was my high school graduation at the bottom of the page, my parents smiling stiffly on either side of me. I barely recognized my own smile. Moving away from that had been such a good change for me.

"Roly?"

I started and looked up from my phone. "Sorry. I just don't know what to think about it."

"Talking to Nate, does it…" Matty's tone changed in the way I knew meant he was going to bring up my brother. "Does it make you feel sad about Brady?"

I shrugged. "It makes me think of my mom mostly. How sad she'd feel seeing my dad call Nate 'son' and roughhousing and stuff."

"Your dad does that with me. Well, he doesn't call me son, so I guess it's different."

It was all the difference. "I want to be happy for him, but I just kept hearing my mom's voice and all the times she accused my dad of forgetting Brady."

"You wouldn't be forgetting Brady if you became friends with Nate. You know that, right? Your mom wouldn't be mad at you."

"She probably wouldn't." Sometimes, it felt like she was trying so hard not to forget Brady, she forgot she had me too. I didn't want this to be what reminded her of me and my lack of memories of Brady. I didn't say that to Matty. "Who can get mad when they're living their best life in Italy?"

"Actually, your mom probably could."

I laughed and Matty hit play, sensitive from a childhood of me changing topics to when I was done with a conversation. "But I will say, I think Nate seems nice and Jack might have been an ass about the spill, but Moonbean is our spot. Don't let him ruin it for you."

"You're just addicted to their peanut butter cookies."

"If we boycott Moonbean I might die from the withdrawal."

"Alright. I'll keep meeting you guys there. Sorry I ditched today."

"It's understandable, but as I said, Jack wasn't there so it would seem at least Tuesdays are safe from him."

"Good." I smiled. It was one of the few school days our schedules matched up for all three of us to meet in the morning. "No Emily either?"

Matty frowned and shook his head. "I wonder if she quit?"

I sighed and turned to the TV.

The movie ended a short time later. Matty woke up Andrew and they vanished into Matty's room. I took a quick shower and put in my headphones. I'd learned early in their relationship that the two of them weren't capable of being quiet. I made them buy me noise-canceling headphones for me after the first week of their dating.

I climbed into bed and couldn't resist opening Instagram again. Jack still hadn't accepted my follow request or asked to follow me back. I sighed and went to my new stepbrother's profile. There were already pictures from the wedding up on his page. He seemed genuinely happy for Stacy and my dad. He and Jack had huge smiles in all the pictures, even the ones I was in. It was strange seeing last weekend through his eyes. Seeing Jack relaxed and joking with the other guests. The only time Jack and I had spoken was right after I ruined Stacy's dress. The guy in these pictures was an entirely different person than the one I'd interacted with.

I stared for too long at a candid of Jack laughing as he talked to my grandmother. What kind of person made Grandma smile like that?

Did I want to find out?

FOUR

I TOOK my time locking up Trevor the bike in front of Moonbean on Wednesday. I was painfully aware that Jack hadn't accepted my request on Instagram. Painfully aware he was just walking back inside after delivering a drink to one of the outside tables. I straightened and hooked my thumbs into my backpack straps. This was my place. Part of my routine here that I loved so much. No stupid boy was going to ruin it for me.

Andrew said he was running late and Matty had class. It was slower than it had been Monday, so Jack saw me as soon as I opened the door. He watched me walk up to the register with a wary look. "Hey, Cheryl."

I rolled my eyes. "It's just disrespectful."

He started. "What is?"

"Refusing to call me by my preferred name."

His mouth opened and closed for a second. "But… *Roly?*"

"Yes. Cheryl is an old lady's name. My dad called me Roly because I loved gymnastics, not because I was a chubby kid. It works with my name and I like it. But I shouldn't have to explain all that. You should have just called me what I asked you to call me. That would have been the respectful thing to do."

Jack frowned. I waited for more protests. There were far too many people who still called me Cheryl after this conversation. Jack surprised me though. He nodded decisively. "You're right. I'm sorry. What can I get for you, Roly?"

And that was it. He said Roly with a serious expression and no more hesitation. My shoulders relaxed and I dropped my hands from where they'd clenched my backpack straps. "Oh, um, just an iced London fog with some lavender."

"Lavender?"

"Yeah, it's really good." The fight had left me after his acceptance of my nickname. Especially since he didn't seem to be questioning me but the computer as he looked for the right button. I shrugged. "Emily, the girl who used to work here, and I called it a Lavender fog."

Jack smiled. "I've heard a lot about this Emily. I guess she's studying abroad this semester in Italy."

What was it with Italy? "Oh, I hadn't heard."

Jack glanced up. I was suddenly arrested by his eyes. It was that look I read about in romance books. Somehow his head was angled just right so I noticed how long his eyelashes were. Long enough to curl gently upward. The green in his eyes was more noticeable today against the green aprons the staff wore here. "You okay?" he asked.

I cleared my throat and dropped my eyes. "Yeah, I'm fine. She and I just…" Maybe things hadn't been going as well as I thought. With all our flirting, she never once mentioned a semester abroad. "Never mind. Doesn't matter. Here." I held out a ten to pay for my drink.

Jack pushed my hand back. "On me."

"No, let me pay."

"I get a free drink each shift, Roly. This one's on me."

"But… why?"

"Because we're going to be friends."

I blinked at him. "But…why?"

He laughed and clutched at his chest as if it hurt. "Brutal. Why wouldn't I want to be friends with you?"

"You don't like me. You made that pretty clear. And I don't like you."

"Well, maybe after a few free coffees you will."

I snorted. "You can't buy friendship, Jack."

"But how else am I going to win you over? You don't seem to like my charm like everyone else does."

"I'm sure they're just humoring you. But you were a dick at the wedding and now you didn't even accept my follow requ—" I shut my mouth, blushing. I did not mean to bring *that* up.

Jack looked as surprised as I did. "Accept your follow request?"

I rolled my eyes, desperately trying to hide my embarrassment with annoyance.

"Sorry, I just rolled out of bed this morning and came straight here. I didn't check my phone."

"Whatever. It doesn't matter. We aren't friends."

"Not yet." He took my drink from his coworker and held it out to me with a smug grin.

"Not happening." I dropped my ten in the tip jar and took my beverage. I didn't exactly feel confident I'd won that round as I found a table, but it would have to do.

By the time Andrew found me, I still hadn't focused on my homework. I let him distract me with his chatter, only half paying attention as I watched Jack work and finish his shift.

Andrew was smirking when I returned my attention to him. "I'm thinking this will be interesting," he said.

"How so?"

"It's just a feeling. Now, as I was saying, we should do something for your birthday."

"I don't want to."

"But what if we just saved it for the weekend after? Then we won't actually do anything on your birthday, but we could still use the excuse to party."

"I doubt I'll feel like celebrating."

"Matty and I will plan something small."

"It'll already be small considering you're my only friends."

"That's not true. You're friends with Lynn. And you have Priya at work. And now Ja—"

I held up a hand. "Don't you dare. Jack isn't my friend. And *you're* friends with Lynn. She and I just talk when we're all hanging out and you and Matty disappear into each other's eyes."

"But she likes you! And she has lots of other friends we could invite. Nothing huge, but just something fun for you that doesn't take place on your actual birthday."

"What is it with you and making these plans this year?" My birthday wasn't until December. It was way too early for me to like thinking about it.

"I'm just excited! You've had a hard summer and I can tell your mom being gone and your dad getting married has you down." Andrew grabbed my hand, sincerity shining in his blue eyes. My irritation vanished at that look. "I just want to have things we can all look forward to this year. Have you talked to your mom about winter break?"

A bit of the irritation came back. "Not yet."

"Okay. But I did find some tickets. I could buy three and we'll just make sure they're refundable if we decide not to go."

"Fine. Buy them and if you don't mention it again until I've talked to her, I'll think about a party after my birthday."

"Deal." Andrew offered me his pinky and I hooked my own around it. I hated my birthday, but maybe something like what Andrew planned could be fun.

I took a sip of my ten-dollar drink. I didn't want to have this connection with my family in Denver, but I found myself staring at the way Jack had written my name on the paper cup. It was nice handwriting. My mom always said nice handwriting spoke of careful minds. I didn't know if I believed that, but I felt it might be true in Jack's case.

Maybe Andrew was right and I'd have another friend to invite to my party by December. One with long eyelashes and pouty lips. Who was just taller than me and took care to style his hair in the morning. One who looked tired and made me wonder what time he had to get up to be here.

One who had accepted my follow request almost as soon as he left work, smiling and waving his phone in my direction outside the window. Somehow knowing I was watching him. It should have been embarrassing, but the way he was grinning… it was sweet.

My classes hit full swing by the end of the second week of school. Approaching the weekend, the Study Room got even crazier. I was called in for the lunch shift Friday and ended up powering through a double and skipping class. The decision was hard to regret when I went home with over four hundred dollars. Saturday wasn't much better, starting strong with a busy lunch rush that had us just laughing at the chaos as the tension in the kitchen kept escalating.

Priya and I hit a slight loll around four. She turned from the computer after putting in a six top of volleyball players' orders and fanned us both with the menus she still carried. "What is even happening?"

"I don't know." I bent to tie my shoelace. It kept coming untied and the lunch rush had been so intense I hadn't even felt like there was time to fix it. I'd just stuffed the laces into my white sneakers and ignored how they poked the sides of my feet. I'd probably have blisters. "But I've had to pee for like three hours. Will you take table two's appetizer out if it comes up?"

"Of course."

I hurried to the bathroom and fixed my insane ponytail before going back onto the floor. I stopped short when I saw the two guys seated in my section. I plastered on my best fake server smile and went up to the table.

Jack spotted me first. "Hey! Missed seeing you at Moonbean today."

Nate and him both looked far too happy to see me.

"So you decided to stalk me at my place of work instead?" I meant to make it sound like a joke, but I missed the mark. Nate's smile fell.

I hated this. The guilt only family can press on me. I was supposed to be free of it once I left Denver. Fort Collins was my perfect escape into adulthood. Why was it following me now?

I tried to recover and softened my tone. "How have you been, Nate?"

"Can't complain. It's nice having the house to myself. Rent is too expensive in Denver to make getting my own place make sense and I appreciate Tom and my mom letting me stay at home but living with parents at our age is tough."

Jack nodded. "Which is why I'm convincing him to transfer to CSU so I don't have to keep living with my horrible roommate. Please, Nate. You owe me."

"I don't think I do, but I'm considering it."

"Great." My voice was weird, my smile frozen. He could *not* live here too. "Can I get you guys some drinks?" The sooner I put their orders in, the sooner they would leave.

Priya jumped on me once I got to the kitchen. "I'm so jealous you get those cute boys! Did you see the one? With the curls. I died when he smiled at me. Sexy green eyes."

"Ew, Priya. That's my, uh, stepbrother." The title felt strange.

Her eyes widened. "The looks just run in your family, huh?"

"Priya, they aren't actually related." Our kitchen manager laughed and waited for me to put the two waters in one hand so I could grab the fried pickle appetizer my other table ordered.

"I know that, but I bet their parents are hotties and that's how they ended up together," Priya said defensively.

I pretended to gag as I kicked the swinging door and went back to the floor. I couldn't decide if I'd rather be hiding in the kitchen with Priya going on about how cute Nate was or staying out on the floor with Nate. I dropped off the fried pickles with a smile to the three older women at table two and was about to walk away when one stopped me.

"Dang it. Um, excuse me, honey. We ordered the artichoke dip."

"You did? I'm sorry. I was sure you said fried pickles."

"Well, you didn't hear me right," the woman said, crossing her arms and staring at the pickles in disgust.

"I'll put you in for the dip, then. I'm sorry."

"How long will that take? It already took forever for us to get these."

My smile was hurting. She'd said pickles. It took seven minutes for them to come out. "It won't take long."

"I'm sure it will be quicker if you don't stop to flirt this time."

Oh, my grandmother would love this woman.

I reached for the plate of fried pickles, but another one of the women stopped me. "We'll just snack on these while we wait."

Of course they would. Because they ordered them.

And I wasn't flirting.

But it also was not worth the argument. I barely stopped myself from slamming Nate and Jack's waters down and went to the kitchen without a word to them. My manager rolled her eyes so hard it looked painful when I told her what the women said. She asked the kitchen for some rushed dip and told me for the millionth time she was too old for this job. I laughed. As annoying as customers could be, I would be bored out of my mind here without the excuses to talk shit.

The dip barely took two minutes to plate with the chips and veggies. When I brought it out, the woman smiled at me. The fried pickles were gone. "See? Doesn't take long when you focus on your job."

I should have spat in her dip. The sandwich she ordered wasn't safe.

Jack and Nate watched me approach with wide eyes. "What did she say?" Nate asked, voice low.

"Nothing. You guys ready to order?"

Nate looked hurt, but they each got a burger and some fried pickles to start. I nodded and headed to the computer to put their order in. Jack called to my back, "And by fried pickles, we obviously mean FRIED PICKLES! Get it right the first time, dang it!"

I stopped halfway between my two tables and turned with my mouth hanging open to stare at him. He tried to keep a straight face, but it broke quickly, and he and Nate dissolved into laughter. I couldn't stop a snort. I avoided making eye contact with table two as I hurried into the back before I lost it. Priya and my manager were already in hysterics, Priya having heard everything and relayed it to the kitchen. "Oh my god, you should have seen those old white ladies' faces! You should have seen *your* face!"

Without Jack here to see me and feel encouraged, I joined them in laughing at the women's expense. It probably didn't happen often enough.

The women were sullen for the rest of their meals, glaring at Jack and tipping me less than ten percent. I couldn't be bothered to care when every time I went in the kitchen, someone made a joke about fried pickles, which my manager comped off Jack's meal for his "act of service to food workers everywhere."

Jack looked too proud of himself. When I stopped by their table it was slightly less painful to ask Nate how his classes were going and make small talk. They were delighted by the free pickles.

"See, I knew those free drinks would come around," Jack said.

"Don't get used to it." I pointed in his face and couldn't quite hold my glare.

When my grin poked through, his smile turned brighter, eyes less guarded. I realized then how much uncertainty he usually looked at me with. That might have been the first genuine smile he'd given me. I turned to swipe their cards feeling far too shaken from it.

"So, any plans tonight?" Nate asked when I came back. "Jack and I were going to see a movie if you want to come."

"I do have plans, but let me know when you're next in town

and maybe we can do something then." My plans involved a movie night with Matty, Andrew, and Andrew's roommate, Lynn, but I felt I had already done my part where family obligations were involved. I could sit this one out.

Another table was sat in my section. By the time I'd turned again, Jack and Nate were gone. Jack had left a ten-dollar bill for a tip and I smiled. I knew exactly where it came from.

His number was also scrawled across the top of their check. I looked around and made sure no one saw me pocket it.

I managed to avoid Nate the rest of the weekend he spent in Fort Collins. There wasn't a specific reason. Seeing him and Jack hadn't been that bad at work, but I experienced an uncomfortable sense of overwhelm every time I thought about reaching out. It was easier to pretend he wasn't in town and that I was too busy to hang out anyway. I didn't even tell Matty and Andrew my stepbrother was around. Andrew would probably encourage me to give him a chance and Matty would be torn. He was good about being firmly on my side, but I knew Andrew had told him before he enabled my unhealthy habits too often. Mostly because I enabled his. It was mutual and it had worked for us for years, but Andrew was slowly turning us into more thoughtful people. It was probably for the better.

But also, I just didn't tell Andrew certain things because of it.

Still, it hadn't been so horrible seeing Nate. Even Jack's presence at Moonbean was becoming an enjoyable constant. I missed my total independence from family drama, but it hadn't been unmanageable. At least it wasn't my dad and Stacy coming to visit. I was getting a better sense of who Nate was as a person too. Jack had a ton of followers on Instagram. Most of his pictures were with fellow soccer players and friends. Nate was only in group shots if Jack was there too. I could tell it took him effort to reach out and was now putting it together that my stepbrother was shy. I didn't spend a lot of time around shy people and each proof this was the case softened me toward him.

Monday morning my phone rang and woke me up. It was early enough to send a flare of panic shooting through me. I fumbled for my phone and saw it was my mom. After all these months I should be used to her disregard for time differences.

"Hello?"

"Hey, bug. How were your first couple weeks of classes?"

She remembers what week of school I'm in, but not that it's four in the morning here. "They're fine. I'm in a couple of business classes that appear to be more math than I bargained for, but I'll just have Matty do that homework for me."

My mom's laugh was distracted. I swallowed a sigh and settled back into the covers. "How is Italy?"

"Oh, sweetie, it's incredible. I could just stay here forever."

This time my laugh was forced. "Yeah?"

"Well, of course, I won't. It's just... the quiet. And the food and..." I zoned out, letting myself close my eyes again as I half-listened. "...My Italian is getting so much better. Marco says he barely notices my mistakes anymore because my accent is so good."

Not even my warm covers could fight the chill that swept over me. "Marco?"

Mom hesitated and let out a nervous laugh. "Just a friend I made. He's been so good, listening to me talk about how your father's wedding made me feel."

Stacy had been my dad's friend too. This was exactly how it started. My mom hadn't answered any of my calls when I tried to reach out to talk about the wedding. To ask how she was and hope she asked me.

She was too busy talking about it with Marco apparently.

"Did you really spill wine on her dress, Roly?" I hated the malicious laughter at the edge of my mom's question.

"I have to go."

"Where? Isn't it early there still?"

So, she did know what time it was. It was too early for tears of frustration. Or maybe that's why they were so quick to well up in my eyes. I swallowed hard. "I'm going to the gym with Matty."

"You hate the gym ever since you quit gymnastics." It was still an accusation five years later.

"Bye, Mom. Love you."

"Bye. Call me soon, okay? I miss your voice."

She wouldn't if she'd answered her phone. "Miss you too." I hung up.

Pressing the heels of my hands into my eyes, I took deep breaths. It burned, knowing how much of a hypocrite I was being. I loved disappearing to Fort Collins. I loved the escape from my parents and forgetting about them. Making a life for myself without them tugging me away from each other. My dad liked for me to show him total sympathy and comfort him when it came to my mom. My mom liked making digs and trying to get me to laugh at my father. I hated it. I separated myself from our broken mess of a family for a good reason.

So why did it hurt so much when they did the same?

I pushed away from the frustrating pain. It was chased by the panicked certainty that my mom wasn't coming home. She and Marco would live happily in Italy. I'd wake up to emails from him that mention in the last line that my mom says hi. I'd have new stepsiblings and a new Italian family to explain myself to. Everyone would think I was so lucky to have a place to stay in Italy, but I'd never want to go because—

No. Family mattered, but it wasn't my future. I was here now and when I graduated, I'd get a well-paying job somewhere far away to live happily. Matty would always be there for me. He couldn't marry and forget me because Andrew loved me too. I was happy. Here, I was happy. I loved riding Trevor around Fort Collins. I loved my job and living with Matty with a Taylor Swift shrine in the living room. I loved going to Moonbean and seeing Ja— I loved the coffee there. I was happy, even if my parents were living their own lives without me. I was an adult, so it didn't matter.

It didn't matter.

I knew how to take care of myself. I had been for years, nothing had changed. I was just freer now than I had been living in their loveless house.

When I finally heard Matty getting up, I considered actually going with him to the gym. Maybe a good workout would get rid of this emotional build-up. He and Andrew spoke in low, gentle voices. I couldn't hear their words through the wall, but the cadence of their speech stirred something quiet and hollow in my chest. I absolutely wasn't lonely. I loved being alone too. But no one spoke to me like that. My habit of keeping things to strictly fun hookups didn't allow for many early mornings together.

Matty left. When I couldn't shake my conversation with my mom or the feelings in my chest, I knew it was time to stop lying in bed with my thoughts. I readied for the day quickly and quietly so I didn't wake up Andrew again. I gathered my materials for the classes I had today and put on a sweatshirt to fight the morning chill.

The streets were peaceful at this hour. I biked without fear of cars, going fast enough for my breathing to turn heavy. Fort Collins was a sprawling city, but it didn't have the skyscrapers of Denver or the insane traffic. Matty and I lived near the well-kept campus and Old Town, the stretch of downtown sporting breweries, independent bookstores, local shops, and more tattoo parlors than any town this size could need yet each seemed to be successful and fully booked anyway. I stayed away from the chaotic parking in that section of town though, following mostly neighborhood streets and well-marked bike lanes to the other side of campus. I peddled hard, working out my emotions and barely paying attention as my favorite podcast played in my ears. I was panting when I stopped in front of Moonbean. I already felt better, and coffee would only help.

Jack and one other girl were the only people working at the counter. Jack was idly pushing a Pluto that hung too low back and forth. The sight reminded me of a lazy cat. Noises drifted up from the bakery behind the counter wall with the smell of fresh-baked pastries. A few people were out this early, but it was slow enough that the girl didn't bother looking up from her phone when I came up to the counter.

"Hey!" Despite it being 6:30 in the morning, Jack's smile was bright.

"Hey." I mustered a close-lipped smile and tried to think of what I wanted. I was cold from my bike ride and unable to think of anything creative to drink. "Um, I'll just take a vanilla latte and a blueberry muffin."

Jack tilted his head as he looked at me. Not even his long eyelashes could get to me today. "Sure." He typed it in and waved away the money I handed him.

"I know you don't get a free muffin every shift," I said.

"No, but you do."

I rolled my eyes and sighed. "Just let me pay for it, Jack."

My face must have betrayed something because for once, he grabbed the money. I know he only charged me for the muffin though. I almost said something when he took two from the case.

"I'm going to take my break now, Jen," he told the girl now making my drink. She nodded without looking up from the steamer. Jack went around the counter with the muffins and waited for me to accept the situation and find us a table. I sighed and led the way to a two-top by the window.

"So, what's up?" Jack asked. "You seem off."

"Just say it, I look like crap."

"I would never say that. And I've learned not to say you look tired. But you do."

I began unwrapping my muffin. I wasn't very hungry. "My mom just called me pretty early and I couldn't go back to sleep."

"Is she okay?"

"Yeah, she just doesn't care about time differences." Jack looked confused. "She went to Italy pretty soon after my dad and Stacy announced their engagement."

"Really? How was that for you?"

"Well, I can't blame her for wanting to get away."

"Sure you can. Do you miss her?"

I shrugged and broke off a bite of muffin. "Yeah. I kind of wished there was someone besides me and Matty there who…" I stopped, remembering whom I was talking to.

"Who what? It's okay, you can say it."

I blushed but forced the words out. When Jack was like this, open and soft-spoken, I felt like I could tell him anything. He was so far from the boy who looked at me with disgust after spilling on Stacy's dress. "Who cared that it was the end of my family. Officially. Before the engagement, my parents still sometimes talked. They were separated, but they took a long time to sign the official papers. But then Stacy posted about the engagement. My mom signed the papers and got on a plane."

Jack's face was perfect, a sad smile that wasn't quite pitying but showed he felt for me. I wondered what my dad talked about with Stacy and Nate. Did Jack know the whole story? About Brady and why it was so hard for my parents to be around each other? Probably not if he didn't even know my mom was in Italy.

"So you still had some hope before then. Why did they take so long to sign the papers?"

We waited while Jen set my latte on the table. I didn't know how Jack had already managed to eat half his muffin. I took off the lid and blew on the liquid inside, making a tunnel in the foam. When I looked up, Jack was staring at my lips. He shifted in his seat and directed his gaze back at my eyes. Were his cheeks turning red or was that the brake lights of the car driving out of the lot outside?

"How do you like working here?" I asked, trying to redirect the conversation.

He frowned at me slightly but allowed it. "I like it. Last year I worked at—" he dropped his voice to a conspiring whisper "—the coffee corporation that won't be named. But I like that this place is local. Fewer rules and cameras."

I smiled. "Less evidence of you going rogue while making caffeinated beverages?"

"You wouldn't believe what I can get away with. We can't let The Man see me add an extra pump of lavender to a pretty girl's drink."

Usually, a comment like that made me want to wrinkle my nose. But I couldn't with Jack looking at me with a perfect mix of teasing, embarrassment, and… admiration. There wasn't another word for that look in his eyes.

"Shut up," I mumbled, fighting a smile. He grinned at me, that genuine, unguarded version that made my breath catch.

The doors jingled as a group of professors walked in. Jack sighed. "I should probably get back to it."

"Have a good shift." I gave him a finger wave and he returned it with enthusiasm. I hid my laugh by taking a sip of my coffee.

I took out my homework and had a productive morning, feeling lighter than I had since my mom called me this morning. Every time I glanced at Jack, he was looking back, taking the time to smile.

My chest was warm and fluttery from more than the strong espresso.

Jack called me pretty.

FIVE

BEFORE I KNEW IT, the weather was changing. One of the servers quit at the restaurant and we were all pulling extra hours to fill the gap, making even more people talk about quitting with the extra workload. I begged Priya to stay after she dealt with an especially difficult table and only got a four-dollar tip on a sixty-dollar order.

"But the people! I could just drop out of school and find a job as a stripper somewhere. Who needs to be a doctor?"

"Don't be a cliche. If you hate serving tables for tips, I bet you'll hate lap dances more."

Priya raised her eyebrows and pursed her lips. "I guess you're right."

"Plus, if you quit, we won't get to hang out anymore."

"Why do you think I want to quit so badly?"

"Hey!" I smacked Priya with the money I'd just picked up off one of my tables.

Priya laughed. "You know, we could always hang out outside of work."

"I'm weird outside of work," I said as I tucked the money into my sticker-covered black book. I loved the sight of it nearly bursting with cash and tickets. A physical sign of my hard work.

"How weird?"

"I have a Taylor Swift shrine in my apartment."

Priya laughed almost as hard as she had when Jack yelled about the fried pickles. "I have to see that." She looked at the schedule taped above the computer and pointed to a day. "We're hanging out after we get off lunch shift on Sunday."

I felt the familiar hesitance I experienced when people tried to make their way closer than arm's length. But I'd known Priya for months now and I liked spending time with her. Maybe I didn't need to work on going further than fun hookups. Maybe I just needed to work on letting people in on a platonic level to start. "Okay, but don't say I didn't warn you."

Priya loved the shrine. She solemnly knelt in front of it and vowed to always shake it off. Matty approved of her immediately. Andrew and Lynn came over too and we ordered pizzas. Matty distributed blankets. I hadn't laughed so much in a long time. We were trying to decide on a movie when my phone buzzed.

It was a text from Jack. I'd texted him after he'd talked with me about my mom to say thanks, but hadn't heard much from him since. My heart most definitely did *not* skip a beat.

What are you doing?

Movie night. You?

Plans fell through and I am desperate to avoid this party my room-mate is throwing.

It's Sunday

Alas, my roommate doesn't care about how restful this day is supposed to be or school nights.

Alas?

It felt right in the moment. What movie are you watching?

"Who are you texting over there, miss secret smiles?" Matty asked. Alas, before I could answer, he'd plucked my phone from my hands. "Oh my god. Can I *please* respond?" The percentage of times I let Matty handle my over-text flirting was nearly one hundred.

Did I want to flirt with Jack? We'd barely talked since that early morning when he took his break with me and if I was being honest, I'd missed interacting with him. That meant I wanted to flirt, right? And he did text me first. Wasn't that him—

"Oh look, he already replied."

"Wait, Matty, what did you say?" I reached for my phone, shocked Matty hadn't waited for my permission.

"I could tell from the look on your face you wanted to do it, so I did it."

"But…" I had lots of reasons why I didn't want to date Jack. The first one being his connection with Stacy. The second one being… well, maybe I only had the one.

Matty passed me back my phone. My palms were sweating as I read the last two texts.

Come over and help us pick one ;)

I would if I knew where "over" was :)

Four pairs of eyes watched me expectantly, even though Matty was the only one who knew what was happening on the screen. Matty and Andrew shared a look, Andrew asking who it was and Matty mouthing back Jack's name. Andrew mouthed back *who?* Matty exaggerated the shape of Jack's name. Andrew looked confused. They caught me staring at them. Why I could read both their lips so easily and they never seemed able to communicate?

"Who?" Andrew asked out loud.

"Jack."

"From the wedding?"

"From the coffee shop?"

"With the fried pickles?" Andrew, Lynn, and Priya asked at the same time.

"Jack gets around," Matty said, laughing.

"Invite him!" Andrew shook my leg. He sat on a pile of blankets in front of me. Matty clasped his hands as if begging, going on his knees next to Andrew.

"Please! We're tired of you living your love life through us!"

"I do not!"

"We know you listen."

"I put in headphones!"

"*Sure,*" Matty drew the word out. I knew what I would have to do to make him stop. I typed out the address of our apartment.

Matty clapped and sat back down. "I told Jack he could help us pick a movie so now we have to wait for him. Shouldn't be long. He seems eager."

So, we sat and waited. We probably could have talked, but I was busy trying to think why Jack texted me to start with. Lynn was on her phone, emailing students who had questions about the lab she taught as a TA. Priya was in the kitchen, snooping in our fridge as she ate another slice of pizza. Andrew and Matty pretended they weren't doing God-knows-what under the blankets. Turns out they were thumb wrestling. When the blanket had slipped, I had been terrified for a second about what I would see, only for it to be two thumbs sticking up in the air instead of something far less PG.

It took Jack ten minutes to knock on our door. Matty and Andrew turned to look at me, expecting me to open it even though I'd have to crawl over them to get there. When they didn't move, I sighed and did just that.

Jack's cheeks were still red from the cold outside. He'd been wiping his nose on his sleeve when I opened the door and dropped his hand quickly. "Hey!"

"Hey." I was blushing. And felt awkward. Because his brown hair looked ruffled from the wind and his bulky hoody looked soft and his cheeks were still red. His eyes looked a perfect mix of brown and green. Bright and a bit timid. I tried to remember how he'd looked at the wedding, staring at me with disgust after I spilled on Stacy's dress, but that guy and the one that stood in front of me waiting to be let in were two entirely different people.

I swallowed and stepped back. "There's pizza." I gestured to the counter. The open box contained a smattering of crusts and a single slice of cheese left, folded from Priya grabbing her slice.

Jack huffed a laugh. "That's so generous but I did already eat."

"Thank god." Everyone laughed at my relief. "So, you know Matty. That's Andrew, Lynn, and Priya. Everyone, this is Jack."

Greetings were exchanged and I took stock of the seating situation with new eyes. Lynn and Priya were sitting on the big couch, Priya smiling with her legs taking up any possibility of free space. The chair I had been sitting in could fit two. Matty and Andrew often made it work at least. But it was a tight fit and…

I looked at Jack. "You can take the chair." I went to sit on the ground next to Matty. I yelped when Matty pushed my butt and practically threw me onto the chair.

"There's room for two!" he sang.

I was too embarrassed to look up as Jack came and sat next to me. He perched on the edge of the cushion and angled his body so only our knees touched. "What are we watching?"

We picked a horror film and Matty got the lights. Jack carefully eased back. I'm not sure how we managed to sit as long as we did barely touching. I could feel his heat between us. I felt it when he relaxed back into the cushions, finally allowing his thigh to press against mine. I snuck a glance his way and barely stopped a laugh when I saw him blinking slowly only a few minutes into the movie. The next time I looked, our bodies were pressed together from knee to shoulder and he had fallen asleep, head resting back and mouth slightly open. Even when Lynn let out a small shriek and Matty jumped hard enough to rock our chair, Jack didn't stir. The only time he moved was to shift closer to my warmth.

Why the sight of Jack sleeping and leaning close made my chest tight, I didn't know. I just knew I would be happy not to move until the movie was over. Maybe even longer.

At one point, the demon in the movie appeared on the ceiling. I couldn't stop myself from jumping and yelping. Jack shifted but didn't fully wake up. He turned to me and put a hand reassuringly on my thigh, muttering, "S'okay." He went still again, the heat of his hand seeping through my thin leggings and his minty breath fluttering against my neck.

Matty looked back and laughed at my wide eyes. He helpfully

passed me one of their blankets and I spread it over us as well as I could without waking Jack up.

The movie ended with one final jump scare we all reacted to loudly enough to finally wake Jack. He gave me a sheepish smile and pulled his hand away quickly. "Sorry." He cleared his throat; it was rough from sleep after that nap. "What are we watching next?"

"Well, *we're* going to watch a romcom so we can sleep tonight. You didn't even watch the last one so we'll see what happens on your end," Matty said.

Jack grimaced. "Sorry. I had an early morning at work."

"How early do you have to get there?" Lynn asked.

"I've been doing some opening shifts this week so around five. It wouldn't be so bad, but my roommate is a bit of a night owl and isn't that quiet so it's hard to go to bed early."

"Yeah," Andrew agreed, laughing, "Clearly you can sleep with noise around so he must be really loud."

Even in the lights of the credits, I could see Jack's blush as he admitted, "I'm usually a pretty light sleeper. I just got too comfortable I guess."

Did he mean being with me helped him sleep? Or the chair? Of the cozy atmosphere let off by our Taylor Swift candle and the smell of the woods? Maybe—

Jack found my hand and squeezed it. I smiled in the darkness, not caring if Jack could see it. He meant being with me.

Jack managed to stay awake through the second movie. I could tell Matty was trying to discreetly watch him, especially whenever Andrew nuzzled closer or snuck a kiss. Matty was protective of Andrew and when I brought over a boy, we judged his reaction to Matty's relationship quickly. It was usually very telling about the type of person he was.

As far as I could tell, Jack was completely comfortable. We stretched and I stood quickly to get out of the bubble of his heat and smell that I had fallen into. I went to the bathroom and when

I came back, they were all talking about Halloween plans for the following weekend.

"My friend Dee is throwing a big party! You guys should come," Lynn said.

"Dee's house is huge and he's on the track team," Andrew said, wiggling his eyebrows at Matty. They had initially bonded through their admiration of the track team.

"Roly and I are down!" Matty would do anything Andrew was excited about. I would have to come along. "Want to come with, Jack?"

"I wish I could, but my dads called this morning and told me my little sister was sad I wouldn't be there for trick-or-treating. She's only eight and I can't disappoint her, so I'll be in Denver."

"Your dads?" Matty asked, eyes widening.

Jack just nodded, clearly used to having to clarify.

I sat on the arm of the chair, feet on the cushions. I stuck my cold toes under Jack's thigh and he shot me a smile. "Matty thinks kids raised by same-sex parents are the only reason the future has hope," I told him.

Jack snorted. "Obviously. Look at me making the world a better place one latte at a time."

We laughed.

Andrew turned around to fully face Jack. "Can I ask, I mean tell me if you don't want to talk about it, but as a gay man hoping to raise kids one day, what was it like? I've never met someone with two dads before."

"I don't mind, it's just hard to explain sometimes. It's all I've known, you know? My biological mom and biological dad, who I call Dad, tried to make it work for a bit when she was pregnant, but she didn't want kids and isn't in the picture now. They were super young, you know? My dad was happy to raise me, and he moved to a more inclusive suburb than the rural town he grew up in. That was when he started dating my pop. By the time I have memories, it's only of their happiness together and being a family."

"Were you ever bullied or anything about it?"

"Not really. Dad's a teacher and Pop is one of the soccer coaches. He's a big guy and kids didn't mess with him and my school district had a strict policy against bullying. There were a few jabs, but nothing that would have made me wish I had a different life."

Andrew was nodding. He and Matty kept exchanging looks. It was adorable. Jack answered all their questions and even talked about how when he became best friends with Nate, his dads and Stacy became close friends as well. Matty remembered a gay couple at the wedding and was thrilled to realize those were Jack's dads.

The night grew late. Priya was the first to leave, complaining about a paper she put off until the last minute. She hugged me tight at the door and made me promise we'd hang out again outside of work soon. Lynn got up to go next and after a brief discussion, Andrew and Matty went with her to spend the night at Andrew's place. Matty gave me an encouraging look as he left with his backpack. I cleared my throat, finding myself very alone with Jack.

"I should probably head out too." He didn't sound excited by the idea.

"You think your roommate is still partying?"

"I do. He's… not easy to live with. That's why I've been trying so hard to get Nate to transfer here for next semester so we can find a place."

I looked away.

"You don't like him?" Jack asked softly.

"It's not him," I said, sighing. Jack looked confused, but the guy from the wedding was still far away so I was encouraged to keep talking. "It's just, school and my life in Fort Collins have always been my escape from the family drama. I love being my own person here. And now, Nate comes here to see you. Then, if Nate moves here, Stacy and my dad come to see him."

Jack looked even more confused. "Won't Stacy and your dad come to see you?"

I almost laughed. "My dad and I aren't close like that. My parents don't come to visit me."

"Why not?"

I shrugged. Because they were too busy making their own lives? Because as a family, there was too much hurt between us? Because even in high school, I had to parent myself and didn't need them now? "We just aren't and I like it that way."

Jack didn't look like he believed me, but he nodded anyway. "I guess if you're happy with things like they are, being resistant to change is understandable. I can give you space if you wa—"

"No, it's okay." The thought of Jack leaving me alone wasn't nearly as pleasant as it might have been a month ago. "I don't mind you and I'm sure I would like Nate if I got to know him better."

I received a smile for my effort. "I can work with not being minded. But I would prefer a step further." Jack paused. He bit his lip, and I couldn't look away from the sight. One of his canines was a bit crooked and he dragged his lip, pink and full, under it. I wanted to pull it out from between his teeth and catch it in my own. Crap. I wanted to kiss him. I *really* wanted to kiss him. "Would you want to get dinner or something this week? Before I go home on Friday?"

Even with the heat and looks between us, I wasn't expecting this. A big part of me just expected us to fuck and then I'd lose interest and that would be that. Just like all the partners before. The heat was the fun part, and I wasn't in the practice of drawing it out.

I couldn't remember the last time I went on a date that wasn't scheduled over a dating app and left unrepeated. Sometimes I daydreamed about situations like this, but they never worked out as they did in my head. The person turned out to be an asshole. Or left for Italy. Or I lost interest.

"I… I'm kind of busy this week." I paused, about to leave it at that. Yet I remembered Andrew telling me I didn't need to be afraid of commitment, that it was almost always worth a heartbreak if that's what it came to, and that it got easier with practice. I thought of my dad and his emails and his therapist saying I shut people out. I thought of Matty, telling me sometimes it made him sad that I didn't let anyone else in because he loved me so much and thought the world would be better if I shared more of myself. I thought of lying in bed after a phone call with my mom and hearing soft voices on the other side of the wall. Maybe I did live my love life through Matty. "But I don't work next Wednesday," I finally said. My heart was beating like crazy and my palms were sweating. It was just dinner, just a suggestion of a free night.

I was terrified.

Jack smiled, showing his crooked tooth fully and I calmed slightly at the sight of his happiness. He wanted this and I had to admit to myself I did too. Maybe it would be okay. Maybe I could trust his interest in me. "Wednesday it is. Want me to pick you up?"

I shook my head quickly. "I'll meet you. We can figure out where over text." The mention of driving set my anxiety off and suddenly I just wanted to be alone to think this through. To make sure this was what I wanted without Jack looking at me.

"Okay." Jack took a step back. I hadn't realized how close we were standing. "I'll text you. Thanks for letting me crash movie night."

I nodded and watched him leave, locking the door behind him. I breathed in deep and tried to think of a nice way to word a text to cancel the date.

But I couldn't think past the fluttering in my stomach. His absence was supposed to make me think more clearly, but the last couple of hours flooded my head. I could still smell him on me. Feel his body pressed close to mine. His hand on my thigh. I could hear the cadence of his deep breathing and his voice rough as he assured me it was okay. I'd done a good job ignoring the heat all this had stirred low in my stomach, but it had been building, and now, alone, all I could think about was release.

I brought the blanket we'd been using to bed with me, thoughts full of Jack as my hands drifted lower and his smell filled my head. I could still feel the heat of his hand on my thigh and to start, I imagined him dragging it upwards. Even just picturing it, my breath caught.

When I finished, I knew it had been too easy to get off. I knew my body had been wanting him since he sat next to me on the couch. Since he texted me first. Maybe even since he yelled at me at the wedding because now, I had to agree with Matty, it was hot.

His smell in my nose and my body not quite satisfied, I wished I had invited him into my room instead of out the door.

I curled up with my head resting on the blanket. I'd never felt like this before. When my phone pinged with a goodnight text from Jack, my smile was for me alone in the darkness of my room.

"Don't get used to it." Habit alone reminded me to whisper the words. People were meant to be enjoyed, but not relied on. Not trusted. I had Matty and that was all I needed.

Yet I still couldn't think of a good excuse to get out of Wednesday night. Instead of canceling, I sent a goodnight text back.

SIX

ANDREW, Matty, and I were a hit when we walked into Dee's party as the three Belcher kids from Bob's Burgers. They were simple costumes and so fun. I was Gene, Andrew was an adorable Louise, and Matty the perfect Tina.

Matty was way too in character and got hilariously sloppier as we drank. His monotone ramblings about boys, butts, and unicorns before dropping into a terrible twerk had tequila coming out of my nose at one point. The party was bright and loud. Crowded and humid. I was buzzed enough to ignore the people who thought a costume gave them an excuse to act like assholes. Andrew kept us hydrated, refilling our waters and reminding us about the realities of hangovers as he drank twice as much as Matty and me and handled his alcohol way better.

In little time, it was Lynn and me talking while Andrew and Matty disappeared to find a corner to make out in. "Can I have a drink?" she asked. I offered her the tequila bottle Matty and I had been sharing. We'd been sharing with Matty and Lynn and it wasn't even half empty, but my head was pleasantly light. I could probably even keep up a conversation with the girl dressed as a half-assed cat I kept looking at all night. I told Matty she was one drink, and I was far beyond one drink. But I was also perfectly content right here. It was a content drunk.

I wasn't thinking about the boy who would only be a half sip or checking my phone for messages from him.

"I hate tequila. It gives me headaches." Lynn grimaced as she lowered the bottle.

"Want some water?" Thanks to Andrew, I'd been double fisting all night.

Lynn grinned. "Nah, water is meant for chugging right before bed. My hangovers aren't that bad yet to need to pace myself."

I lowered my voice. "You lucky son of a bastard."

Lynn laughed. "You sounded just like Gene."

I giggled. "I hadn't meant to."

We both fell to the freedom of drunk laughter, reminding each other of funny scenes from the show until we were acting said scenes out and barely exchanging words between laughs. Lynn twerking like Tina was even better than Matty's and might be the funniest thing I'd seen this year.

I looked around for Andrew. He'd told me to slow down, and without him near I took another drink of tequila. My phone buzzed in my shorts pocket. A text from Jack. *What are you wearing?*

My cheeks had felt numb, but they were pleasantly warm now. I sent him back a gif of Gene dancing.

Hot.

Thanks, that was clearly the goal of the night.

So, Amelie went to bed early. I'm almost back to Fort Collins.

Come!

Where?

I'm not sure, I'll ask someone.

I looked up. Lynn was talking to one of the track players, hip-cocked and smile wide. I didn't want to interrupt that. I stumbled off, clutching my bottle and too far gone to panic when I couldn't find Matty and Andrew right away. I went to look for them upstairs.

I mumbled apologies as I bumped into people in the hall. I said hi to Dee, remembering it was his house and thanking him for the invite. We did shots together and I complimented his Power Rangers outfit. I found a bathroom and decided it was a good idea to stop for a second. While peeing, I checked for my phone. I'd just had it, hadn't I? But it wasn't in my pocket or my hands or on any of the bathroom surfaces, which were in desperate need of cleaning. I finished peeing and went in search of my phone, wondering if Jack was still texting. He'd probably just go home when I didn't respond. I tried not to, but the drunk was quickly shifting, and I felt my eyes well up. What if he didn't see my funny costume?

I was too drunk. I needed more water. I went to the kitchen and was refilling my water when I felt a hand on my shoulder. "There you are!"

I turned and it was Jack. "Thank god." I didn't hesitate. I stepped close and wrapped my arms around him, resting my spinning head on his shoulder. He smelled so good. His red flannel was soft under my cheek. I pulled back a bit.

"Are you a lumber-Jack?" I laughed too hard at my own joke.

Jack chuckled. He leaned in close. "Every year."

I laughed even harder. Jack rubbed my back and called something over my shoulder. I heard Matty respond and released Jack, turning too quickly in my dizzy state. Matty caught me in a hug and we both stumbled. "Matty! I *lost* you! Then I lost my phone. Then I remembered hangovers and came to get water, but I couldn't find you!" I held up my water and Matty grabbed it to take a drink, one arm still around my shoulder.

"I'm sorry. I thought you would stay with Lynn. Andrew was just looking so delicious. I think I found a pink bunny ear kink."

I pouted, stepping out of Matty's arm. I poked the hickey darkening on his neck. "You can't leave me alone with a bottle of tequila. Asshole."

"If you guys are ready to leave, I can drive you back," Jack said. He had that concerned look of a DD surrounded by drunk people at a house party. An underage DD, I just remembered. I went back to his side and smiled when his arm went around me.

"But I can't find my phone."

"It's right here, Roly," Andrew said, handing it to me. His hair was a mess and he'd lost his bunny ears somewhere. Matty looked put out about it. "You gave it to Dee to put in the address."

"I did?"

Jack laughed, his arm solid and warm around my waist. "Shall we?"

I let him lead me out of the party, Matty and Andrew holding each other and following sloppily, calling out goodbyes to Lynn.

It was annoying that Andrew was still the second most sober when we got to our apartment. He answered Jack's questions as Matty and I sucked down more water and ordered pizza off Matty's phone.

"How much did you guys drink?" Jack asked.

"I don't know about me, I had a could other drinks but we were just sharing that bottle Roly has and I told them not to drink anything else."

I looked down and realized I was still holding the tequila bottle. It was a little over half empty.

Jack laughed. "Suddenly their behavior at the wedding makes more sense."

"Yeah, they're a couple of lightweights."

I narrowed my eyes at them.

"Roly, focus, this is important!" Matty said, drawing back my attention. "Do we need cheesy bread or just the two pizzas?"

"Matty, don't be dumb. Of *course* we need cheesy bread."

"But do you ever think about how we're just paying more for a smaller pizza with one less ingredient?"

I considered that. "But it's got more cheese than pizza so it's more ingredients. More special ingredients than marni...mara... marinara." Matty high-fived me when I got the word out.

Jack and Andrew were laughing where they sat on the couch. I went toward the sound and sat next to Jack, far closer than I meant to. Oh well. I put my head on his shoulder, breathing him in.

"How are you feeling?" he asked quietly. Andrew was in the kitchen now, laughing as he helped Matty put in his card information.

"I feel a bit dizzy, not gonna lie."

"Pizza will help with that."

"I feel like puking might help more. Then pizza."

Jack considered this, then stood, holding out a hand. "Let's go hang out in the bathroom just in case."

"Not you. Just me. Gene Belcher puking is *not* sexy."

"If anyone can pull it off, you can."

I went with Jack to the bathroom. He sat on the edge of the tub while I puked and offered me a water glass as soon as I was done. I sat back against the wall. I sipped the cold water and caught my breath, thoroughly embarrassed. Jack flushed the toilet and stepped around me to sit at my side. "It's okay, Roly. Happens to the best of us."

"You probably regret leaving Denver early now. Why did you come back tonight?"

Jack smiled and brought out his phone. He pulled up messages from Matty. It was a lot of pictures of the three of us and progressively more misspelled texts telling Jack I wanted him there. I pushed his phone back and groaned. "He's drunk. You didn't have to."

"It looked like fun and it has been. When you aren't spilling on Stacy's wedding dress, you being drunk is pretty funny."

Faster than I thought possible, my eyes filled with tears. Jack made a horrified noise and pulled me close. "I ruined her dress! It was probably hundreds of dollars and I ruined it!"

"No, no. It's okay. She didn't want to ever wear it again. No one is mad. It's okay, Roly. I'm sorry I brought it up."

Now I was hiccupping and crying into Jack's chest. "Now I'm not even fun anymore!" I wailed.

Jack laughed. I think I felt him kiss the top of my head. "You're just fine. I'm really happy I'm here."

"You don't hate me? You hated me when I spilled on her."

"I don't hate you. I just thought I was standing up for Stacy, but I should have let her handle it. Especially since she wasn't even mad. I'm sorry I yelled at you. I'm sorry we started on the wrong foot."

"Me too. You smelled too good for me to keep hating you."

"I've been driving and trick-or-treating all day. There's no way I smell that—"

The doorbell rang. I sat up quickly, grateful the puking had taken the edge off of my dizziness.

"Pizza!" I whispered in excitement. Jack let his head fall back as he laughed. He didn't bother to help me as I scrambled over his legs to the door.

I hadn't seen Jack since I passed out on the couch with a half-eaten stick of cheesey bread in hand, so on Wedsnesday night I was already blushing as I braked in front of the bistro style restaurant we were meeting in for dinner. It had been a twenty-minute bike ride from my place. I wiped my sweaty forehead and hoped my deodorant wouldn't fail me as I locked up Trevor and went inside.

I found Jack sitting at one of the center tables. He stood with a smile as I got close. Then seemed to not know why he stood and sat back down with a wave.

Why? Why did he have to be so cute?

"Hey!" he said loud enough to turn heads. He lowered his voice. I smiled at his evident nerves and felt my own settle. "I missed seeing you at the Moonbean."

"Yeah… I was honestly too embarrassed about Halloween to come in Monday. You're lucky I showed up tonight."

Jack smiled. "I really am."

I melted. "Shut up."

Looking around to avoid him seeing my renewed blush, I took in the small, intimate place. The walls were dark green with gold swirls that matched the little lamps on every table. It felt like an old-timey movie. Like women should be in flapper dresses and men should be puffing cigars. Instead, it smelled clean, and people laughed easily as they sipped wine or craft beers. I watched the servers move casually from table to table, only two of them needed in the small space. Longing stirred in my chest.

"I like this place," I said.

"Me too. My dads and I came here after we moved me into the dorms last year. Pop liked the beer." He patted the beer menu and sighed with all the longing of a nearly-twenty-one-year-old. "One day."

I laughed. "Should I get one just to make you jealous?" Then I cringed at the thought of drinking. "Never mind, too soon."

Jack laughed. I loved making him laugh. "Did you feel just awful the next day?"

"Not so bad. I think the pizza and puking helped."

Jack nodded seriously. "It usually does."

"I don't really remember why you came back."

"Amelia went a little hard. She had her candy bag full and was crashing from the sugar by nine, so instead of staying the night, I came back when Matty texted."

"Is it a long drive?"

"Nah. We live about five minutes away from Stacy's house."

I didn't tell him I had no idea where in Denver Stacy, and now my dad, lived. I just smiled and nodded. Between exchanges with the server, Jack told me about his little sister's costume, Sponge-Bob, and trick-or-treating with her. Then he told me more about Amelia in general. His dads adopted her when she was three and

Jack was fifteen. It was clear he loved being an older brother and his sister sounded like such a character.

"Do you have any siblings?" he asked.

As always, the question stabbed a little. I never knew what to say. Saying no felt like a betrayal of my brother. Saying that I used to made for awkward and painful conversations and pitying looks. I just shook my head and took a huge bite of the chips and cashew queso we got for an appetizer.

"Oh right, I guess they would have been at the wedding. It's good you have Matty. He seems close enough to be your brother."

I nodded, ignoring another crack of pain in my chest. The guilt I sometimes felt over my closeness with Matty was hard to swallow. "He's been my best friend since third grade."

"I think it says a lot about a person when they hang onto their friends."

What did it say about me that Matty is the only friend I have from before college? "Are you just saying that because you and Nate have been friends so long?"

"Yes. I'm trying to make you understand how great I am."

I was starting to. "Eh, we'll see."

The conversation turned to our interests and hobbies. Jack loved playing soccer and did it on the intermural team here. He was impressed to learn how I grew up doing gymnastics. He loved cats, hated Tuesdays, refused to pick a favorite color, wanted to be a teacher, and grew up baking with his pop. He was working in the back of Moonbean more on the pastry side, which was why I hadn't seen him some mornings.

The food was amazing and conversation only paused when we were taking bites. We were both relaxed in our seats. I felt at ease like I did joking with Priya at work or talking with Andrew. It was rare for me to grow this comfortable with someone so quickly. I found myself eating slowly just to try and make the meal last longer.

By the time we finally left I knew Jack a hundred times better, but I'd kept a lot of my answers to his questions vague. I didn't want to scare him off or tell him how much I hated talking about my family or remembering my childhood. Matty was my one bright spot and Jack already knew him. Maybe one day I'd let Jack in more, but for now, I liked that he thought I was normal. That my parent's divorce was my biggest scar.

When the check came, I reached for it and Jack smacked my hand away. "I have money just for this. You can get the next one." His words were a bit confusing. Did he have to save money just for this? I felt guilty watching him pay. Still, warmth fluttered in my stomach with the promise of a second date.

We went outside and I stopped at the bike rack by the entrance. Jack kept going and turned when he noticed I wasn't with him. "You biked?"

"Yeah. This is Trevor. Got to get my exercise somehow, right?"

He frowned. "But you live so far away."

"Not that far. You can bike almost anywhere in this town."

He still looked skeptical. I willed him not to offer a ride. I hated telling people no and trying to get them to understand how much I loved the freedom of my bike and how I hated leaving it behind.

And how little I trusted people behind the wheel.

"If you want, it could fit in my car and I can give you a ride."

"No, thanks." I started unlocking Trevor, avoiding Jack's eyes.

Jack came up behind me. "But if we go by my car, I was thinking it would be a little more private if I were to kiss you."

We were right in front of the restaurant's windows and cast in their warm light. My inhale was a little shaky and my tone wasn't right when I said, "Who said I wanted to kiss you?"

"I'm sorry, I shouldn't have—"

I winced and grabbed his arm. "I was teasing. I do want to kiss you, but just, not yet."

My gut was telling me to wait, to move slow. The faster this went, the faster it would end. And as much as my feelings for Jack terrified me, I wasn't ready to let them go. I wasn't ready for him to find out so much about me that it became too much. To look into my raw eyes and see who I was and find out I wasn't for him.

Jack smiled sweetly, looking maybe even a little relieved? He kissed my cheek. "Okay."

I watched him walk to his car, enjoying the view of his ass and the way he kept glancing back at me. On my ride home I felt light as a feather cruising under the streetlights.

SEVEN

EVERY THURSDAY after the lunch rush, our favorite regular comes in. Priya and I always work the shift in an attempt to see her. We were "keeping her relevant" as she liked to say about our lessons on pop culture. Harry Styles played in the background as I brought Maya her standard iced tea with two lemons. Priya sat at the table, showing Maya Harry's google images when I sat down.

"He looks very nice."

"Oh, he is," Priya said.

"You've met him?"

"No, it's just his thing."

"I see."

I laughed at Maya's sincere tone. She turned her attention to me as Priya rolled her eyes and went to seat the young couple who walked in. They were the only other table. "So, Miss Cheryl, how are classes going?"

I let Maya call me Cheryl because she told me it was her late sister's name. She called me by name as often as possible, like she missed the sound of it. "They're fine."

"What are you taking?"

"Just some business classes."

"You know, when I asked Miss Priya that question, she listed off every course."

I looked down, struggling to remember what names each course had. I swear they all blurred together. "Priya is interested in her classes. They're all different and she likes them."

"Do you think someone interested in business would say the same thing?"

"No one is actually interested in business."

Maya scoffed. "Check your privilege there, Miss Cheryl. Remember, I had two kids at your age and never even thought college was an option. I would have given my arm to take business classes."

I winced and nodded. I was lucky to be in school, I knew that. I was lucky that it was a necessary evil I had access to in order to have the future I wanted.

Maya's thoughts went in the same direction. "You know, Priya also talks about how excited she is to become a doctor. You've never mentioned what you want to do."

Here I shrugged. "I'm just trying to get a job somewhere new. I've been thinking about taking more marketing courses, but I don't really care what job that is." The hollow panic at the thought of the office job I would most likely end up in was easy to swallow. "I just want to be able to afford the life I want."

Maya laughed. "You ever consider marrying rich?"

"Maya!" I joined her in laughing and heard my name called from the back. As soon as Maya walks in the door, Priya or I put in her order. I got up to get her BLT with red onions and a side of sweet potato fries.

When I came back to Maya's table, Priya was reseated and clearly gossiping. She winked at me as I sat down.

Maya pounced. "You have a boyfriend? What happened to Emily?"

I glared at Priya, set down Maya's sandwich, and took a seat. "Emily went to Italy. And Jack isn't my boyfriend."

"Would you like him to be? Will he be your rich husband?"

I laughed. "No, he isn't rich. At least, I don't think he is."

Maya was insistent. "But would you like him to be your boyfriend?"

I fiddled with the pepper shaker. I was trying to stay open-minded with Jack, trying not to fall back on old habits, but the thought of it made my stomach flutter with nerves.

Maya leaned forward, concern creasing her wrinkled forehead further. "Did you get your heartbroken, Miss Cheryl? Is that why you look so scared right now?"

"No. Well, not romantically. I just…" I spilled some pepper on the table. Priya's table waved her over and she reluctantly left. I took a deep breath. Maybe practicing with opening up started with a nosy regular who loved to ask personal questions. She already knew about the wedding and my mom being in Italy. Maya was incredibly easy to talk to. "The suburb I grew up in was pretty close-knit, but I had a hard time making friends. My brother died right before I started kindergarten and my home life got… well, I was a sad kid. I was avoided like being sad was infectious. I have one friend I made when I was young, but other-wise, I learned I didn't need a lot of people in my life. That they tended to let me down or leave when I did let them in and they couldn't handle it."

"Have you ever had a significant other?"

"No."

Maya frowned. She took a bite of her BLT and let the word sit between us. I thought of mornings alone with quiet murmurs on the other side of the wall. The loneliness the gentle moment stirred.

But what would happen to Matty and Andrew if they broke up? The nights would be spent crying and wouldn't it hurt so much more to wake up alone after love like that?

What if they stayed together even when the love ended and they spent the next decade hurting each other?

Was it worth it?

"How will you ever know if you don't try?"

I didn't realize I wondered the question out loud. I swallowed. "But people always end up hurting me."

"Not your Matty or Andrew or Priya. You've told me before you love waiting tables, Cheryl. You see so many people in so many different relationships. You love interacting with them, I've seen it. I don't think other people are the problem." I froze and Maya let me take that in. "If people hurt you, it's a matter of learning what you can forgive and what you can't. When to give second chances for the sake of companionship. People aren't perfect, but we weren't made to be alone."

I sighed and sat back, sweeping my small pile of pepper onto the floor. "I'm not alone." Only in the mornings.

Maya pressed on. "Think about this Taylor Swift you had me listen to. How many times do you think she's been let down? Does she let it keep her down? Does she let a bad experience stop her from chasing happiness? Even if you don't know her, think about the woman she is in your head and ask yourself why you admire her and if you could ever try as she does."

Her words rose goosebumps on my arms. I wrapped my arms around my stomach. "This is why everyone needs a wise old lady in their life."

"Don't call me old."

I laughed and got up to refill her tea. The woman chugged it like it was the elixir of life. I thought about her words as I walked and came up with a new refrain in my head that I later wrote on a piece of notebook paper and put on our shrine.

What would Taylor do?

I was sitting in Moonbean the Monday before Thanksgiving. Andrew just left for his class, but I was skipping my next one. The professor didn't take roll and posted most of the material online. I was happier here, doing other homework and talking to Jack each time he came by my table. He kept dropping off origami animals made of receipt paper. I already had a collection growing on my nightstand. He made me bats, frogs, and cranes. He liked making the jumping frogs most though. Sometimes, if he had time, he'd write little notes before folding up the papers, but I liked the animals too much to unfold them. It made him laugh that I refused to ruin his little creations to find out what he was writing.

My phone rang with a call from Matty. "My sister is pregnant," he started as soon as I picked up.

"Matty! That's gr—"

"My mom packed everything and they're already driving down. They want me to meet them in Grand Junction for Thanksgiving."

My heart broke at how guilty he sounded. He should be happy and celebrating, not worried about me. "You should go! She's been trying to get pregnant for forever. I can just hang out here for Thanksgiving. Priya is doing a Friendsgiving thing with some of the other people at work. Honestly, I might prefer that."

"But you were saying last week that Stacy was already calling you to see what you liked to eat."

"Yet another painful reminder of how little attention my father paid to me. He should know what I like on Thanksgiving. I don't want to go to Denver."

"But he's trying, Roly."

"If I change my mind, I'll figure something out. If I want to, I can find another ride. Do you know how many people go to Denver just for the airport? Don't worry about me! Be excited for your sister!"

Matty took a deep breath. He worried about me too much. I knew he was biting his bottom lip on the other side of our call. He took his job of being my person very seriously and I loved him for it, but I knew we needed some boundaries. Probably. "Alright. She better name it Matty."

I laughed and he told me more about the news. Apparently, Lizzy was already five months in but wanted it to be a surprise. She wasn't going to find out the sex and didn't want to enforce any harmful gender stereotypes. I could practically hear Matty's smile as he talked. He and his sister went through a lot when he came out. Now, she was his biggest supporter in his family.

He sighed. "She's going to be the best mom."

"She really is. And you'll be the best uncle."

"Shit. An uncle! Are you sure you'll be okay without me giving you a ride? I could still drop you off."

"No way. You don't have class after today. Go to your sister's."

"Alright. I'll probably leave early tomorrow. See you at home?"

"I work but I'll get up early to say goodbye."

"Love you bunches."

"Love you too." I hung up and sat back. My phone pinged with a message from Stacy. It was a picture of the groceries she'd just purchased. *Can't wait to see you!*

I would have to tell her sooner than later that I wouldn't be coming. Despite my assurances, I didn't trust anyone but Matty to drive me.

"What's that face?" Jack asked, sitting down across from me. He slid a chocolate croissant my way. Fresh from the oven and gorgeous.

"Thanks." I smiled and bit into it, catching the chocolate as it spilled down my lip. My stomach warmed noting how closely Jack watched my tongue. We still hadn't kissed and were too busy to find time alone.

I thought about kissing him at least once an hour. My vibrator was getting way too much use at night with all my dirty thoughts of Jack and his constant flirty texts. I wanted him so badly it made my breath catch and heart race even when he wasn't sitting beside me watching my lips.

I cleared my throat. "You look tired."

Jack gave me an affronted look. "We don't tell people that."

I laughed. "Did you forget to put on makeup?"

"No." Jack sniffed with mock indignation. "I just didn't sleep much."

"Roommate being loud?"

Jack nodded. He stretched and twisted his head a bit to pop his neck. "I had an early morning too. I'm very ready for vacation. What day are you and Matty heading down?"

"Oh," I looked down, brushing off a few crumbs. "I don't think I'll be going to Denver now. Matty has to go to Grand Junction instead."

"But why does that mean you have to stay?"

"I don't have a car."

I knew the offer was coming and barely contained my wince when he said, "I'll give you a ride."

I took another bite, considering my words. "I know. It's just, I don't really like driving with people I don't..." Trust, is what I wanted to say, but I couldn't' get the word out with Jack looking at me like he was.

"You could drive if that makes you more comfortable."

I hated driving. I did it as rarely as possible. The lack of practice equated to me being one of the worst drivers I knew. I didn't trust myself either.

Jack put his hands on mine, stilling my nervous fingers as they picked at the pastry he probably worked hard on. "I won't pressure you, but I'm generally considered a good driver. I think we would have fun road-tripping."

"It's not even an hour. That's hardly a road trip."

"We'd have fun." He winked. He was keeping it light, but I could tell he wanted this. He wanted my trust and time.

I bit my lip again. His hands were warm and there was still flour around his nails. And in his hair. He had purple bags under his eyes and his mouth, those perfect lips, were quirked in a half-smile and... I would miss him if he left and I stayed here. He already told me his family usually spent Thanksgiving at Stacy's. If I stayed here, everyone but Priya would be gone. My mom would forget to call and she'd probably stay away for Christmas too and then that be my first holiday with Stacy and my dad. Without Jack as a buffer.

Fear climbed up my throat. Anxiety had me flipping my hands to interlock our fingers. I wanted to trust him. He could probably feel how sweaty my palms were.

I nodded, unable to get the words out.

"Great." He smiled down at our hands. I made the right choice. Taylor Swift would have accepted the ride. I just had to keep remembering this moment and how firmly he was holding my hands back. Like he didn't want to let go. I tried not to think about the drive to come. "I was going to leave Wednesday around four-thirty. Does that work for you?" he asked.

I nodded again.

"Alright. I'll see you then. I have to get to class." He kissed my cheek and smelled so wonderful. I wanted to bundle him up and take him home and do dirty things to him. It was hard to let go of his hands.

I watched him leave, paying attention to how well he pulled out of the lot and the complete stop he made before turning into traffic. He used his signal and everything. I blew out a shaky breath.

Matty and I were making coffee the next morning when his phone rang. He raised an eyebrow at me as he answered it, putting his phone on speaker. "What's up, Jack?"

"Hey, Matty! I just was calling because Roly seemed pretty nervous yesterday when she agreed to go to Denver with me."

"Oh, did she?" Matty raised his eyebrows at me. He leaned his hip against the counter, facing me fully with his phone held out between us. I hadn't told him I agreed to let Jack drive me.

"Yeah, and since she trusts you, I was just wondering if there was anything I should do to make her more comfortable on the drive?"

Matty and I melted together. He put a hand on his chest as if it hurt how sweet Jack was. He had to clear his throat to talk. "For sure. She's fine with speeding as long as you're staying with traffic and not going too crazy fast, but always keep space between you and the car ahead. Try not to look away from the road. Ever. Let her play music and directions if you need them. And talk to her enough to distract her, but not so much that she thinks *you're* distracted."

This whole conversation was going to kill me. That Jack would call and Matty would be so ready with an answer. I always liked driving with Matty because he never looked to see how nervous I was. I didn't realize how much he saw and altered his driving to make me more comfortable. I stepped forward and wrapped Matty in a hug. He balanced his phone on my head and hugged me back.

"Okay. Yeah, that makes sense. Anything else?"

"Not really. Just be careful and you should be fine."

"I will. Thanks, Matty! Drive safe, okay?"

"You too. See you after the break!"

"Have fun at your sister's."

They hung up. Matty rubbed my back because I might have been crying a bit. "I think that proves how much Jack deserves a chance."

I nodded. "I know. I haven't even kissed him yet. I'm so scared I'll mess this up."

Matty laughed. "Honey, you would have to mess up astronomically at this point. I don't even know if *you* would be capable."

"That sounds like a challenge."

Matty kissed the top of my head and went to finish packing and say goodbye to Andrew, who had yet to leave Matty's bed.

Eventually, Andrew left too so he could catch his flight home to California. I spent the rest of Tuesday battling my anxiety over the drive. It was less than an hour, but that stretch of I-25 was filled with fast drivers who refused to acknowledge Denver's recent boom and how treacherous the often congested road now was.

I worked the Wednesday lunch shift and biked home quickly so I could be ready by the time Jack arrived. I usually liked to keep my ears free when I biked so I could hear if a car was behind me, but today I put on my favorite podcast, Hooked Up, and tried to distract myself. Riley was telling her cohost Alma about her latest disaster of a date that ended with the guy leaving his number for their server and warning Riley that he was polyamorous and if she couldn't handle stuff like that, he wasn't her guy. Alma was in disbelief until Riley pulled out a picture she took of the check. They dissolved into laughter. The sound was familiar enough to relax my shoulders and I let out a giggle of my own. They went on to debate if polyamory was a good enough excuse to pull a move like that on the very first date, Riley coming to his defense just to make Alma laugh more.

They moved on to their topic for the episode, talking with a renowned therapist about attachment theory. Half an hour later, I was so engrossed in their conversation, I jumped away from the bag I was packing with a yelp when Jack knocked loudly right on time. I pulled out my headphones and took a deep breath before I opened the door.

"Hey!" He smiled. I liked how Jack said "hey" like he was surprised and delighted to see me. Every time.

"Hey yourself." My smile shook a bit. I turned in an attempt to hide it and grabbed one of my bags.

"This all you have?" Jack asked. He was teasing, so I shoved my pillow and black Doc Martins into his arms to make him help carry it all. I had packed with every ounce of anxiety I possessed, meaning three pairs of shoes and an extra couple of jackets, and enough clothes for a trip twice as long. My smaller bag barely zipped.

I caught Jack smelling my pillowcase as he turned for the door.

We loaded everything into the backseat of his burnt-orange Jeep. "You doing okay?" Jack asked, stopping me with a hand on my arm before I could get in.

"Yeah, I'm fine."

"Anything I should know or that you want to talk about before we go?"

I shook my head, grateful he'd called Matty so I didn't have to try and explain. So grateful that I stepped forward and wrapped him in a hug, pressing my cheek into his shoulder. His cologne or deodorant was like a pine forest.

Jack hugged me tight until my body began to relax. "I promise I'll be careful." He ruffled my hair. "Precious cargo and all that."

We both laughed and blushed as I stepped back. "Shut up."

Jack settled himself behind the wheel and handed me the aux cord. "Wanna play music?"

I nodded. "Any preference?"

"I want to hear what you like."

I picked a song and Jack asked me what I liked about it. I never realized how much I associated music with memories, but it turned out I had a story to go with a lot of the songs I listened to on repeat. Most of the Taylor Swift songs I remembered hearing for the first time with Matty. I explained how we used to make dances and how we'd send lyrics to our crushes in middle school. I told Jack about those puberty-heightened small heartbreaks, even telling him I was bisexual and girls were included in the list. It wasn't something I liked talking to most straight guys about, but Jack didn't even blink. I wondered if being raised by two dads taught him how to be a safe space or if he was just naturally so accepting.

Eventually, we found a heartbreak song that Jack admitted he sent to his ex-girlfriend. I laughed and asked for all the details, laughing harder when he blushed and told me it was only three years ago. "You sent a girl a Taylor Swift song when you were *seventeen*?"

I was still nervous about cars passing by too fast and the sudden stop and go of rush hour traffic, but it was almost easy to give Jack my full attention. To stare at his profile and take in his sharp chin and slight Adams Apple. Those pouty lips and how he spoke more out of one half of his mouth. Even though he could probably feel me staring, he studiously kept his eyes on the road, never once forgetting Matty's words.

The drive ended up being twice as long as it should have with the Thanksgiving traffic on the roads. We eventually pulled into an unfamiliar neighborhood. I wished for a useless moment that I could go home instead. My mom still owned the house I grew up in. I had a key and the house sitter's number. I could go there. I didn't have to face this place that contained my dad's new life without us. Jack parked in Stacy's driveway in front of the double garage. It was a typical suburban house, blue-gray in the jeep's headlights with small pine trees dotting the lawn and a mailbox painted to match the siding. I took it in silently.

Did I go up and knock? Text my dad that I was here and see if he came out to get me? Just walk in like it was my new home?

"You okay? Did I traumatize you?" Jack asked, genuine concern pulling at his brows.

"No, you did great. I just… don't want to be here." I admitted this without looking at him and waited for him to jump to Stacy's defense.

"It's not home yet?"

"I've never been here before."

"Oh!" Jack sounded surprised. "Your dad didn't bring you? He's always over here."

I sighed. I didn't want Jack to know how disconnected my dad and I were. How even with my dad trying harder now, our conversations rarely moved past work and my classes. "I met Stacy at the rehearsal dinner."

Jack fell quiet. I stared at the house that was my dad's home. Stacy already found or made a sign that hung over the front door that said, "The Rossi's." I was a Rossi. My mom, my dad, and I were the Rossi's.

I wanted to cry just looking at it.

"I'll go in with you," Jack said.

I nodded, not trusting myself to speak.

"Hey. Look at me." I turned in the seat, biting my lip. His face was shadowed in the light coming off the garage. "This is bullshit for you. I didn't realize how bad it was, but your dad should have at least made sure you knew Stacy before proposing or even making the decision to get serious. You might not be a little kid anymore, but you're still his responsibility. He and your mom made the decision to bring you into this world. You're allowed to be sad they haven't done everything in their power to make it a great place for you."

A tear fell. People didn't come this sweet. "You don't know the full story."

"I know who the parents are and who the kid is. That's enough to tell me whose fault it is that you look more terrified to go inside the house than you were to get in my car."

"You'll come in with me?"

"Yeah, I'll text my dads and let them know. I was going to go in and see Nate anyway. The three of us can go hide in the basement. Stacy will be thrilled we're bonding. We can just leave you alone too if that's what you want."

"I don't want that. I'll hang out with you guys."

Jack smiled and I hated the distance between us. Sucking in a breath, I leaned closer, over the console. I paused. No matter my feeling, consent was impor— Jack tilted his head and closed the distance, hand coming up to cup my jaw.

It was just a light peck before Jack drew back. I could barely see the green in his eyes under the overhead light. His pupils were huge. He looked uncertain. I wanted to wipe the nervous expression from his face forever. I wanted him to trust me as much as I wanted to trust him. I felt everything in me start to warm. I grabbed the front of his hoodie and pulled him close again. I heated to a boil.

He made the perfect sounds. Heavy breathing, little groans, gasps. He was following my lead and I fucking loved it. Everything I did seemed to catch him off guard and excite him further. I unbuckled my seat belt and shifted closer, my hands circling his neck, thumbs catching the movement in his throat as he swallowed. I hummed in approval and his other hand came up, finding my waist, fingertips trailing over the strip of exposed skin.

It was a good kiss. Maybe the best I'd ever had. "Jack," I whispered his name, a desperate prayer that this moment never ended. He moaned, tongue sweeping in and—

The porch light burst to life, startling us both. We were breathing hard as I hastily sat back in my seat, fixing my sweater and patting down my hair.

Stacy and my dad stood on the porch. Ruby started barking at their feet. My dad looked slightly scandalized. Stacy looked the most excited I had ever seen a person. Which was sad considering I just recently attended her wedding. Jack's hand found mine. His words were shaky when he spoke. "I can't even be embarrassed. That was so…"

I smiled and nodded. The kiss was a bit indescribable. "Now I really don't want to go in."

Jack cleared his throat. "I need a second for sure."

I smirked as he shifted his jeans. "The things I want to do to you," I said, his current state bolstering my confidence.

He groaned. "Roly, stop. I'm trying to think about my grandma."

I laughed. Then sighed as Stacy waved impatiently for us to come in. I got out and grabbed my things from the backseat. I had most of it gathered by the time Jack came around to get anything left over.

With my arms so full, Stacy couldn't give me a proper hug. My dad gave me a strained smile before looking back at Jack. "Where's Matty?"

"His sister is pregnant so they're doing Thanksgiving there."

"You could have called me, Roly-Poly. I would have come to get you." My dad was well acquainted with my fear of being in the car.

"It's fine. I had Jack."

Jack looked between us, likely sensing how much more there was to the story than just my nerves about being in the car with someone for the first time. My dad nodded and stepped aside, gesturing for us all to go in.

My dad took most of my things and led the way upstairs and to the guest room.

"Not the guest room, Tom. Roly's room," Stacy interrupted, smiling at me. "It's important she knows she has a place here."

"Uh, thanks." I dropped my stuff by the door. The room was simple, done in green and yellow mostly. Took much paisley. It wasn't great, but it wasn't my room, so it didn't matter if it was my taste or not.

"You have a bathroom right across the hall. It's all yours since Nate has one downstairs and we have the master. I took the liberty of stocking it, but if you don't like any of the products let me know and we'll grab what you're used to. Your father wasn't sure."

I nodded, swallowing the familiar sting. I've been using the same brands I used when we lived together. The same products my mom used. I wondered if it was reasonable that I expected him to know. Matty would be able to pick them out and had before when I asked him to grab things for me from the store. I couldn't excuse ignorance when a man made no attempt to learn. Not once. I was his daughter, and he didn't know anything about me because he never bothered to learn. Didn't even think to go through the effort of asking me when Stacy had brought it up.

"Can I see the rest of the house?"

Stacy was an enthusiastic tour guide. My dad followed, smiling at her in a way that brought up foggy childhood memories. I thought maybe he used to give my mom that look. Jack stayed close to my side, holding my hand even when Nate joined us. Nate raised an eyebrow at it but didn't comment.

"Are you staying for dinner, Jack?"

"If it's cool with you, Stacy."

"Of course. I figured you'd make an appearance at some point tonight. We made enough for everyone. I'll just go call your dads and let them know you're here."

There was a familiarity of long-established habit in their conversation. It reminded me of my parents talking to Matty, including him in plans without a blink. "Sounds good. Mind if we go show Roly the basement?"

"You kids have fun," Stacy said, distracted and already on her phone.

"But leave the door open!" My dad called at our backs.

I rolled my eyes and made a point of closing it when we got to the bottom of the stairs. Jack and Nate wisely kept quiet.

EIGHT

I WOKE up to the sun shining bright outside my window. Rudy had found her way into my room at some point, leaving the door slightly ajar. I couldn't be mad when she was so sweet curled up at my side. She was a beautiful golden lab, still enough of a puppy that her feet and ears were hilariously disproportioned. I scratched her tummy and ignored the smells of breakfast beckoning me from downstairs. This time alone was necessary if I was going to face the day. The first family holiday with my mom gone. The first Thanksgiving I didn't spend in my childhood home with both my parents present. At least, as present as they could be.

I sighed, my stomach rumbling and my bladder telling me it was time. I'd slept in but still felt tired after staying up late with Nate and Jack. The main room of the basement sported a huge TV with two recliners in front of it. It had made my chest tight to see Jack's chair waiting for him and I wondered how often Nate sat down there alone and missed his best friend. I could practically smell the hours of video game playing that had taken place between them growing up.

We had shifted things around to pull the couch against the back wall closer to the TV. Jack and I sat there, not nearly as close as I wanted to sit by my stepbrother was in the room. Jack had held my hand as he and Nate caught up. The stress of the day didn't leave me feeling very social, but I enjoyed listening in on this aspect of Jack's life as he interacted with his best friend. He was pushing hard for Nate to transfer, showing him apartments on his phone. I didn't know Nate well enough to say for certain, but it did seem like he was hiding something. Like he was letting Jack go on but already made his decision. If I had to bet, I would have a stepbrother living in Fort Collins in a few months.

We watched TV and snacked on the food Stacy brought down until midnight when Jack had to leave. Jack hesitated but whatever expression I had on my face encouraged him to kiss me again. Too briefly with Nate there. With a promise to see me tomorrow, he went up the stairs. An awkward silence had followed his exit until Nate asked me if I wanted to watch another episode before we called it a night. I had agreed and it had been surprisingly easy to sit alone with him. He asked me how my semester was going, and we stayed up another hour after the show ended just talking about school. Nate didn't love most of his classes either and asked me if I regretted switching majors. I could tell he was listening closely to my descriptions of CSU and it only made me more certain he was planning to transfer.

I took my time showering and readying for the day. A big part of me dreaded going downstairs and acting like this was a special holiday with the special people in my life. I wondered briefly what the chances were of Jack coming over early if I texted. His family was already planning to come by for the actual dinner, but I wanted my buffer around sooner.

In the end, I didn't have to worry. I heard his laugh as I was going down the stairs and the weight lifted like magic from my shoulders. The kitchen was already bustling with dinner preparations. The little girl sitting at the counter peeling potatoes must be Amelie. Stacy was standing next to her, smiling as the girl chattered away, the beads at the end of Amelie's braids clicking each time she turned her head. A bald Black man was chopping carrots and a big man with Jack's hazel eyes was talking to my dad. They both already held beers and stood over the turkey, debating something. I almost rolled my eyes at the sight. After my childhood of dry Thanksgiving turkeys, my dad had no room to voice an opinion.

Jack was stirring something on the stove, Nate giving him shit and saying that it didn't look right.

"Look who *finally* got up! I was about ready to go check for a pulse," my dad exclaimed, drawing appreciative laughter from the other dads in the room. I fought the urge to roll my eyes like I would have as a teenager.

Jack handed Nate his wooden spoon and crossed the room to my side. "Roly, this is my dad, Steve, my pop, André, and my sister Amelie."

"Roly?" Amelie asked in that tone people used when they heard it.

"Yes, Amelie. Roly," Jack said firmly.

Amelie still looked skeptical but turned her attention back to the peeler when Stacy cautioned her.

"Come help me with the cranberry sauce," Jack said, saving me from awkward small talk for the moment.

I could have kissed him. I was happy to be meeting his family but already overwhelmed by the full kitchen. Jack steered me toward the stove to a very watery-looking cranberry sauce. In time, Jack had saved it and Nate and I started on the stuffing. Then mashed the potatoes when Amelie had finished her task. Stacy was thrilled to see us all getting along and working together. By sticking with Nate and Jack by the stove, I was able to avoid the adults in the kitchen for the most part. The two of them sandwiched me between them so nicely that I felt almost as comfortable as I would have with Andrew and Matty. It didn't hurt that Jack kept touching me. Just small brushing of his fingers or a bump of his hip. Enough to be distracting and make me hyperaware of his presence.

To my surprise, my mom remembered to call at an appropriate

time. We were just waiting on the turkey when my phone rang. I excused myself and went back upstairs to answer.

"Hey, Mom."

"Hey, Cheroly! How's your day going?" I could hear the sympathy in her voice, but no regret for her absence. That would have been too much to hope for.

The screen door to the deck beneath me slammed. I went to my window and shamelessly watched Nate and Jack start passing a soccer ball between them. Jack wore his hoodie and I remembered the smell of it from last night. I loved watching him bounce the ball expertly, inner foot, knee, knee, forehead, and right to Nate's chest. Rudy ran between them happily, not even trying to get the ball, just content to chase it. I knew very little about sports in general, but I could tell Jack was good. Watching him gave me feelings I did not need to be having while talking to my mom, but I didn't look away.

Maybe I could understand a bit more why she would be excited about Marco and Dad would be so quick to marry Stacy. The pain was so dull when I saw Jack laugh at something Nate said.

I was smiling as I talked to my mom for the first time since she left. "So far it's been pretty good."

There was silence on the other end for a moment too long. "Oh. Well, good. Is your new mom a good cook?"

I rolled my eyes and flopped back on the bed. It was a family joke how bad at cooking my mom was, something she had always laughed about. *Now* it bothers her. "Mom, I've barely talked to her."

"So it's been good hanging out with your father?"

Nate laughed loudly in the backyard. I rolled to my side and looked outside again, catching sight of Jack getting back to his feet and brushing off his side. I'd missed him falling, but no doubt it had been ridiculous.

"No, not really. I haven't talked to him much either."

"I see. Then you're… making friends with… her son?" She sounded almost choked up.

"What?"

"Your new brother. I suppose it wouldn't be too hard on you. You probably don't even remember Brady."

I froze. She so rarely said his name. "Mom… it's not like that. That's not fair. I—"

"I have to go. Happy Thanksgiving." She hung up.

I stared at my phone, feelings I couldn't name rising hard and fast. I didn't want to be here. I didn't want to celebrate a racist holiday with people who stood on the opposite end of a void. No matter what I did, I was hurting someone. I was picking between my parents. Maybe even hurting the memory of my brother.

It wasn't fair. What did my mom expect? What was I allowed to do to be happy? She wasn't here for me to spend the holiday with so was I just supposed to be miserable and alone?

I called Matty. He heard my shaky inhale and I didn't even have to tell him I was upset. "It's okay, Roly. I'm here." He found somewhere quiet and sat on the phone with me while I cried and tried to explain the conversation with my mom.

"That's fucked, Roly. You know it is. She just doesn't want to be alone in her pain, but she's also unwilling to do the work it takes to move forward. Your parents needing a therapist is no reflection on you. You would never hurt anyone purposefully. She's letting you down, not the other way around."

I hugged my pillow close and smelled our apartment. That was home. Not here. I let his words wrap around me. I sniffed back the last of my tears. "Matty, have I told you lately how much I adore you?"

"I could stand to hear it more often." His voice was teasing. I missed him like crazy.

"How is your sister? Tell me all about your day."

He allowed the distraction, going on about his sister's bump and how insane their mom was acting about it all. I could hear the smile in his voice. He talked until my cheeks were dry and my dad was calling for me.

"I should probably go too," Matty said. "Hang in there, champ."

I laughed. "You too, bud. Love you!"

"Love you, Roly."

I checked my mascara and went downstairs feeling more like myself.

"I know Tom just called you down, but he got distracted playing with the boys outside," Stacy said when I entered the kitchen. She, Amelie, and André were sitting at the overfilled island. The adults were holding glasses of red wine and André was quick to pour me one. I liked him immediately. Amelie was sneaking bites of the mashed potatoes when they weren't looking and seemed happy just to be included in the adult talk.

Stacy and André looked natural and sophisticated. I learned they worked in the same office. They gossiped like Priya and I did about their coworkers. The scene was exactly how I pictured Matty and I sitting in our expensive, shiny kitchens after long days at the office in the future.

Minus the aprons and turkey grease splattered on André's front. "How was your mom?" he asked. "Jack said she's in Italy. I'm so jealous."

"She's fine. Busy. We didn't talk long." I took a rather big drink of wine.

"Who were you chatting with so long then?"

"My friend Matty."

André was interested immediately. "Just friend?"

"Just friend."

"Good. I'd hate to see Jack heartbroken." He leveled me a significant look and I blushed. Jack had talked about me. It couldn't be clearer. His pop was papa-bearing me for him. Because Jack liked me *that much*.

I smiled into my wine glass. Stacy gave a delighted laugh. "I don't think we need to threaten her. You have a very pretty blush, Roly."

"Why is Roly blushing?" Amelie asked.

André turned to her with a teasing expression I'd seen on Jack's face plenty of times. "Because she has a crush on your brother."

Amelie rolled her eyes. Too serious, she turned to me, "He probably wouldn't be good at being a boyfriend. He likes school and soccer too much. He's boring."

I glanced up at the sound of the screen door closing. Jack stood there, looking startled. His smile was tight while André and Stacy laughed. I turned to Amelie and widened my eyes. "You'll understand one day how nice it is to watch your crush do something they're good at."

"You've watched him play?"

"I was just creeping on him in my room."

"Weird." Amelie lost interest and returned to her origami, calling Jack over for help. His smile was easy again as he went to her side, touching the small of my back as he passed.

"Amelie, you know I can only make three things and *you* taught me how to make them."

"Just see if you can tell what I'm doing wrong."

Amelie may not recognize Jack's appeal, but he was obviously a great brother. One day she'd realize how lucky she was to have him. How lucky I was to have his attention. André and I shared a smile over their heads, him looking as proud as he should be of his two kids.

My dad and Steve came in with the turkey, avoiding stepping on an eager Rudy who was circling their feet. Chaos ensued as we grabbed plates and filled them before going to the table. Some of the food was a little cold, but I'd never experienced such a perfectly cooked turkey. Conversation ended for the most part as we ate. Any remarks made were about the food. It wasn't as bad as I thought it would be to sit at the table. Even when we finished, they talked about things and people that were part of this community and I just settled back in my seat. Did I spend most of the dinner staring at Jack and ignoring everyone else? Maybe.

It was too easy.

The meal ended with Jack bringing out the pie he'd made from scratch. It was almost as delicious as the darkening of his eyes as he watched me eat it. Maybe Jack had a bit of a food kink. I scooped some whipped cream off my pie and stuck my finger between my lips, keeping eye contact with him as I sucked it off slowly.

Jack shifted in his chair, swallowing. I could practically hear his thoughts about his grandparents. Smirking with satisfaction, I looked away and saw my dad staring at me like a strange creature he'd never come across before. André was trying so hard not to laugh, he was wiping away tears with his napkin. Amelie was staring up at him in confusion.

"I have to pee." I fled the kitchen. I was burning with embarrassment.

My dad had just seen my sex eyes.

But I struggled to fully regret flashing them at the table. The memory of Jack's expression made everything worth it. I couldn't wait to get him alone and receive the full version of his dirty looks.

The long weekend passed more quickly than I could have dreamed. I spent every moment not with Jack trying to think of a way to get more time with Jack. Time *alone* with Jack, more specifically. Every day I took Ruby for a walk to get out of the house. My dad and I went to lunch on Saturday and it was nice. He was doing agility classes with Rudy once a week and had hilarious stories about it that took up most of the hour. I had so many questions, so many worries, but I couldn't voice them when his mind was clearly on more pleasant topics. He was the happiest I'd ever seen him. A calm in his eyes that was never there before. He was proud of himself for making this effort for me, but it was only because Stacy pushed us out the door together to get some time alone.

It stung that it hadn't been his idea, but I tried to feel grateful. The diner hadn't been far from Stacy's house, but my hands were slicked with anxious sweat by the time we pulled into the driveway again. My dad was equally tense. We didn't say a word about it. We never did. I went straight to the basement once we got inside. It had become my hideaway here. Stacy and my dad weren't allowed downstairs, making sure Nate felt like it was his space. He even had his own entrance and kitchenette.

I knocked on the door at the base of the stairs and he called for me to come in.

"Jack's not over," he said, catching me looking around for the familiar head of brown hair.

I was tempted to turn around to go hide in the guest room. Nate pointed to the other recliner and I couldn't tell him no. I watched him play his game for a moment before he found a good stopping point and paused it.

He took a deep, bracing breath. "Okay, I can't take it anymore." I was surprised by the force of his tone. He was normally so soft-spoken. "Why do you hate me? Why does your dad get so weird when my mom asks him about your mom and the divorce? Why does he sometimes get teary-eyed when we go play soccer? And why can't you *look* at me? Jack's trying to convince me the wedding was just a bad day for you and you're actually really great, but all I get is coldness from you. I *want* to be friends. I want it not to be awkward when you come over. My mom has always wanted a bigger family and I hate that whatever your problem is is getting in the way of that. Please, just talk to me and we can try and work it out." Nate froze at the end of his rant, anxious.

I picked at the worn-out seam on the arm of Jack's recliner. My face burned. I thought I was doing better, that we were getting comfortable with each other, but he clearly hoped for more from me. The chair smelled like Jack.

I was nearly certain Nate was planning to transfer. I needed to start making plans. Maybe add another course to my workload and take summer classes so I could graduate early and leave Fort Collins before it was no longer my escape.

The thought filled me with dread. I didn't want to rush away from Fort Collins faster than currently necessary. I didn't want to take classes as it was. I still wasn't excited about my major. I didn't want this onslaught of change. Well, that wasn't completely true. I wanted more time with Jack. That I couldn't deny. If only he and Nate weren't a package deal. But that would be like someone wanting to date me and not see Matty. Off the table.

I sank into the cushion, pulling my legs up to sit sideways facing Nate. I didn't like hurting him and I wasn't willing to risk Jack by not trying with Nate. "We don't talk about this. Well, my dad doesn't talk about this. My mom will bring it up and sometimes I talk to Matty, but it's really hard for my dad still so don't tell anyone. *Anyone*," I started. I still wasn't ready for Jack to see my broken pieces. Nate frowned but nodded. I spoke quickly like I could get the words out faster to stop the lifelong ache. "I had a brother and he died. His name was Brady and he died when he was seven. My mom thinks my dad is replacing him with you. She said I was doing the same when we talked on Thursday." I cleared my throat. "There's just a lot of hurt there."

Nate's mouth had dropped open. "I didn't..."

There were quick, light steps on the stairs. I gave Nate a warning look as Jack came down with a bright smile. "Don't you look comfortable!" he said lightly, eyes heating at the sight of me curled in his recliner.

Before I could respond, he bent, lifted me with a slightly insulting grunt, and spun us both so we were sitting on the recliner together, me neatly on his lap. The chair rocked hard enough that I grabbed at Jack, but he just laughed into my hair.

Nate rolled his eyes and muttered a half-hearted "Gross." When I turned to look at him, he searched my face but didn't say anything more. I was careful to keep my expression clear with

Jack here now. I still cringed from the thought of laying my baggage at his feet. What we had now was light and easy. A slow burn that would explode when the heat of our bodies finally got to collide. I told myself that was all I was looking forward to. It wouldn't do to get too deep.

I knew I was lying. I ached for things to get too deep with Jack.

We settled in to watch a movie. I had never been one to enjoy being lifted. I always felt too big to fit comfortably on a person's lap. I liked cuddling side by side in bed but struggling to find a good position on couches and chairs usually gave me anxiety. Especially when someone tried to put their arm around me in the movie theater. That was the best way to have a sore neck and a miserable couple of hours.

But Jack wrapped his arms around me so tight, that I couldn't even try to keep my weight off him. He welcomed it. It was almost like he wanted to add to it, to make me really crush him. When Nate wasn't looking, Jack would smell my hair or nip at my neck or press his lips to my shoulder. Our kiss in the car had unlocked his physically affectionate nature and I wasn't complaining.

I pried one of his hands off my waist and he let me examine it. He bit his nails. He had pretty soft skin and little callouses from his infrequent gym visits. His fingers were long and perfectly rounded. His knuckles just the right amount of bulge. I traced the veins on the back of his hand and fell for him even more. I pushed my fingertips between his tendons and slipped them between his fingers, curling them into his palm. He folded his fingers around mine and brought our hands up to his mouth, tracing the same lines and dips with his lips on my hand that I had just explored with my fingertips on his.

I pulled his hand back and kissed the base of his palm, the sides of his wrist. I wanted to kiss every inch of soft skin. I wanted to bite him, to tease him, to make him beg, to make him laugh, to pull him into my heart and feel like this forever.

My stomach swooped. I had never wanted anything like I

wanted Jack. The intensity of the feeling and the nervous fear that accompanied it rose the hair on my arms.

His eyes softened. He was wearing an olive sweater today and it brought out the green spiking around his pupils. Jack glanced at Nate, but I was lost in the sight of his face. He kissed me right on the corner of my mouth. He dragged his lips up to my ear and I shivered. "If you don't stop looking at me like that, I don't think Nate will be very happy with us."

I stuck out my bottom lip in an exaggerated pout. Jack's laugh was full of something close to wonder. He put our hands back against my stomach, wrapping me up tight against him, and winked. He mouthed the word later and forced his attention back to the television.

Later. Later I would make sure he was fully addicted to me like I was to him. Later, I would make him understand what I was feeling and he wouldn't be able to walk away from me even when he learned all the hurt inside me. I could do it. I had to. Because right now, the thought of ever losing Jack made me want to shrivel up and blow away in the wind.

NINE

I UNCLENCHED my fists as Jack put the car into park. We exhaled as one. He'd done everything right again, but there was no way to prepare for other drivers on the road and that was the main problem. Traffic had been aggressive and congested and I had trouble focusing on Jack's attempted conversation the entire drive.

"Hey." He reached for my hand in the sudden quiet. "You okay?"

I blew out a breath and let my head fall back into the seat. "I'm okay." I rolled my head so I was looking at him and attempted a smile. "I know you called Matty when I was nervous to drive with you. It means a lot that you would do that. And that you followed his advice."

Jack's answering smile was almost shy. "It means a lot you trusted me to drive you."

It was midafternoon on Sunday. The parking lot was busy with students returning home from the short break. I didn't care. All I saw was the space between his lips and mine and how badly I wanted it gone.

I wasn't all that graceful when I closed the distance between us. Our teeth clicked and Jack huffed a laugh. He'd just unbuckled his seatbelt and I felt the buckle get caught between us as he reached to meet me.

Alright. It wasn't graceful at all. It was downright sloppy. But I couldn't care. I unhooked him from the belt, breaking our contact for only a second. I kept him close with one hand to the back of his neck and ran my other hand through his hair, down his arm. In a circle around his stomach, up to his cheek. All the while tugging him closer still. I couldn't get enough of him.

He caught my hand from his neck and held it tight. He pulled his lip from between my teeth and nudged me with his nose, tipping my head back. He made the slightly frantic kiss gentle, sweet, and slow, holding my hand tight even when I made a half-hearted attempt to pull it back. "Breathe, Roly. We made it back okay. The weekend is over."

A breath shuddered out of me and washed over his lips. He kissed the corners of my mouth as I sucked in another breath. His lips found the tip of my nose. Then he ducked his head and went to work on the line of my jaw, my neck, behind my earlobe. I shivered.

"Come inside? Matty won't be home for a while still."

Jack froze. He knew exactly what I was offering. The way he tensed made me do the same. It wasn't the eager agreement I had expected. Had I read this wrong? I cleared my throat. "Never mind. You probably want to get home."

We had just spent the whole weekend together. I was being clingy. Me, clingy. Unheard of. Maybe he needed his space. Maybe I was being too eager and smothering him. I started to pull away, but he still had my hand caught.

"No, Roly, no... I want to. I just, I'm not ready yet." His face was still down and pressed into my shoulder.

I frowned, my stomach turning, my mind trying to convince me it was my fault. But that wasn't it. I knew that wasn't it. This was about consent, and I needed to accept no's without explanation or making it all about me. But I was glad Jack wasn't looking as I worked to calm my mind and remind myself of all this. He said he wanted to. It wasn't even a no.

"Okay." I swallowed an apology for suggesting it. I was allowed to offer and he was allowed to say no. There didn't have to be hurt feelings here.

He looked up quickly. This close, I was glad I'd taken a moment to control my thoughts. I met his gaze steady. Jack relaxed a bit. "I'll be ready, but I want it to be special."

"Jack, you can just say no. You don't need an excuse."

"But I want you to understand I do want you. So bad. Just—"

"Okay." I kissed the corner of his mouth like he'd done to me. It was a sweet place to kiss. No obligation to return it, but a true kiss nonetheless. "I want you too. When you're ready."

"Do you want to go to dinner tomorrow?"

I sighed, shaking my head. I had work. It was back to our sporadic schedule of seeing each other. This was where sex would help. Then we'd have the nights. The soft morning murmurs.

But was I ready for the late-night conversations when the truth always came out? Maybe Jack was right to wait. I knew somehow I wouldn't be able to separate sex and emotion where Jack was concerned. My body wanted him badly, but I was too far gone already for casual.

"I'm working every night this week to make up for the nights I took off this weekend."

He pursed his lips. I had to laugh at the expression on his face. It was close to the look he'd given me after the wedding dress incident. Displeasure, nearly disgust. He didn't want space at least. Just wanted to wait for sex. Relief made my head light. "And I work every morning but the ones you have class," he said. "I hate capitalism."

I laughed, fully relaxing against the seat and playing with the pulls on his hoodie. "You could come up and just hang out for a bit. No sex."

He looked a little startled to have the word out there, but he nodded. "We could get something delivered for dinner?"

"We definitely could."

Jack smiled, his genuine smile with nothing held back, and kissed me. Then we went up to my apartment and he kissed me through most of the movie. I hadn't had a make-out session this long and intense since high school. He always stopped us at a certain point, leaning back in the cushions with a breathless laugh. The pauses always came when my skin was crawling with need to lose my clothes and touch him everywhere. Jack jokingly led us through breathing exercises. Two minutes later, his hands would be back in my hair, his lips caught in my own, and I would be fighting the urge to rip his shirt off and crawl into his lap.

I tentatively edged a hand under his shirt, giving him time to pull away. He leaned into my touch, deepening the kiss, his fingers toying at the base of my own shirt. I almost growled, wishing for his touch on my bare stomach and higher. And especially lower.

A light skim over the hard bulge in his pants earned me a sexy, little yelp. He brushed his knuckles over the front of my sports bra, perking my nipples almost painfully. He pushed back, panting. His eyes were so dark with wanting. I knew it was mirrored in my gaze.

"Fuck, Roly."

I wished he would.

Yet, there was something about teasing ourselves like this. The buildup was so bitterly sweet and sexy. I hadn't been this turned on in... ever really. I felt like even shifting around enough against the seam of my jeans might be able to get me off in moments. I was sweating with need. My face warm and my body a strange mix of relaxed comfort and desperation for release.

And I could tell Jack was loving it. He liked the teasing. The pull back as he thought of the eventual payoff. I loved watching the disappointment in his eyes and the light in them as he focused on the future.

Jack liked being teased. I tucked the knowledge away. I couldn't wait to use it.

Eventually, one unwatched movie rolled into the next. Matty came home and we caught up, the sexual tension in the room draining away. Matty showered and went to see Andrew. Jack pulled me close again and we ordered food and ate too much. We fell asleep tangled together on the couch. It was close to midnight when Jack kissed me goodbye at the door, drawing it out with playful nips and pulling my hips close, not wanting to let me go. As soon as the door shut, I ran to my room and dove for my nightstand. With Matty gone, I took my favorite toy to the couch and pressed my face into the pillow that was warm with Jack's smell.

I ran through our make-out session, preparing to imagine a different conclusion to get myself off. Ready to picture him naked and sweating beneath me.

I only got as far as the real memory of brushing his erection before I shuddered with release. It was a hard push, harder than usual. I moaned as it rocked me.

When I finally sat up and went to shower, my cheeks burned from having done that in our shared space. Embarrassment was hard to hold onto as I washed away the weekend, head light and buzzing with thoughts of Jack.

I stared at the ceiling and tried to calm my heart. I was a bit obsessed. It wasn't like me. It was terrifying, but I couldn't stop my excitement either. Especially seeing his text when I got out of the water. *I'm really glad we had this weekend. Goodnight, Roly.*

Me too. Goodnight, Jack.

I stared at his name typed out on my scene. The feeling that overcame me was nearly possessive. Jack, my person to text and kiss and feel wild about. To obsess over, confident that he felt at least nearly the same about me.

I had never loved my routine more, though I wished I had more time in the afternoons when Jack was free. Mornings were filled with Moonbean, free drinks, and Jack's smile. He now always stopped at our table for a bit when we were there. Slowly, he learned our inside jokes, he asked Andrew about the stresses of being a TA, he and Matty were playing a video game together at night, and we all were regaled with stories about his crazy roommate. He always smelled like pastries and coffee. I wanted to eat him up in his green apron.

Classes were harder than usual, my distraction and texts with Jack making it extra challenging, but the semester was passing by quickly at least. Nearly another one down until I had the freedom to apply for jobs and move far away from my family. I didn't let myself dwell on how this thing between me and Jack had dimmed those plans. Winter set in fully and servers kept asking for me to cover shifts. I often did, just waiting for the time I would finally catch whatever bug was going around as I biked to and from work in the cold. I fantasized about Jack bringing me soup, us finally having an afternoon to ourselves on a weekend when homework wasn't getting harder with the dawning of finals.

Instead, I stayed healthy and pulled in more cash than usual. Priya and I shouldered the extra shifts together and I heard daily about her great aunt she lived with and benefited from her cooking when Priya started bringing us both dinner. Samosas and curries that made my eyes water and think about later at night when I just wanted more.

One night, she and Lynn came in while I was working. I was only slightly surprised to see them. I had my suspicions that Lynn missed having Andrew around since he spent most of his time at my apartment. We were slowly becoming closer, and my Jack-induced good moods meant I was trying harder to include her. I sat with them when it was slow and the three of us made plans for the next weekend to help Lynn find a dress to wear to her cousin's wedding. As I went to greet the next guests, I had the dispiriting realization it was the first plan I had made with only girls since... well since Matty and I became friends.

My stomach swirled with nerves at the prospect.

That Sunday I braved a ten-minute car ride with Priya behind the wheel. Luckily, I was in the back, so they didn't notice me clutching my seatbelt and the panic in my eyes. We shopped in the outdoor mall of Loveland, walking around in the cold and then running when it was unbearable, laughing at the looks we drew. Eventually, we found a lavender-colored dress that went beautifully with Lynn's dark complexion.

We sat drinking hot chocolate sometime later in a coffee shop I wished was Moonbean. I was like Pavlov's dogs, the taste of coffee making me crave Jack's presence.

"So, are you excited for the wedding?" Priya asked Lynn.

Lynn shrugged. "Yes and no. It'll probably be pretty emotional. My Uncle Will died last year from cancer. Jessie was pretty ruined by it, especially since it was right after the engagement. I think it'll be good for us all to be back together, but it's the first time since the funeral and it'll be hard sharing it without Uncle Will there."

Priya patted Lynn's arm. "My grandpa died right before Christmas two years ago. We all still got together, but there was lots of crying. But also, lots of laughter and joy. We remembered him together and I felt at times like he was there with us. My grandma said we should just remember the look he'd get on his face whenever we cried and remember he wouldn't want to see us sad."

Lynn smiled a little and nodded.

I was struck. This was shared, adult grief like I had never experienced before. I couldn't imagine my mother sitting with two friends and talking about my brother. I couldn't imagine my mother talking about my brother with anything but a dead voice and haunted eyes. From my parents' example, I thought *that* was grief. Silence and lashing out. I thought mentioning Brady was something I could only do when I was willing to press deep on the bruise.

But this was different. This was mourning with happiness. I tried to think of what Brady would say about my family's version of grief and cringed at the thought. He would hate it. He loved making people laugh. I didn't have many specific memories, but I knew that. He had been just plain silly.

He wouldn't want me thinking of the shadows his death cast. I had had a brother who taught me to tie my shoes and loved calling me Roly-Poly-Guacamole in a singsong voice I could still hear in my head when I thought of him. Maybe I didn't remember much else, but those at least were happy memories I could smile at instead of cry.

"Are you okay, Roly?" Lynn asked.

I tensed, ready for the pity, but her eyes only held concern. She didn't know about Brady anyway. I wiped my eyes and nodded. "I think I just needed to hear that. Do you guys ever think they're watching us? Like still out there somewhere?"

I felt the shared grief and understanding envelope me as they realized I'd lost someone too. Priya shrugged. "I still feel my grandpa's love sometimes. Even if it isn't *him* somewhere, it's an echo of him and I like it."

"I don't think I believe in anything like an afterlife, but I like thinking we carry memories and that they continue on through us."

I nodded, strangely settled by the conversation. It took me a moment to realize it was because I felt less alone. I had known separation from my peers because of my grief nearly my entire life. I wished then my parents had been able to lean on each other or even found friends who understood what was happening. Grief can be so solitary, but I felt so much better with the burden shared. Maybe it was only possible to feel this light because I barely remembered my brother and so many years had passed, but I wished there had been a moment like this for my mom and dad.

"Maybe we should talk about something else," Priya said, forcing a laugh at the heaviness around the table.

She and Lynn shared a smile and turned to me. "Andrew is super excited about your party next weekend," Lynn said.

"My party?"

"For your birthday!"

"Oh," I laughed uncomfortably. "Right. I forgot he mentioned planning that."

"Well, he didn't. Do you have a favorite alcohol or cake we should bring?"

I laughed at Priya for mentioning drinks first. "Just no tequila after Halloween. And we're still just keeping things small, right?" They shared another look, this one wide-eyed. I groaned. "It's not going to be small, is it?"

"I'm changing the subject slightly," Priya said. "When I found out your birthday was Tuesday, I requested the day off for you. Make Jack take you to dinner."

I tried to smile. It was a sweet thing for Priya to do, but I had been looking forward to the distraction of work. "I have my birthday off?"

"Yes! And you know what you're going to do? Finally?" Priya wiggled her eyebrows and I did know. "Maya and I are still waiting to hear all about it. This build-up has been hot and all, but we're ready for all the juicy details."

"Gross. And I don't think it'll happen Tuesday. I'm not a huge fan of my birthday."

"Yeah, but are you like, oh I hate my birthday but go home and secretly count how many people posted about it, or are you an I hate getting older kind of birthday hater?"

"We just didn't celebrate it growing up. It feels weird to want to now that I'm an adult and it doesn't matter as much." Only slightly a lie.

"Of course it matters now. Any excuse to drink matters!" Lynn said.

Priya laughed and they cheersed with their hot chocolates. I was able to hold my smile as the conversation changed to upcoming holiday parties, thankful when I only had to contribute a little. I didn't want to think about next week, but dread was crowding in. I hated my birthday.

I woke up on December 14th feeling cold. My phone already had several notifications wishing me a good day. I forced myself out of bed and dressed in Jack's hoodie and a pair of black leggings. Hair in a bun, I had no energy for makeup. I looked longingly at my bed, but I had a test today. It was especially cruel because we would also be having a final soon in the same class. But today was just a day. I had to tell myself this every year.

I opened my door but paused when I heard Matty talking beyond the open door of his room. "No, Andrew, I'm serious. Don't let Lynn bring anything over. Don't make her breakfast. Don't give her a present until this weekend. The more we can do to pretend it isn't her birthday, the better. Just trust me, okay?"

"But I didn't even know it was her birthday last year! I completely missed it!"

"Exactly. That's what she wants."

"Why?" Andrew was practically whining. He loved birthdays.

Matty dropped his voice. I waited for the words, my heart freezing in my chest. "Babe, her brother died on her birthday. Her family always mourned today and she doesn't feel comfortable trying to celebrate."

Silence in the other room. I felt sick. It shouldn't hurt so bad this many years later, should it? It was just another day. I tried to recall the feeling I had talking about grief with Lynn and Priya, but alongside the hurt was guilt. Especially today. As much as my adult self knew I had just been a kid when the accident happened, the story didn't change.

I didn't remember very much about my fifth birthday. I didn't think many kids did anyway, even without the trauma I went through.

But I remembered my ninth birthday. We went to my grandma's to try and celebrate for once. My parents were always tense with fear in the car. Their fear had infected me from such a young age it was the reason I hated driving to this day. We only managed to have a quiet dinner before my mom asked to leave. Said she couldn't do it.

I cried in the car. My dad tried to make comforting noises and promises to try celebrating again next year. My mom sat with a tight jaw in the passenger seat, clutching her seatbelt. We hit a patch of ice and slid briefly, just a slight fishtail. My mom lost it; screaming at my dad to be careful and yelling at me to shut up and stop crying. I'd been shocked into complete silence. We got home and they went into their room. My dad looked back before shutting the door. I couldn't read his eyes but I remembered wishing he'd come back and hug me. I clutched the stuffed dog my grandma had handed me before we left her house instead. It smelled like plastic. It was the only present I'd gotten that day. My dad hadn't remembered to give me the rest until we were leaving for school the next morning.

I ran up to their door once it shut and settled on the floor, ear to the gap underneath so I could listen.

"You can't yell at her like that, Helen."

"I can't *stand* it, Tom. I can't stand her crying or the cake or driving in the winter. I can't smile or be happy or celebrate *anything* today. If we hadn't gone out to eat that night, if she hadn't been so tired and crashing from the sugar, if she hadn't been throwing a tantrum while I was trying to drive…"

"Helen. The accident wasn't Roly's fault." I rarely heard my dad so firm with her nor so present in a conversation.

"It was an accident, that doesn't mean I'm blameless. It doesn't mean we wouldn't have crashed if she'd just *stopped crying.*"

Every year, I'll remember the screaming. My childhood brain was gracious enough to block everything else about the accident out. That was what trauma does. But my mom screamed my brother's name for days, so while I might be able to forget sitting next to my brother's dead body in the back of the car, I couldn't forget the screams. Or my mother's words four years later.

I went to class. I took my test. I skipped going to Moonbean and ignored my phone. I didn't have my birthday posted anywhere, at least not accurately. Facebook thought I was 112 and born in January. Someone had spread the word though and my phone kept pinging. Jack, Nate, Study Room staff, Andrew, Lynn. Phone calls and texts I didn't bother reading.

I went home and got back in bed. I turned on Bob's Burgers. I pulled up the hood of Jack's sweatshirt and let the smell of him engulf me. I knew today was hard for my mom. I knew it was hard for my dad. I thought about them and guilt churned and I wished my brother wasn't dead. I wished it wasn't snowing just like it had been on that day. I wished my mother's screams and father's silence weren't ringing in my ears. I wished I could outgrow the grief.

I wished my brother wasn't dead.

Matty came in and got under the covers. We cuddled and watched together, making jokes about the show to try and make each other laugh, ignoring the fact that anything was out of the ordinary. I felt better than I had all day with Matty near. I wished my mom would call but knew she wouldn't. My dad didn't either. I pulled Matty's arm tight around me and just tried to imagine their voices.

I gave Matty my phone and he responded to the messages so I didn't feel guilty tomorrow for ignoring people. He knew I wanted to know if my parents called and that was it.

It was dark out, that early winter dark that touched your soul, when the doorbell rang. Matty sat up and frowned. "I'll get it."

I just nodded and pulled my covers back up after he left. My eyes slid shut when I heard Jack's voice. It rose just a bit after a beat, loud enough for me to hear through my open door. "Matty, I like you and I respect you know her better, but unless she tells me to leave, I'm going to go talk to her."

"She shouldn't have to tell you. She likes being left alone on her birthday and always feels guilty when people take that personally but it's her day to spend it how she likes. It's not about you. Come back tomorrow."

They were closer to my open door. Jack's voice lowered. "Is she okay?"

Matty didn't answer. I sighed and shut my laptop. I got up and went to the door of my room. "You can come in Jack. Thanks, Matty."

Matty nodded and gave Jack a warning look before he went to the couch. Jack came in slowly, looking confused. "I was going to ask if you wanted to go to dinner."

And he looked so nice. Hair combed, fresh save, a soft sweater, and black jeans. Any other night, I wouldn't have been able to keep my hands off of him. Tonight, I was tired. "No, thanks."

"Do you want me to go? I won't be hurt."

"No, just… will you come in?"

Jack glanced back at Matty and came into my room. I shut the door behind him and took a deep breath, eyes closed. He stepped near and put his hands on my cheeks. "Did you sleep at all last night?"

"Are you saying I look tired?" I attempted a smile.

"Have you eaten today?"

Good question. "I don't think so."

"I missed seeing you at Moonbean. I mean, I don't want to make you feel bad, but I…"

"It's okay, Jack. Today is just a hard day, okay? I just can't believe I'm feeling twenty-two." I sang the last of that sentence poorly. I didn't even sound like myself.

Jack's face softened. "You don't have to try and make me laugh right now. It's okay to be sad."

"Oh." I didn't have a response to that.

"Okay. Get back in bed. I'll be right back." And then the warmth cradling my cheeks was gone and Jack wasn't in my room anymore. I drew in a shaky breath. I didn't want him gone. Not at all. But I did as I was told. I sat on my bed in the soft light of my lamp. Jack talked to Matty briefly and I felt the jolt in my body when the front door shut as he left.

I didn't know what else to do, so I opened my laptop and

watched another episode. Then another. I didn't force any laughs and tried in vain to let it distract me. What if Jack didn't come back? What if he looked at my face and realized how damaged I was and didn't want to deal with it? I'd tried so hard to keep things light and easy between us. I never even told him about my brother.

This was why I didn't let people close. They didn't deal well with pain they couldn't understand. I needed to wait until tragedy caught up with them. I remembered the hot chocolate with Priya and Lynn. I didn't want bad things to happen to people, but it made it easier to let them in.

My chest hurt. Another episode started and I debated just turning it off. Making myself fall asleep. It seemed unlikely to happen, but it had to be better than this.

The door opened. I told myself it was just Andrew. But Andrew wouldn't open my bedroom door without knocking. Jack came in dressed in sweats now and holding a familiar bag. "I picked up some food. Want to eat out here with Matty or in your bed?"

I hated eating in my bed. I got up and went silently to the couch. Matty was eating the Rambler, a burger with jalapeños and cream cheese on it. He offered a messy smile. Jack sat next to me. "Priya said you always get the hot wings, so I got you those."

Matty was watching all this carefully. I took the box Jack offered. "Why did you go to Study Room?"

"Because you didn't want to celebrate. But you need to eat. So, I just got food somewhere that didn't feel special." He opened another box, offering the pretzel bites I ate when wings didn't sound good. I took one and dipped it in the cheese sauce. Matty sank back into his chair with relief when I started eating. My throat burned as I fought tears.

Jack talked about his day. Classes and some new work drama including a mystery involving wooden spoons. Matty asked all the right questions and they carried out a completely normal conversation. I ate the hot wings I got every other shift. Max must have been in the kitchen because they were perfectly sauced. Priya must have done expo because there was a drawing of a penis on the inside of my box's lid.

Matty suggested the wooden spoons were being stolen for a certain purpose that made Jack laugh hard enough to choke on his burger. I slapped his back and laughed. Neither one of them made a big deal out of my smile.

I was comfortable and warm. Jack was as perfectly sweet as always, not overdoing it but grabbing me a blanket when I kept pushing my toes under his thigh for warmth. He asked Matty if he wanted to put on a movie and they picked one out without my input, not demanding I choose anything just because I was the birthday girl.

When they fell quiet to watch some stupid action movie, I shifted on the couch until I was lying with my head on Jack's lap, facing his stomach. Jack worked the hair tie out of my hair and released my bun. The taste of buffalo sauce still burning faintly on my tongue, I fell asleep with Jack's fingers running through my hair.

It was the best birthday I had in my memory.

TEN

I WOKE up in my bed to Jack's phone alarm. He groaned, turned it off, rolled over, and reached for me. I smiled into his chest as he pulled me close. When their movie ended, he'd woken me up late last night and ushered me to bed. I asked him not to leave and he'd agreed.

I think falling asleep next to Jack might be my new favorite pastime.

"Go to work for me," he muttered into my hair.

I shook my head, still smiling. I hugged Jack tight and thought about asking him to call in sick. It was so early, that I doubted even Matty was up for the gym yet. "Sorry for making you stay. I should have realized you had work."

"Yes, that's all I thought about as you held me at gunpoint and forced me into bed."

I laughed. "Thank god I'm so persuasive."

His arms tightened around me. "It's worth it. But I do have to go home and grab a change of clothes."

"Wear some of Matty's."

Jack kissed the top of my head. I shifted closer and felt him hard and ready. Heat flooded my core quickly enough to raise goosebumps on my arms. I shifted again, bringing a leg up between his knees and higher. He let out a noise, half groan half a surprised huff. He edged his hips toward me, rubbing against my thigh. I pressed closer still and tilted my head, looking for his lips as he ground against me again. He gasped into the kiss and broke it. "Tonight. Can I come back tonight?"

"Stay now."

He ground against me again. I started to reach downward but he caught my hand against his chest. "I can't. I should go to work. But tonight?" His voice shook on the last word. He wanted this, I knew it with certainty as he pressed his hips toward me yet again, but I could hear his nerves and it was enough to make my heart melt. I pressed a kiss to his lips and brushed my free hand down the front of his pants, drawing a smile and delicious noises from him. "Tonight." I untangled our legs and pushed him away. "I'm first cut at work. Be here at nine."

"Okay," he said, eager. I could feel it coming off him, that desperate, excited energy that came from our stop and go teases. I burned with the need to draw it out. To play with his desire in a way that made him crazy. He stood and I crawled to the edge of the bed and got up on my knees so I was kneeling in front of him. In the moonlight, I looked up at his eyes and reached, putting my hand firmly over his hard, ready bulge. He froze, eyes on my hand.

"Don't touch it when you're alone. Wait for me."

He swallowed. He was shaking and tense and so excited. "But... I won't last even a minute tonight then," he admitted, sounding miserable.

I stroked him with my thumb. He let his head fall back, breathing strained. "You will. Don't touch it."

"Oh my *god*. You're so fucking hot."

I smiled, filling with pride and power and need for him. Not many of my male partners let me play these games with them. They wanted the control, to prove themselves. Jack was puddy in my hands and it was going to drive me insane.

"Nine tonight."

"Yes. Nine."

I gave him one last squeeze and he yelped. I let him go and gave him a soft kiss. He sighed into my lips. "I'm not going to be able to focus on a single thing today."

"Yes, you will. It'll be me." I bit at his lip. "And I love it."

"Fuck."

"See you later." I laughed, pushing him toward the door and taking in the excited torture in his eyes.

He loved it too.

When he left, I fought the urge to reach for my nightstand and take care of myself with my face pressed into the pillow he used all night. But that wasn't fair. If I wasn't letting him get off until tonight, I would have to wait too. My hands strayed, but I never let myself get to the point of release. Eventually, I fell back to sleep, waking to a text from Jack. *This morning was hands down the hottest thing that has ever happened to me.*

I smiled, feeling invincible. *Just wait for tonight then.*

By the time he responded, I was in class. *I don't know if I'll survive. But if that's how I go, I won't complain.*

I left the classroom. *No, you won't.*

I got dots and no response by the time I got to Moonbean. As usual, I was there first. Jack was already sitting at a table with my coffee, his leg bouncing. I didn't like the look on his face or his clear nerves. I wanted him to always be comfortable with me. But he looked more anxious than normal. My steps slowed. What if this was bad? What if he was ending things? What if I was too miserable yesterday and he thought about it and it overshadowed whatever sexiness passed between us? I focused on his words this morning and his bodily response. Jack wouldn't have teased me that cruelly. He wasn't ending things. That wouldn't make sense.

I sat down slowly, unable to think my way past the dread curling at the base of my throat.

"Good morning," he said, sounding as if he was addressing a professor. Where was his usual excited hey?

"Hi. We okay?" I meant to ask if he was, but our relationship was my main concern and raced to the forefront of my mind.

"Yes! Of course." He leaned in and kissed me hard enough to ease most of my doubts.

But when he backed up, I still didn't like the nervousness pulling at his features. If this was about this morning, I wanted him excited, not afraid.

I kissed him quickly again to steady myself. When he returned the kiss willingly, I relaxed slightly. He worked here, so I couldn't do what I wanted and kiss him until his leg stilled and I'd burned all the nerves away with want.

When we broke apart, he pulled in a deep breath, no longer meeting my eyes. His leg was bouncing faster now. "Can I talk to you? About… sex, um, without ruining the excitement for tonight?"

"Of course."

He was fiddling with my coffee. I smelled the lavender London fog. He glanced around before he spoke. "I had a girlfriend all through high school. We lost our virginities to each other my senior year and she… she didn't like it. She broke up with me after. I know we were pretty young, but she said it was boring and that it made her realize I was, um, boring. That our relationship didn't excite her. I had a couple of hookups last year too, but I don't think I did very well then either. It spurred me to do a *lot* of research, but I haven't had sex since then and I don't think I know what I'm doing and I just don't want you to be disappointed or, or to think I'm bor—"

I put a finger over his lips. "I'll teach you. I like teaching." And I did. Guys, girls, myself. I loved sex. I'd been reading smut since an inappropriate age and listened to podcasts about sex and relationships all the time. Just this morning, Alma and Riley did an episode on Hooked Up about blowjobs and I was dying to try one of Riley's suggestions. "I have fun trying new things with people and I think being open and talking about this stuff is always good. I like the basics and don't expect you to get me off right away, but

I also like taking control. If you're okay with that and trust me, I'll show you tonight."

"But what if I'm not good at it?" he asked in a whisper. I remembered his face when Amelie called him boring over Thanksgiving. I knew this was about more than sex. I was waiting for Jack to see I had too many issues. He was waiting for me to grow bored with him.

For some reason, this made me more hopeful about a future together than anything else. He cared enough to be afraid, just like me.

"Jack, you've already shown me you're great at it. Sometimes, I feel like I'll explode just from the look in your eyes when you're turned on." I leaned in, resting our foreheads together. "You're the furthest thing from boring."

Jack breathed me in. He slowly relaxed, knee going still. The look of want kindled in his eyes and I bit my lip. He let out a little laugh. "Okay. Tonight then." His smile was more ready than any other time we'd broached this subject.

"Tonight."

Jack took my hands. We were still sitting so close. "And you're okay, right? You were pretty down yesterday, and I don't want this to be hard for you."

"I'm down every year on my birthday. Today isn't my birthday."

"You sure?"

"Jack, I can't wait to fu—"

We started when Andrew cleared his throat above us. "If you're done with the sexy eyes, I have party news."

"What party?" Jack asked. His hands were tight on my own. He knew what I had been about to say judging from the way he was shifting in his seat. Thinking about his grandma. I smirked.

"A party you're invited to that only happens to be planned the weekend after Roly's birthday and definitely isn't a birthday party."

Even I had to laugh at that. Andrew turned to me. "Tequila again or are you turned off of it from last time."

I cringed at the memory. "Something else."

"Alright. I'll figure it out. Otherwise, Lynn and my place at ten on Friday night. You got it off, right, Roly?"

"No, but I'll be off before that. I hope. I'm not closing at least."

"Good. Okay." Andrew went on about more details, being vague about the party size and how wild he expected it to get. Jack sat holding my hand until his break ended. He kissed my cheek, eyes blazing with thoughts of tonight, and left.

"Okay. That was hot. There's no way Matty and I are wearing headphones during whatever goes on tonight."

"Nope, because Matty is staying at your place."

Andrew pouted. "But—"

"No buts. For our first time, you won't be listening in."

Andrew smiled. "So it's the first time? Look at you taking things slow. You really like him?"

I caught Jack's eye behind the counter. "I think I really do." My blood rushed just from admitting it.

"Amazing. So what about the second time? No headphones?" Andrew asked.

Someone called me while I was biking home at the end of my shift. I still had messages and missed calls from yesterday. It wouldn't hurt to let it go unanswered one more day. I had only checked my phone a few times to see if my mom tried to call me.

My thoughts were full and my core too molten with anticipation. I left work a little late, so I wouldn't be home right at nine like we'd planned. I liked the idea of Jack waiting for me. I liked every idea I was having about tonight. This build-up was like nothing else. I just wanted to pull Jack in and never let him go. Every piece of himself he shared with me I clung to. This was going to be a huge piece. And I'd given him a big piece, letting him see my grief. We hadn't talked about it, but I was now confident the conversation about my brother wouldn't scare Jack away.

Hope was a powerful thing and it made me want Jack that much more.

I turned into my parking lot and frowned. I didn't like that Matty's car was still in his spot. I'd asked him to stay with Andrew tonight, but maybe he was just held up talking to Jack. There was an unfamiliar car parked next to Matty's in the spot that was meant for me but usually held Jack or Andrew's car these days. With a flare of panic, I checked the rest of the lot as I swung my leg over my bike. I spotted Jack's Jeep in the small guest lot and the panic settled. Nerves of a different nature danced happily in my stomach at the confirmation that he was here. With Matty here too, I could take a quick shower while they hung out. I didn't want to smell like beer and burgers for our first time.

I hurried up the stairs, a smile already pulling at the corners of my mouth as I worked my key in the front door.

The smile died on my lips as I stepped into the apartment.

"Roly! We were so worried when you didn't answer your phone yesterday!" Stacy rushed forward and wrapped me in a hug.

I couldn't breathe. My brain couldn't process her presence here, invading my escape and routine and plans for the night.

Stacy let me go. I hadn't even returned her hug.

"What are you doing here?" I knew I sounded betrayed as my eyes landed on my dad standing awkwardly in the kitchen area. Jack sat with Nate and Matty on the couch. I felt ready to crawl out of my skin.

Jack looked apologetic. Matty looked bewildered. Nate looked embarrassed. It was a Wednesday night. I just got off work and had class in the morning. A full day tomorrow. What was happening?

"Well, we came to help you celebrate! I didn't even know it was your birthday until your grandmother called me." Why was that woman so awful? "Your father tried to tell me you wouldn't want to do anything, but I remember being your age." Stacy laughed. No one else did.

My father seemed to be on a different planet entirely. His eyes were distant and pained. The expression horribly familiar. It was how he looked up until the divorce.

"We tried calling," he offered, as if that made it my fault they came here. Of course. Why not?

"If we'd known you had work, we wouldn't have come tonight. Do you work tomorrow night?" Stacy asked. Did she not feel the cold in the room? The gut-churning anxiety?

I nodded.

"What about classes? Can we do a family lunch?" I winced at the word. Stacy's face started to fall. "I just wish I hadn't missed your birthday."

"You should have listened to my dad."

Stacy blinked, her smile finally slipping. "I know this marriage hasn't been easy for you, dear, but it's okay to accept love. Your mother is in Italy and you only get one birthday a year. Let us spoil you a little. Because we love you."

I was staring at my dad, trying to see the words echoed on his face. He was a million miles away. He was keeping it to himself. Not telling Stacy about what happened even now. Talk about needing to accept love.

I could feel the task falling to me. The responsibility settling on my shoulders to take care of myself. I'd have to say something.

"We might have rushed our plans since we were so worried," Stacy was still talking. Each time she said "we" I wanted to roll my eyes. Clearly, she should be saying "I." My dad had no part in any of this. "We didn't get a hotel room. Nate can stay with Jack, but do you think you could find room for us here? I can change sheets or whatever else is needed. Also, if you're hungry, we can make a food run. Here, Jack, take this and go pick us up something."

Jack took the twenties Stacy handed him without question. The ease of his acceptance caught me by surprise. Nate stood with him and when his mom didn't say anything, they left. Just like that. I stared at the closed door for a beat too long, my throat getting tight.

My only spot of warmth remaining in the room was Matty. I hurried to sit next to him on the couch. I didn't want to let Jack's departure hurt alongside everything else I was feeling, but it did. It really did.

Matty grabbed my hand and I sucked in a breath. "I just changed my sheets," Matty said. "You two can take my room tonight."

"Oh, Matty. You don't have to sleep on the couch for us," Stacy said.

But I did?

"I was already planning to go to my boyfriend's."

"Who's your boyfriend?" Stacy latched onto the topic, perching herself on the armchair. Our apartment had never felt so small.

Matty talked about Andrew for a while, but an uncomfortable lull wasn't long in the making. Stacy turned back to me and I tensed. "What did you do for your birthday?" she asked.

Once again, my eyes sought my dad as if he'd step forward and save me from this. He cleared his throat and my heart jumped, but he just settled back against the counter, not meeting my gaze.

"I don't like my birthday."

Matty squeezed my hand and leaned forward, blocking me partially from view. "We're throwing her a party this weekend."

Stacy smiled. "How fun!" She leaned around Matty to keep me in view. "But why don't you like your birthday?"

I was getting mad. Why couldn't she just read the room? "I just don't."

"But everyone likes their birthday!" Stacy laughed. My dad winced at the sound. "Why don't you like it? Birthday cake mishap? Did your dad not get you the presents you wanted one too many times? What's the story?"

She wanted to get to know me better. She wanted to be part of my life and family. I knew that. I told myself that. I tried to swallow the irritation that she was here and Jack wasn't. That she was in my apartment and my mom was silent in Italy. That she was reaching for my hand and my dad was standing stiffly across the room, not coming to my aid. I couldn't swallow it. I couldn't take it. I moved out of Stacy's reach, gripping Matty like a lifeline.

"My brother died on my birthday." I spat the words in Stacy's face, gratified by her jump but not by my dad's flinch. The room went still. Silence stretched.

I couldn't be here. "I'm going to bed."

I got up and rushed to my room, locking my door behind me. I wouldn't cry. I wouldn't cry. I was embarrassed and I hurt my dad. In my anger, I'd thrown out the pain of my brother's death like a barb meant to strike Stacy. Just because she was worried. Because she wanted to celebrate my birthday with me. Because she interrupted the night I had planned with Jack and threw off my week.

And I couldn't stop thinking about Jack just leaving. Leaving me after seeing how hard my birthday was. This was why Matty was the only one I let in. If I asked him to, he'd kick out Stacy and my dad and stay with me all night. Since I didn't ask him to do that, I knew he'd make sure my dad and Stacy were comfortable before leaving. Matty was the only one I could trust to do what I needed. Why couldn't I learn?

I couldn't focus on my dad and Stacy and hurtful words when Jack was so much easier to be angry at. To be disappointed in. I replayed him slipping out the door over and over and fumed alone in my room, disaster in my wake but not caring what kind of conversation my dad was having with Stacy now.

What kind of a person did that make me?

ELEVEN

WHEN I LEFT my room in the morning, Stacy was the only one in the living room/kitchen area. She looked tired and her jaw was slightly clenched. I tried to walk by her for the front door without making eye contact, but she stopped me with a hand on my arm.

"Roly, I am so sorry. I know none of this has to do with me and the hurt has been around far longer than I have... I just can't believe your father never mentioned..." She looked a little lost. A lot hurt. I didn't want to have to comfort her, but I still felt bad about my outburst the night before.

"We don't talk about Brady."

"Brady," she repeated the name softly.

"And we pretend my birthday doesn't happen. You couldn't have known that, but maybe try to follow our cues better in the future."

"I will, but I also can't read minds. I'm trying, Roly. So hard."

Too hard.

I just nodded.

"Can we still do a lunch today if you have time? I think we have some things we need to discuss as a family."

Dread was cold and pressing, but I forced myself to nod again. "I can meet you at one, but I have class now. I have to go."

"Would you like a ride?"

She didn't know anything. "No, thanks."

I practically ran out of the apartment. I wanted to call Jack. But he was at work and a big part of me still wasn't happy with him. He'd just taken Stacy's money and left. I had Matty and that had helped so much but... I had been thinking maybe Jack could be someone to lean on too. It hurt realizing that wasn't the case. That he didn't understand what I was feeling. He didn't read it on my face. He was still Team Stacy and did what she wanted over offering me comfort.

The more I thought about it, the angrier I became. Last night was supposed to be ours and he did nothing to defend it. He didn't say a word to me. Hadn't even texted to check up on me.

I went to class but barely paid attention. I was angry with myself now too. I needed to focus as finals drew near. My future and escape from all this depended on my success.

I went to the library instead of Moonbean and nearly cried when Andrew found me there. I loved him and Matty. I loved being known and seen and predicted. Andrew didn't even have to text me, he just put in the effort to find me.

He set down a coffee cup from Moonbean. There was a heart drawn on it, likely from Jack. I took off the lid so I wouldn't have to look at the heart every time I drank.

"Matty and I can come to lunch if you want. I'm good with parents," Andrew said.

It was true. Matty's parents adored Andrew. Probably called him more than they called Matty. Matty loved it.

"I think this is just one of those adult things I have to do alone. Thanks, though."

Andrew nodded. "Do you want to be alone? Or to talk? Or to sit together and not talk?"

I smiled and bumped Andrew with my foot under the table. "I think the last one."

"Of course. First, can I just say, Jack seemed upset? He asked me to let you know he thought he left his phone at your house."

"Okay. Thanks." It made me feel slightly better. At least it was a good excuse for him not checking up on me. But Jack wasn't here now, and he didn't stay last night when I needed him. Texts weren't as important as actions.

Andrew and I worked on homework in silence, headphones in and coffee sipped. The clock moved too quickly toward my next class. Toward "family" lunch. I kept glancing at Andrew, debating taking him up on his offer. Every time I swallowed the words.

Class passed too quickly. Before I knew it, I was biking to a nearby Mexican restaurant. My dad, Stacy, and Nate had already been sat. I slid into the space on the booth next to Nate.

We shared stiff greetings and I picked up a laminated menu. Its border was decorated with yellow and orange flowers, much easier to look at than my dad and Stacy.

In my periphery, I saw Stacy elbow my dad. My heart hurt. It shouldn't take reminders and effort for a dad to talk to his daughter. "How was class, Roly?" he asked.

"It was fine."

"Finals coming up?"

"Yes."

"Think you're ready?"

"I should be. After the party, I think I'll just use the rest of the weekend to study."

"Good plan. What kind of party are we talking about, though?"

I swallowed a sigh. If my dad still wanted to pretend I didn't drink or go out after my showing at his wedding, I didn't want to explain it to him now. "Just a small get-together at Andrew's place."

The server came by with a basket of chips and a round of waters.

"So, I think we need to talk about what happened last night," Stacy said. I couldn't tell who was more uncomfortable. My dad, me, or Nate.

I looked at my dad, willing him to speak up. To explain our

family so I didn't have to. He proposed. He made the wedding vows. He invited Stacy into our life. He was the parent.

But he didn't speak up and silence fell. I clenched my fists and forced myself to break it. "I don't like celebrating my birthday and I don't like being on my phone that day. Now you know not to bother calling or worrying on my birthday. I also like my space and being able to separate my life here from family." I ignored my dad's flinch. "I felt like you invaded my boundaries last night and I don't appreciate it. Next time, if you can't reach me, call Matty. I'm twenty-two. I have a life and a busy schedule. I don't like surprises like that and I hope in the future you'll respect my space enough not to do this again."

Stacy visibly fought her tears. What did she expect? My father was staring at the brightly colored tablecloth like a chastised child. He would never have sprung this on me. He knew the unspoken expectations of our family. Why hadn't he stopped Stacy?

"Thanks for telling us," Nate said. "I didn't even think to call Jack first, but I should have known he'd be around and would have warned you. I'm sorry." He was also staring at the table. I wanted to assure him his presence wasn't as bad, but I didn't know how to do that without making Stacy's tears spill over. I didn't want Nate to feel like he couldn't visit his best friend without asking for my permission.

I relaxed with his apology though. When the server came by again, we all ordered hastily. No one had really looked at the menu so we went with the basics, chicken quesadillas for my dad and me. Beef tacos for Nate and a cheese enchilada for Stacy. I sipped on my water after the server left. It became clear we were waiting on Stacy to gather herself.

Finally, she drew in a deep breath. "I'm also sorry for barging in on you last night. My mother and I are very close. She surprises us with visits all the time. I didn't take into account the differences in relationships you might have with your parents." She sent my dad an accusing look. He didn't meet her eyes.

I sighed. We picked at the basket of tortilla chips and salsa. Stacy leaned forward and lifted a hand like she wanted to touch me and thought better of it. "I'm not trying to be a second mom, Roly, please understand that, but I do want us to be family. Please just give me a chance. Keep up this communication and I think we could, we might, well, I'm hoping one day you won't feel like you have to escape us." She gave a shaky smile.

I struggled to find a response and was saved by the door opening. A rush of cold air accompanied Jack's arrival. He was still wearing his apron and had flour on one of his eyebrows. I tried not to feel as happy as I was to see him. But his eyes went right to me as he hurried over. I scooted down on the bench to make room and Jack slid in next to me, pressed thigh to thigh even though there was space for him to keep his distance. He pulled off his coat, noticed his apron and took that off, then settled into the seat, cold hand settling between my knees. I pressed them together, trapping his fingers there.

"Sorry. I just got off," he said.

I tried to hold onto my anger with him, but I was too relieved that he was here. I wrapped a hand around his wrist, holding him in place even more. I felt his rapid pulse. I could confront him later.

He ordered a water and some tacos when the server stopped by. His knee was bouncing, and he didn't meet Stacy's disapproving stare. She had planned for this to just be family. For once, Jack put my needs first. Did that make up for last night?

At this moment, yes.

Jack turned to me, cautious. "So I was thinking Nate should stay for your party, if that's okay with you. I'll drive him back home Saturday or Sunday."

Nate tensed on my other side. I turned to him and smiled. "You should stay. It'll be fun."

Though it meant him staying with Jack at Jack's house. Our plans from yesterday were put on hold even longer. Jack ran his thumb over the sensitive skin on the inside of my knee. Even just that rhythmic contact was enough to thaw out any remaining chill toward him and pool heat in my core. There was a certain amount of trust broken between us, maybe just on my end, but I couldn't deny how badly I wanted to ignore it all and pretend this was enough.

Stacy was smiling now. She liked seeing us getting along. All the disapproval for Jack was gone from her face. I felt another moment of doubt then. Was Jack here now for me or her? Did he throw out the invite in front of everyone for Nate's sake, my own, or Stacy's?

The warmth in my stomach twisted into something a bit uglier.

***

"So, they just showed up? And Jack left without saying goodbye?" Maya double-checked.

I nodded miserably. "Well, he came back with food but by then I was hiding in my room."

"And he didn't come in to see if you were okay?"

"No." But by then my door was locked and my headphones had been in.

"Hmm." Maya took a long drink of her tea, sucking on the air between the ice cubes loudly. Priya sighed, not wanting to be left out, and hurried off to refill it.

It was so slow Maya was the only table in the restaurant. It was nice to be able to sit and chat about this. I wanted her stance on everything as a woman who had learned decades ago not to take any shit.

"I think you did good setting boundaries with your stepmother. I also think that this is only between you and your family, not Jack. Imagine how awkward he must feel caught in the middle. I think it would be good for your relationship to keep him separate from the family drama. Maybe let him know how you feel, but don't make him choose. Not when things are so new."

My shoulders lowered. Maya was probably right about that. Maybe I was projecting more on Jack than I realized. It wasn't fair to him.

Priya set down the refilled tea. "You just want them to work out so Roly will tell us about it when they finally bone. You're such a gossip, Maya."

Maya sniffed but didn't deny it. We laughed and I felt a bit lighter. "I think you're right, though," I said. "If I was Jack, I probably would have wanted to leave. And he did show up the next day. I just wish he would have at least said goodbye."

"Well, like you said, he left his phone," Priya said, eating one of Maya's sweet potato fries. "And maybe he's the only one respecting boundaries and didn't want to intrude when you'd closed your door."

Maya smacked Priya's hand away from her plate. "Alright then, Miss Cheryl. It sounds to me like you quite like this boy."

My stomach turned with nerves when I admitted, "I think I do." I might not be as hopeful now, but I wasn't ready to let Jack go.

"So, if that part of your life is going well, what are you going to do about your future?"

I laughed. "What?"

"Well, I worry about you. I want you to be excited about the future, but you hate the classes you claim will get you there and you don't even know what you want to do. I'm wondering if having a boyfriend is making you think more seriously about where and what you want to be in the future. Especially if you picture him in it."

I sighed, rubbing my temple. "I just want to make enough money to move."

"If you had enough money, what would you be doing?"

I looked around the restaurant, the answer there but it wasn't the right answer. "Sitting here and talking to you."

Maya snorted. "I think you need to talk to your advisor about a gap year. It's never good to waste money, especially on an education many people want. You're taking up someone else's seat in all those classes you don't care about. Figure out what makes you passionate, then invest."

I looked down, the guilt hitting me. I knew I was privileged to come from a high school that pushed its students to college. It seemed like the only and best option when I applied. Now here I was, three years later, and still unsure what I was doing.

"I'll think about a gap year," I said. My skin crawled at the thought of staying here another year though. Especially after Stacy's visit. I had savings, but it wasn't worth moving just to finish school somewhere else. When I finally left Colorado, I wanted it to be a move forward, not just a shift in schools. I wanted to get my future started.

But half of me relaxed at the thought of another year. Jack was here for at least two more years. Matty loved Fort Collins and Andrew was applying to get his masters at CSU. Priya had three more years of school. If I could set the boundaries I needed to with Stacy and Nate, maybe things would get easier. Maybe Fort Collins could still be enough of an escape.

"Good. And without class, you'll have more time for Jack and we can hear more about—"

"Don't say it, Maya."

"It's not like you to be a prude, Miss Cheryl. You always have the best stories."

"Jack's different."

I ignored the smile that Maya and Priya shared. It was true and I refused to be embarrassed. I liked what I had with Jack, and I liked how much we kept just between the two of us. He wasn't a drunken one-night stand gone hilariously wrong. He wasn't a story to tell the next day. He was special and mine

I suddenly couldn't wait to see him. His leaving to grab food at the back of my mind as the heat rekindled in my core. With our schedules, I wouldn't be seeing him until Friday. It was the first time since Andrew started planning the party that I was excited about it. Priya's mind went down a similar path and we started planning outfits with Maya's outrageous input.

Friday work was insane. Priya and I did our best to keep ahead with our side-work despite the rush, but tables camped for far too long as they drank and avoided the snow outside. I wasn't looking forward to riding Trevor home. I would need to get there quickly to change, then Matty and I would drive to Andrew's for the party.

By the time I stopped taking tables, Matty was calling to see where I was. Priya was second cut but helped me roll silverware so I could leave sooner. She sent me off as if she were my fairy godmother and had just saved the night by helping me. She had a change of clothes in her car and makeup already done. Chances were she'd get to Andrew's before me.

I called Matty back as I pulled on my coat and clocked out, a wad of cash in my pocket. Honestly, the money had been worth it. Matty didn't bother with a greeting. "I'm outside. We'll come get Trevor tomorrow but it's too cold for you to bike tonight."

"I love you." I tucked my gloves under my arm and waved to Priya as I left. As promised, Matty was circling the lot and when I got inside his car, my seat was warm. We drove home, me with my eyes closed, and raced each other up the stairs and into the apartment. Matty and I listened to Taylor Swift and talked as I curled my hair and did my makeup heavier than usual. A full-face that changed the girl staring back at me in the mirror entirely. I wanted to let go tonight. To drink away the birthday stress and enjoy my friends. I wanted Jack to stare at me all night until I couldn't remember why I ever doubted him. Maybe we'd even slip away and… well no, I didn't want our first time to be impeded by alcohol, but I did miss kissing him.

I wore a cropped black shirt, no bra, and high-waisted jeans that had enough holes to show off basically my entire legs. I cuffed them and stomped into my black Docs. Matty whistled his appreciation when I left my room.

"You look pretty good yourself," I told him. His jeans were black with holes of their own at the knee. His sweater was a burgundy that looked so warm I couldn't help hugging him. He pulled me half away and we took a few selfies.

"God, we look like a boring straight couple from the waist up."

I laughed. "It's a good picture. Save it."

We were slightly more than fashionably late by the time we pulled onto Andrew's street. The lights of his house were lit, but his neighbors' windows were dark. Hopefully, they weren't home. The music pulsed into the night as we walked up his drive and into the garage. A round of cheering went up at my arrival even though I maybe knew a third of the people there. A lot of Lynn's track friends. A few people from classes I'd shared with Matty or Andrew. People from Study Room who got off before me, including an already tipsy Priya.

Jack jumped out of the crowd and swept me off my feet in a tight hug. "I missed you," he said into my hair.

I pulled back and gave him the kiss I'd been craving. Tongues and all in front of everyone, drawing another round of cheering. When we broke the kiss, Jack was blushing and grinning like an idiot.

Nate came forward with drinks and the night got started in earnest. Apparently, Jack's party-loving roommate had invited himself. While I didn't like him from Jack's stories, his enthusiasm for drinking games did shift the party into full gear. Soon my cheeks were numb, Andrew was on Matty's lap on the couch, and Jack and I were undefeated at the beer pong table.

The game got harder the more I drank, and I convinced Jack we should quit while we were ahead. We went back to the drink table where Nate was flirting with a girl I'd hooked up with last year. She took in my outfit with appreciation and Jack's hand on my hip with a pout. But then she took Jack in with appreciation. The look she turned on me was suggestive.

"We're not going there, Abby," I told her, laughing.

"What? I wasn't thinking about anything. Unless you want me to…" She winked. Nate looked startled. Jack took it all in a stride.

"I'm flattered, but at this point in my life, I'm not into sharing," I said, putting my hand over Jack's. Abby shrugged and turned back to the party.

I tensed, waiting for the usual threesome comment that my sexual attracted for some reason. I didn't mind it as much when a girl hinted at it, but it felt reductive from men in a way that made me want to hit something.

Instead, Nate and Jack started making fun of Jack's mess of a roommate, who was already slumped in a chair near the door and laughing at nothing in particular as far as I could tell. Despite his joking, Jack didn't look happy about it.

He made another comment about Nate moving to Fort Collins. Nate glanced at me and cleared his throat. "I'm actually thinking I should just finish the year in Denver."

"But you got accepted here! We found a place!"

"I know, but I just feel—"

"You should come here, Nate," I interrupted. He was only planning to stay away for me, and I didn't like that. "I mean it. It would be fun. Jack needs to get out of his current living situation. If I hear him complain about it much more, it'll probably be over between us."

"Oh, no! You *have* to come here, Nate! I'm incapable of not complaining."

Nate laughed, looking unsure. Meeting my steady gaze, Nate nodded and a grin spread across his face. Jack jumped around in celebration, almost taking out the drink table. He was drunker than I thought, but I could only laugh at his excitement. The last of my tension eased out of my chest.

"I need to pee, walk with me?" I asked him.

He took my hand and let me lead the way out of the garage,

through the crowded living room, and upstairs. I went straight to Andrew's bedroom and kicked the door shut. Jack met my enthusiastic kiss as if he'd been waiting all night. He couldn't keep his hands off the skin exposed between my jeans and shirt, even running a thumb under the roll of my stomach where my jeans were tight. I wanted to be embarrassed, but he moaned into my mouth, and I melted in the way only he could make me melt. He backed me up against the door, pressing his hips into mine, his body curved so we pressed together in all the right places.

I brushed my lips up his neck, feeling his pulse in his throat and hearing his quick breaths when I lingered there kissing. I licked him from the base up and his entire body shuddered as I nibbled his jaw. He swallowed hard and I felt him stiffen, then suck in a breath.

He pushed his next words out. "I've still been waiting," he said quickly. Nervously. Cheeks warming with embarrassment. "I haven't touched myself."

"Good," I whispered the word into his neck and nipped at his earlobe.

He let out a breathless laugh and I felt his dick jump between us. Pressing my hips into it and making him gasp, I looked over his shoulder at Andrew's bed, perfectly made and waiting. With some regret, I pulled back a bit. Jack's hands tightened at my waist. "But I want to be sober when we do it," I said.

Jack's pupils were huge. I couldn't make out any color in the dim room. "When Roly?"

"Do you work Sunday morning?"

"No." He pulled me closer again, bending to kiss my neck now. He paused to inhale deeply. Smelling me. More heat pooled and I moved against him again, making him shudder. It was agony not to do more.

"Tomorrow night, when I get off work? It might be late."

"I'm taking Nate home in the morning so that works. I'll wait. I'll keep waiting."

"Good," I said again, brushing the back of my knuckles down

his hard length. He moaned, hips bucking as he searched for more pleasure. His nerves were gone, burned away by the heat between us. I would keep burning it away until he never doubted himself again. I hated his ex for calling him boring and breaking the confidence everyone should feel with a willing and eager sexual partner. "I'm going to take you apart," I whispered.

"Yeah?" I could feel him straining to keep still. I was fighting the urge to reach for myself.

"It'll be beautiful."

Jack froze for a moment, face buried in my neck. He drew in a long, shaking breath. "We should probably stop unless you want me to come right now."

I laughed and wrapped my arms around him. He held me back and we stayed like that, simply hugging until some of the strain began to ease. Jack took a deep breath, shifting the hair at my ear. "Fuck, Roly."

I wanted to hear him say that every day. "I'm so wet right now."

He stepped quickly away. Shook out his hands. Looked longingly at the bed. Down at the bump in the front of his jeans. Back at the ceiling. "I think I'm having a heart attack."

I laughed, leaning against the door and just staring at him. "You're so gorgeous."

"Seriously, stop. I'm going to make a mess." He glanced down at his dick again.

"Should we go back to the party?"

"Well, obviously not at this moment."

"One time I walked in on my grandma naked. She just met my eyes and said, 'Take it in, Cheryl. You don't appreciate it until it looks like this.'"

Jack stared at me, horrified. "Why would you say that?" he whispered.

"Are you picturing her? All proud and saggy and mean."

He shuddered. The bulge in the front of his pants started to ease. "She really was mean."

I laughed and waited while he thought about her a bit longer. "Ready now?"

"Unfortunately."

Jack took my hand and we rejoined the party. Every look between us for the rest of the night had me squeezing my legs. He kept shaking his head at me, mouthing for me to stop when my sex eyes had him adjusting his pants and thinking about grandparents.

Tomorrow couldn't come soon enough.

TWELVE

I WOKE UP CAREFULLY. I could tell I drank a lot last night, but I'd also paced myself, not wanting to get sloppy at my own party when eyes were already on me. Jack had left around one, him and Nate helping Jack's roommate to his car. I was currently sleeping in Lynn's bed with her and Priya. My nails were a mess. We'd decided around two in the morning to paint them. Matty and I had matching black, but it wasn't done very well. Lynn had her arm around me and Priya was snoring.

I heard noises downstairs and untangled myself. Andrew and Matty were already up. Matty looked miserable at the kitchen table and Andrew was making coffee. We'd cleaned up some last night before bed, but the kitchen could only be described as sticky. I grimaced at the counter as I accepted a mug from Andrew.

"Don't worry about it. Lynn and I will clean it today. You aren't cleaning up your own birthday party."

"I thought it wasn't a birthday party."

"It was a party for you, and you aren't cleaning it."

I smiled into my mug. Andrew sat down next to Matty, placing a coffee cup next to the water in front of his boyfriend.

"Did you have fun?" Matty asked.

"I did. And also, you're going to have to stay here again tonight."

The hungover pain left Matty's eyes as he smirked. "Do you think Stacy will show up again and ruin the mood?"

I groaned and sank down in my chair. "Now I'm just going to be thinking about her tonight."

Andrew laughed. "No, you won't. I couldn't stay off Matty after just watching you too."

"Ew." Matty rolled his eyes and forcefully redirected the conversation. "So, you aren't mad at him anymore?"

"I don't think so. It kind of felt like he was taking Stacy's side but saying that just feels like such an immature thing to be mad about. I talked it out with Maya and she thinks it's not fair to make him choose or involve him in my family issues."

"Your feelings are your feelings," Andrew reminded me.

Matty nodded vigorously, then winced and sipped from his water.

"But also, I don't even know if that's actually what happened. He probably didn't think he was choosing anyone. Maybe he just didn't know how to handle the situation. None of us did."

"That's true. It was *incredibly* awkward," Matty said.

"I wish he hadn't left and maybe that he'd jumped in to make things easier, but my family drama isn't his fault or his problem."

"That's fair, but if you do feel hurt by his actions, that's okay too. Just maybe work on talking to him about it next time instead of avoiding him until your drunk at a party," Andrew said.

"Don't attack me like that!" We all laughed because Andrew hadn't spoken with anything but kindness. His words did hit hard though and I regretted pushing Jack away the last few days. "I'll make it all up to him tonight," I promised.

"Ew," Matty repeated.

I was grateful for the chaos of the busy Saturday night shift at work. I ran around most of the time and it passed in a blur. Before I knew it, I was biking home and showering thoroughly. I moisturized and told Jack to come over, then stared into my under-wear drawer, unsure how I wanted to dress.

I went with my black underwear and triangle bra set. I pulled on Jack's sweatshirt and tight black biker shorts, admiring my freshly shaved legs in the mirror for a moment. It had been three months since I last shaved and I usually didn't, not even for sex, but I wanted to feel extra confident and enjoyed the smooth brush of uninterrupted skin. I wanted every inch of it pressed against Jack.

Fluffing my hair to try and coax it into dry with volume, I walked around making sure everything looked neat. I lit a candle in my room and turned on the lamp, casting a flattering glow. I brushed my teeth. Drank enough water to stay hydrated. Walked another lap.

Finally, Jack knocked at the door. I met my own eyes in my mirror. I looked nervous. Excited. My cheeks were flushed and my hair slightly damp, but I smiled at myself, liking the woman in my reflection. With that boost of confidence, I went to the door.

Jack was running an anxious hand through his hair when I opened it. He swallowed hard when he saw me. "Hey!" His voice was too high.

I regretted then the number of days that had passed since my reassurances at Moonbean. He looked so unsure of himself that I couldn't believe I ever doubted how much I meant to him.

"Don't be nervous," I said softly, pulling him inside. I kissed him as gently as I could and then wrapped my arms around him. "Nothing is going to happen that you don't want to happen."

"I... I want it all to happen, I just want to make sure you—"

"How about tonight, I show you what I like? Then we go from there once you have a better idea. You say you've researched, so you know the basic concepts, I'm just going to show you how they apply to *me*."

"Okay." He swallowed again and I went to get him a glass of water. He sipped on it, eyes darting around the living room. They rested on the Taylor Swift shrine.

"Come here." I loved how quickly he followed my gentle command. I felt a rush in my core, thinking about the other things I wanted to tell him to do. We went up to Taylor and knelt in front of her. Jack relaxed enough to laugh. I asked Taylor for her blessing, making him laugh again. His grip tightened on my hand and he leaned closer so our shoulders were aligned.

"May we do well enough to inspire lyrics of your standard."

Jack's laugh was nervous again. I'd just have to show him he had nothing to worry about. I turned and kissed him. The kiss quickly deepened. Jack set his water aside. I pulled him down on top of me. When we were breathless and our hands on the verge of straying, I felt the shift that came with the confidence of a partner as enthusiastic as Jack. "Go in my room and sit in my chair."

His eyes darkened at the command in my voice. "Okay."

I followed him into my room, admiring his ass in his jeans as we went. He looked unsure again as he turned and sat in my reading chair. How many erotic scenes had I read right there? I couldn't wait to act this one out.

"If you're okay with it, I want to take the lead." I hoped he understood what I meant.

Jack was already nodding before I could finish the sentence. "Okay."

"Just tell me if it's ever too much. And tell me when you're about to come. You don't get to until I say it's okay."

He squirmed in the seat, the front of his pants betraying how my words affected him. I felt a flush of warmth. I was so wet just looking at him sitting there, waiting for me, at my disposal. My hands trembled a bit with need, but they steadied when I reached him. I straddled his lap and grabbed the back of his hair, pulling his head back so I could kiss him deeply and thoroughly.

"Roly," he panted the nickname against my lips. I stilled, thinking of the nickname's origin. A young, chubby girl somersaulting around my childhood home.

"Don't call me Roly right now."

"Okay." His hands were on my ribs, his thumbs brushed the underside of my boobs. My breath caught and I bent to kiss him again, rolling my hips to make friction against the hard zipper of his jeans.

I moaned and he gasped, pulling back. "Maybe we need to… slow down." He was breathing hard. Blushing with embarrassment and need. Even as he said it, he pushed his hips into me.

"Sit still."

He froze. He was sexy and perfect, and I loved how well he listened. I took his wrists and put his hands on the arms of the chair. I put some of my weight behind keeping them there.

"I can't touch you?" There was a needy panic in his voice, but I could also see in his growing pupils how much it turned him on.

"Not until I tell you."

He nodded, biting his botom lip.

"Good." I rewarded him with a kiss and another roll of my hips.

He let out that delicious sound that was all his. Nearly a whine. A high-pitched and swallowed groan. "Cheryl…"

I loved that. Loved the sound of him begging and the use of a name that always felt too adult, too sophisticated. Not now. With him at my mercy and following my orders, it felt right.

I shifted back and he started to move his hands as if to keep me close but caught himself in time. His knuckles were white from his grip on the arms of the chair. I stood and took him in. Hair messed up, lips pink and swollen like my own felt. He shifted his hips again, trying to find some sort of release. I gave him a look and he stilled again with a pleased whimper.

He was falling into this as completely as I was. Soon, it would just be us. Two souls bared by need and desire and pleasure. I wanted to reduce him to his most basic self. I felt it in my underwear, the hot buildup that came just from the thought. "You're doing amazing."

He smiled, staring up at me, soaking in the encouragement. I never wanted him to stop looking at me like that.

"Take your shirt off, Jack."

It was gone between one blink and the next. He took a shuddering breath as I pushed his knees apart and knelt between them. "Cheryl." His voice cracked.

"Put your hands back where they were."

He looked startled, not having realized he was reaching for me. He did as he was told, bare chest shaking with the force of his breathing. He had a patch of hair in the middle of his chest. More pointing out from the band of his underwear. I scratched my fingers lightly through the hair on his chest. He stared at them, then at me as goosebumps rose on his skin. I put both hands on his stomach and ran them up to his shoulders, watching his muscles jump and tighten. He was starting to sweat. I enjoyed the view of it glistening on him, then leaned forward and traced a path from his belly button to his throat with just the tip of my tongue. He yelped, clutching at the armrest. I licked up one side of his neck, bracing myself with hands on his thighs. I kissed under his ear. "Is this okay so far?"

It took him a moment to catch his breath enough to answer. "Cheryl, this is so, so, good. But are, are you? I'm not doing anything and…"

Without pulling my face away from his neck, I followed the length of his arm with my hand, fingers light and trailing down from his shoulder. I found his hand and guided it inside my shorts. He was barely breathing. I shuddered when his fingertips made contact with my clit and then he gasped to find how wet I was. "I'm fucking enjoying myself."

"Fuck. *Fuck*. Rol—Cheryl, fuck." I pulled his hand back out of my pants, tugging when he tried to resist and keep touching me. I put his hand firmly back on the armrest. He was shuddering beneath me, pulling in hard, unsteady breaths.

I drew the tip of my nose up his neck until my lips were at his ear. I barely breathed my next words. "I'm going to blow you now."

He moaned, head falling back and missing the cushion. It

thudded against the wooden frame of the chair. If it hurt, he didn't seem to notice. I kissed his chest some more on the way down, pausing to pay special attention to his nipples until they were reacting to my touch too and Jack was moaning. I went to my knees, sitting back and grinding myself against one of my heels to release just a little of the tension gathered in my clit as I freed Jack from his pants. He pushed his hips out to help me guide his pants and underwear off.

I stopped again to admire him fully naked before me. I loved every line of his body. Every inch of skin. I scratched my nails through his leg hair, ankle to knee, pausing on his thigh. "Look at me, Jack."

He didn't.

I smiled.

I dug my nails in a bit and watched his dick jump. "Look at me, babe."

"I might come," he whispered the words at the ceiling.

"Not until I say." I sat back, grinding against my heel again and leaning away, giving him a moment without my heat. "Look when you're ready, but I want you to watch me do this for you."

His dick jumped again. I hadn't really even touched it, but a hint of moisture was already beading at the top. I wanted to suck it away, but that might be his undoing. He breathed and stared at the ceiling. His body started to relax enough for him to joke, "Just please don't mention your grandmother."

"Clearly you're already thinking about her."

Jack laughed, finally ducking his head so he could look at me, looking proud of himself. I smiled up at him, resisting the urge to praise him again.

"You're so beautiful," Jack told me. "Can I ask you to do stuff too?"

"Depends on what it is."

"As much as I love you in my clothes, will you take off the sweatshirt?" I pulled it up and over my head, throwing it at his face to make him laugh again. I wanted him to last a bit longer. This distraction would hopefully help.

Jack caught it to his face and inhaled deeply. I flushed with more longing. "Put your hands back, Jack." He dropped his sweatshirt to the side and did as he was told. I pressed myself harder into my heel at the sight.

"And your shorts?" Jack asked. I smirked and shook my head, loving how his gaze instantly heated at the denial.

"In just a bit," I told him. In truth, while I was still focusing on him, I was enjoying the placement of the seam with every rub against my heel.

He stared down at me, stiffening up again as a hush fell over us. "What happens next?"

"Now, you warn me when you're close."

Jack nodded. I kissed the inside of his knee, slowly sucking and licking and nipping until my lips were inside the junction of his thigh and groin, his dick against my cheek. I loved its warmth there, loved how when I pressed against it, the hand I could see tightened on the arm of the chair. I kissed the very base of him, my hands coming up to explore. I kept my touch light and teasing on his balls, the skin underneath. One slipped a little lower, only applying a bit of pressure with my fingertips. Jack clenched and whimpered. I checked his face. It was dark with lust and need. I hadn't gone too far. It was all the encouragement I needed to rise up on my knees and take him into my mouth.

Jack wasn't huge, but I couldn't take him in to his base. He was perfect. Every inch. I didn't like the pain that came with big partners any more than I liked the ego that also too often came with size.

Jack grunted and I tasted some of his spill. I sat back as quickly as I'd taken him in. He was breathing hard, hair sticking to his forehead and temples with sweat. Staring at me. Looking undone.

I was close to the moment when all the outside world broke away. He was still too disbelieving, couldn't get over the fact that he was here like this. I wanted him here fully in the moment, just him and me and pleasure.

"You good?" I asked.

He again struggled to find his voice. "I didn't come."

"Good." He looked relieved by my praise again. I ran a finger up his dick, watching it jump. I loved making him twitch like this. Every part of his body reacted to me. I checked his white-knuckled grip on the armrest. Then I licked the same path with my tongue, first with just the tip, then I flattened my tongue and did it again. I paid attention to the head until he was gasping out that he was close. I kissed up and down his thighs, up his stomach, and along his knuckles until he was breathing normally again. I went back to taking him in my mouth, up and down, gagging a bit and making eye contact until he was frantically shaking his head.

Then I stood. He made sounds of protest that he cut off as soon as I said his name low with warning. I went to my nightstand and grabbed a condom and a small bullet vibrator. His eyes lit up at the sight of the condom. "Hold this." I put the vibrator in his hand. He clutched it.

Then I pulled off my shorts. He was silent, reverent, as I got fully naked.

"Can I touch you?" He sounded as if I was strangling him.

"Not yet."

"Please, Cheryl."

"Wait." I straddled him again and rolled the condom down his length. Then, slow enough to torture us both, I guided his dick inside me and lowered myself. We were both gasping and groaning as I got into position. I could probably have come just from riding him like this, but he wouldn't last that long. I sat back on him, the pressure and feel of him incredible even when I was still.

I met his eyes again and there it was. The world was gone. All he saw was me and his lust and animal instinct he still fought at my command. Jack, raw and bare and open.

He was stunning. So beautiful I felt it in my chest, where I'd never experienced the sensation before. I longed for him, hurt with how much I wanted him happy and with me.

I loved it.

I loved him.

"You can touch me now, but don't come until I do."

"But..." The fear crept back. I refused to let it ruin the moment. I took his hand with the vibrator, turned it on, and pressed it into the perfect spot on my clit. Jack felt the jolt of it inside me when it hit. Our breathing picked up at the same time.

I clutched his shoulders as his hand held the vibrator in place, the other coming up to explore my breasts. Down my side. Squeezing my ass. He was panting. I was gasping. We were raw and together and he was so beautiful, so beautiful, so good, and beautiful...

"So are you. I love you," Jack whispered.

I didn't let my shock at his words break the moment. He was too far gone to even notice fully what he said. I certainly hadn't realized I was talking out loud.

"Go Jack." I didn't need to elaborate. He started bucking his hips under us, grunting and gasping, pressing at me exactly where I needed, his hand shaking as it held the vibrator in place.

I broke over him. I didn't know what noises I made, but I felt the pulse of my release blindingly hard inside me and then Jack's and then just simple, perfect, throbbing pleasure.

THIRTEEN

I TENDED to wake up happy, especially here in this apartment. I loved Matty and my little home and knowing what the day would bring. I loved Fort Collins and biking to class. I loved when my feet were still a bit sore from work the night before. I loved the bed I bought with my own money, my biggest and most adult purchase. I thought I was so happy with the life I built here.

None of that compared to how it felt to be woken up by Jack.

I slowly woke, relaxed and warm, his body pressed flush to mine. He was kissing my neck. I hummed and tilted my head to give him more access. He pressed closer at the encouragement. I felt him breathing me in almost as much as he was kissing. I murmured a good morning, but he was already wide awake. Past sleepy mumblings. He was almost desperate, whispering compliments and gratitude for last night.

It was better than quiet murmurs.

"I fucking love that chair," he said, pushing against my thigh with his morning erection. We were both only in our underwear. We'd fallen asleep cuddling after the chair incident. I had planned to keep the night going, but we'd both worked the day before and the chair sex had taken a lot out of both of us. I was still in wonder of these feelings in my chest. I would do anything for Jack right now after how completely he'd given himself to me.

Even his nearing frantic kisses were still so sweet. My heart raced knowing he must be bursting with these feelings too. I lifted my hips, pressing myself into him so he groaned. I pulled off my underwear and reached for a condom. He was panting and compliant as I pushed his underwear down, freeing his hard dick with a bounce that was far sexier than it should be. I rolled the condom down him. He was breathing harder now. "No, wait. Cheryl, I should…"

"You will. I'll still teach you soon. Right now, I want you inside me." I pulled at his arm until he was braced over me. Still, he hesitated. "I want to feel your weight. I want to feel how much you want me. Go, Jack."

He let out a little laugh, closer to a whimper. I pulled up my knees so he fit perfectly between them. I could listen to him moaning all day. He eased himself inside me. I was already so wet for him and it drew out a whispered *fuck*. I smiled when he went slow, teasing himself with his thrusts, drawing it out. He kept looking at me, unsure. I nodded and pushed my fingers through his hair. "Keep going."

He did. Fast, slow, breathing through gritted teeth and trans-fixed by the sight of himself moving in and out of me. He was so consumed by his want for me that I could hardly breathe watching him. Every once in a while he would slow enough to lower his full weight onto me, kissing me deep and slow before rising with a grunt and picking up his pace.

He shifted, crawling a bit closer on the bed in a way that tilted my hips up and let him in deep. He froze when I let out a noise. "Don't stop," I gasped.

He didn't. Now he only stared at my face as he worked his hips, hitting me in that perfect place. A place no one else had found. Something about the way he filled me was… it was… "Oh, god Jack, don't stop."

A couple more thrusts, another glimpse at Jack's raw soul, and I threw my head back into the pillow, grabbing at Jack so hard he hissed in pain and fucked me harder. I came so quickly, the force of it surprising and lovely. Jack didn't last long after, coming with a choked gasping sound. So hot. So raw and sexy. He settled his weight on top of me again, laying on me while I felt his dick continue to pulse every so often. I wanted to smother myself under the weight of him. I could feel his pounding heart. He was slicked with sweat. His smell and my post orgasm blood rush made my head light.

Eventually, he went up on his elbows, just enough to look at me. He brushed my hair back and kissed me quickly.

"What is it, Jack?"

"You really came right? I didn't do anything to help and—"

"Jack, I've never done that before. Come from just penetration, I mean. Well, it wasn't only penetration. Whatever is going on with your bones and form down there, it really works for me. We just fit together like that."

His hands were still on my cheeks. I put my hands on his. I brushed my thumbs along his cheekbones and felt his dick move inside me again. He loved the tenderness.

I felt nothing but tenderness toward him.

"Roly, I really fucking like you."

"I really fucking like you too, Jack."

"And I really fucking like your chair."

"Well, let's eat something and shower and maybe we'll use the chair again."

Jack's dick liked that idea, but he smiled and made no move to get up. He pulled himself out slowly and threw away the condom in the little trash can next to my nightstand. "Okay, but let's lay here for just a bit first."

I was more than happy to roll back into his arms.

My mom called while Jack and I were at lunch. "Do you mind if I answer? She isn't great about calling me often."

"Go for it." He gave me his usual sweet smile and tucked into his gyro.

"Hey, Mom."

"Hi, bug. Sorry I didn't call on your birthday."

"It's alright, Mom."

"I was just a little busy. Marco and I went out to this beautiful vineyard…" She described the whole day and I stared across the restaurant, unable to picture it. Every year on my birthday she had locked herself in Brady's room. My birthday was the sound of my mom's muffled crying. Not her getting drunk at a vineyard.

Jack noticed something was off. He got up and came to sit on my side of the table, sliding his arm behind me in silent support. It gave me the strength to cut off my mom's rambling. "You didn't call me on my birthday because you were off drinking with some guy?"

Stunned silence for too long. "Roly! You know it isn't an easy day for me."

"And you'd rather spend it with a stranger than try to help your daughter celebrate?"

"I don't understand where this is coming from."

I leaned into Jack's chest and lowered my voice. He was blocking me from the view of most of the restaurant. "Mom… I hate my birthday. I barely remember Brady, but I remember you crying every year. I remember you making sure I knew it wasn't a day to feel happy. I remember you making sure I knew from your example I had to be alone every year or I wasn't mourning his death properly."

"That's not—"

"That's exactly what you did. Don't try to gaslight me."

"You don't understand how hard it was," she whispered.

"Was? Damn, maybe you should have gone to Italy sooner if that's what it took for you to stop forcing us to be miserable with you."

It was so quiet, I worried she'd hung up. My heart raced. It felt so good to talk to her like this, but I knew it wasn't fair. That in seconds the guilt would come crashing. I spoke first, "I'm sorry. I'm just feeling… you just left and you said you'd be back for Thanksgiving. Then you said you'd be here for my birthday and now you'll probably promise to be back for Christmas but you won't come."

"I can't come back. Not yet."

Fuck fairness. "I know. Dad and Brady are enough to keep you away, but I'm not enough to bring you back. I get it." I hung up the phone and turned into Jack's chest. He held me until my angry tears stopped, only turning to get the check and ask for boxes. He ushered me outside and into his car.

"What do you need from me?" he asked.

"I need to use your body to forget everything that hurts." I attempted to keep my voice light, joking, but he heard the desperate truth in my words.

"While that may not be the healthiest coping mechanism, I suppose I can take one for the team and let you do that." He drove back to my apartment. I could see how hard it was for him not to speed, to keep from looking at me. His hand moved off the wheel once as if he wanted to offer it to me, but he put it back quickly.

Just watching his care with me, with my fear of being in the car, was enough to settle me. By the time we were a sweating, gasping heap on the floor in front of my chair, all hurt was consumed by my feelings for Jack. I held him tight and he burned away all the pain.

Finals week was spent studying at Moonbean. We claimed a corner table and rotated who guarded coffee cups and bags while the others were taking exams. After each day, we cleared up, sometimes waiting for Jack to close, then we had a movie night at our apartment, often still studying while paying half attention to the screen. I wasn't surprised that Andrew spent most of his time with me and Matty, but Lynn and Priya were also constant presences. Jack spent every night with me to avoid his roommate, who wanted to end the year with a bang. He couldn't wait to start packing next week once his roommate went home. He'd already found someone to take over his lease and on Friday Nate was coming up to sign on their new apartment.

Stacy called me on Friday night. I was surprised to feel no annoyance as I answered and let her pepper me with questions about how my finals were. She told me about Nate's fears over one of his and how happy he was that he didn't have to worry about ever getting that professor again. The conversation dipped after that. The silence moved toward awkward when Stacy cleared her throat. "Do you know if you'll be with us or your mom for Christmas, Roly?"

I swallowed and looked down. Jack was napping, his head on my lap. He'd stayed up too late studying last night and had passed out almost as soon as he got back after his last final. I played with a curl of his hair in front of his ear. It was getting long, and I loved it. "I'm not sure, but it didn't sound like she'd be back when we last talked."

"You're always welcome here."

"I know. Thanks, Stacy." And I meant it. "I'll come there if she doesn't make it." At least I'd have Jack close by.

I could tell she was trying to keep most of the excitement from her voice. I had to admit it felt nice that she hoped I'd be there. No vague promises or half-hearted I miss you's on her side of the phone. "Great! Anything you want in particular? I might have already picked up some things. Because even if you aren't here on Christmas Day, maybe you could stop by the day after or on Christmas Eve? It might be a bit much but... I'll just be honest with you; I've always wanted a daughter. There are just some things my mom did for me that I never got to do for Nate. But please, keep setting boundaries if you need to."

"Okay. I'll let you know." I traced the shell of Jack's ear. Stacy meant a lot to him. Maybe that alone should be a reason to try harder. "Is there anything you want?"

Stacy laughed a bit in surprise. "Actually, I've been seeing a lot of those charcuterie boards on my Pinterest. Maybe if you find something for one of those?"

"Sure. Those are great. We could make one for Christmas, or whenever I come, with what I get you."

There was a beat of silence. My heart dropped. I held my breath, not even sure why I was suddenly fearful. Preparing for the sting of rejection. But then Stacy sniffled. She was trying not to cry. I relaxed a bit. "I would like that, Roly. We'll make one for lunch and have a big dinner after. If you can come on Christmas, that is."

"Okay."

"Okay. I'll let you go, dear. Can't wait to see you!"

"Bye, Stacy." I hung up and stared at my phone for a moment. Jack rolled so he was looking up at me. "Sorry," I said softly. "Did I wake you up?"

He reached up and touched my cheek. "You aren't doing anything wrong when you let people in, you know that right?"

"But what if it only leads to me being hurt?" Looking into his eyes and tracing his delectable lips with my fingertip, I knew I wasn't asking about Stacy. My feelings for him only seemed to grow. Like my chest itself was expanding to contain it all. One day, he might smile at me, and I'll just burst.

It was making me skittish, no matter how much I tried to swallow my fear.

"Sometimes love hurts, but being alone hurts more. I think it's important to give people a real chance. All I know is Stacy adores my sister. Showers her with affection and silly make-up and costume dresses she makes herself. If she does that for Amelie, she'll happily do it for you too. Not such childish things, of course. But she'll also be careful not to push you away. She cares a lot, it's who she is. You wouldn't believe how much she did to take care of me when my pop got sick."

"Got sick?"

"Yeah, when I was in high school. He had cancer, but he's doing fine now. It just took a lot out of us. Amelie and I used to stay with Stacy and Nate for days. Stacy never asked for anything in return for taking care of us. That guest room, your room now, used to be my room. Amelie would sleep with Stacy most nights even though she had a bed made up on the couch." He went quiet, looking up at the ceiling now like he was too embarrassed to meet my eyes. "We struggled a lot financially and Stacy fed us and took care of our school shopping. She probably did more that I didn't see. My dads are good now mostly, but I make sure I can pay for most of my expenses since they're helping me wherever the scholarships don't cover, but it's just nice having someone reliable in our corner, just in case." Jack turned back to me, eyes cautious. "My point is, Stacy's earned my trust and I think she deserves yours. Or at least a chance. We're all a kind of big family when we're together and I want you to feel included in that."

I curled forward and kissed Jack's forehead, ignoring the doubt that swirled in my gut. I wanted him on my side and maybe Jack thought this was what was best for me, not just for Stacy. But I wished he understood my caution more. "I'll try."

"And if staying over there doesn't work out, just come to my house," Jack said, smiling now. "Either way, you should come over at some point. My dads ask about you all the time and Amelie wants to show you how she can finally make that cat."

"You guys all talk about me that much?"

"Of course. I've been talking about you constantly. Even more than I complain about my roomie."

I rolled my eyes. "Impossible." But I couldn't fight a smile. "Let's go to dinner to celebrate being done with finals. On me this time."

"Are we dressing up like a date?"

Since I could tell he liked the idea, I nodded and tried to think up an outfit. "Sure. Go home and pick me up at seven."

Jack wore a green knitted sweater. I couldn't stop staring at his eyes, the green in them popping beautifully. Even our server kept eyeing him, giving me a subtle eyebrow raise when Jack looked down at his menu. I winked back and Jack looked up to catch me smiling.

"What's up?"

"Just smiling," I said and quickly ordered a glass of malbec. The server walked away grinning.

Jack looked around the small restaurant I picked out. There were plants lining the walls and the narrow room was mostly done up in white and silvers. Local artists had paintings on the walls with handwritten price tags. This place had a similar vibe to the restaurant Jack had taken me to on our first date. Only the prices were a little harder to look at.

"I like this place," Jack said, looking up at the multicolored painting of a cow hanging on the wall above our booth.

I was wearing heels despite the cold outside and let one fall off to hook my foot around Jack's calf. "Me too." I bit my lip, looking around. "I would have applied somewhere like this if it was more bike accessible. Fort Collins does pretty well but this area is sketchy."

Jack's eyebrows knotted. He looked so concerned I tried to keep the wistful expression off my face as the server came by. She was in no hurry and wore a cute dress and light make-up. She set down my wine and told us the specials. At the Study Room right now, I would be moving from table to table like a pinball, just trying to keep up with the beer drinkers and deliver all the sides of ranch being requested.

Our server got our order and went up to the cocktail bar. The bartender was wearing a suit and if Jack wasn't sitting across from me, I might have been staring at her way more frequently.

"Do you have a driver's license?" Jack asked.

"Yeah. I just hate driving even more than I hate sitting passenger." I tried to laugh it off but couldn't make my smile fit right.

"You like where you work though, right?"

"Yeah, I like it. It's just hard during the rush sometimes and people get so drunk and care about the games on the TV more than the humans trying to give them good service. And I only make so much because of the number of customers, not because of tips." I eyed the twenty-dollar glasses of wine, quickly calculating twenty percent and hating to realize that was probably the average tip I got at Study Room with all the college students asking for separate checks.

"I would drive you. If you wanted to apply here."

I smiled at the offer. "Jack, I wouldn't ask anyone to drive me to work every day. I like the Study Room enough and one day I'll move closer to somewhere like this or I'll stop being enabled so much by the people around me and start driving. Maybe get into therapy. That would probably help."

Jack idly picked up my hand, still thinking. "You picture yourself serving for a while?"

"Oh, I guess I'd probably have a degree by then."

Jack eyed me. "You never talk about school or class. But you get so excited talking about your ideas for the menu and your customers. If you could, would you just work in a restaurant? Especially somewhere like here?"

I thought about it. I loved serving. I loved talking shit about customers and how well I dealt with difficult ones. I loved messing around in the kitchen, having the cooks show me how to use different knifes and watching the flames kiss my spatula. I loved flipping the frying basket and letting the excess oil fly. I loved helping come up with ideas for specials and talking to owners and solving the day-to-day problems that came up. I loved the rare nights I had off and had the energy to cook at home like I had for myself growing up. Podcast or smutty audiobook in my ears, I could make food way better than I served every night. Matty loved those nights as much as I did. If serving didn't pay so much better, I'd take more shifts in the kitchen. Moving positions would keep me from getting bored and I'd done it before. "I think I would."

"You know, that *is* a career. A future you could be working toward. You can just serve. Or cook or become a manager. One day you could open up a place like this of your own. If you wanted to stick with school, you could look at a culinary one even. You should be pursuing something that makes you excited."

I'd been considering a gap year like Maya suggested so this shouldn't have been a shocking revelation. I'd never considered dropping out entirely. I slumped in my seat. "I fucking hate school. But... if I don't get a degree and find a more consistent job, I'll never save up the money to get out of here."

"I think you could. There are restaurants everywhere. If that's your future, it opens a lot of doors." Jack let me ponder that, then shifted forward. "Do you hate it here so much?"

"I love Fort Collins. I've just always wanted to get away from my parents." I stared at the table as I admitted it. I didn't want to see Jack's judgment as he thought about how much a statement like that would hurt Stacy's feelings.

But he didn't drop my hand. "Maybe I don't know the full story," he started, "but it looks to me like you've been doing better about setting boundaries. Maybe, thinking about therapy and the future, that's something you should focus on regarding your family, instead of letting them chase you away from a life and city that you love."

The server came by and dropped off rolls. Piano music played softly in the background. The server walked away, standing at the end of the bar again and joking with the sharply dressed bartender. She was wearing a bowtie. I would get so much shit if I tried wearing one at the Study Room. The clink of glasses and the smell of garlic filled the air. Outside, people walked in their coats through the gently falling snow. Most of them were dressed up for the high-end restaurants lining this block. There were bright, twinkling lights strung up over the road. This was a dream. Sitting here with Jack, I realized this could be my dream. I could work in a restaurant until I dropped. I could walk this street for the rest of my life. If not this street, every city in the world had restaurants. I might not ever have the money for a huge life, but I might have enough for the life I want to live.

"Roly?" Jack looked worried that he might have overstepped.

"Thanks. I need to think about all that a bit more, but I appreciate your insight. Really."

Jack smiled, squeezing my hand. "I know you could make it work. Whatever you decide. I want you to be happy and doing what you love. I'm sure your family does too."

"They'd lose their shit if I dropped out."

"They've got enough going on. They'll get over it."

I laughed. "Not Grandma, but she probably needs something new to gossip about now that my dad and Stacy are settled. What about you? If you could live anywhere and do anything, what would it be?"

"I think it would be this." He lifted my hand and kissed it. I laughed, but he only smiled gently. I searched for teasing in his eyes, but all I saw was nervousness. Fear that he'd gone too far once again. I blinked hard. This was getting too emotional for appetizers.

"What about a job?" My voice came out soft and nearly unrecognizable.

"I want to coach soccer, like my dad. Maybe teach. Maybe be a professor. I love college and class. I don't want it to ever end."

I laughed at our opposing sentiments. "If we're going to keep doing this for a while, one of us should probably get a job with benefits."

"I'll just take one for the team then."

"Okay. Now I feel like we should take a step back before we jinx things."

"Roly, I'm not going anywhere. You don't have to be so scared. Not even a jinx would keep me away."

I took a bite of my roll, avoiding his eyes. He waited. "Jack, people let me down."

"And people don't. You trust Matty. He isn't the only good person in this world. I want to be here for you. I want to know everything. I want to live in that chair in your room. Let me be here."

"We haven't been dating that long. Just a couple months."

"And it's been the best couple months of your life. You can admit it."

I laughed and threw a crumb at his smug face. But my stomach tilted and warmed. It seemed impossible we could be so entirely on the same page. I felt too young, too messed up in the head, too unsure about the future.

Could I be sure about Jack?

"But what if it doesn't work out?"

"Then we get our hearts broken. I think it's worth trying. I think you're worth it."

He was blushing in the dim light of the candle between us. I was too. "So are you, Jack."

"Good. Then we keep going and figure it out as we go."

"Okay."

"After a conversation like that, it's probably a good time to tell you I love you."

I smiled so hard it hurt. "You already told me you love me."

"Yeah, but that was unplanned. I mean it and have thought about it this time."

I laughed and kicked him under the table. "Shut up." He kicked me back, raising an eyebrow. "I love you too, Jack."

"Nice," he drew the word out and nodded in satisfaction.

We both laughed, breaking the peaceful quiet of the restaurant in a beautiful way.

FOURTEEN

I CALLED my mom while Matty drove us to Jack's apartment. We were on our way to help him pack. He would be stashing his boxes at our place until the first of January. Matty kept teasing me about how Jack was moving in with us way too soon, how much rent he expected Jack to pay, and if Andrew could move in too.

"Hello?" My mom and I had talked a couple of times since my blow-up, but conversations were still wary and stilted. I could hear it in my mom's voice even within her greeting.

"Hey, Mom. How are the travel plans coming?" She'd promised to be home for Christmas. Over and over.

The silence told me she was breaking that promise even before she answered. "Roly... I just don't know if I'll be back in time."

"Don't act like it's something that's out of your control, Mom."

She huffed. "It's your father! He keeps asking me when I'll be back and inviting me to *family* things with that woman. She's putting words in his mouth, making him think it's what's best for you but I don't want to expose you to that tension! If I just stay here a bit longer, I'll come back feeling so much better. Your father will have settled in his marriage and—"

"Where does that leave me in the meantime?"

"Bug, some things just aren't about you. And your dad told

me you have a boyfriend. You'll find a way to fill your time, I'm sure." She sounded… hurt?

"You think having a boyfriend around replaces your absence? Missing Christmas and being gone for months is fine because I'm dating someone?"

"Roly, you're twenty-two years old. An adult. You don't need me around to pretend Santa came in the night. I'll send you something nice."

This time the silence was all me. Because as much as she wasn't around for me growing up, as many times as I had to make myself dinner or ride my bike to practice or call my friends for math help, my mom had been there when I *needed* her. It was rare, but she'd always seemed to know. It was like she snapped out of a fog and noticed me and opened her arms and I would suddenly have a mom. Especially when it came to dating. She was never more present for me than when my love life, or lack thereof, was involved.

She'd held me when I was crying over small heartbreaks and talked about girls and boys with me with genuine excitement. It was the topic that made me feel closest to her because it was fun and easy and emotions different than the messy family ones. She was the one who got me started reading romances, though we never once broached the topic of whether or not she loved Dad. My crushes were her escape. My moving from partner to partner supplied us endlessly with conversation. I didn't know how my mom really felt about love, but sometimes she said things that made me wish I could find it for real. And I'd never felt like this for anyone before Jack. I wanted to see her face while I told her about him. I didn't want to talk about this through a screen and a time difference.

I missed her.

I reached for Matty's hand. He held it tight as I spoke through my tight throat. "You don't get to say that just to make yourself feel better about leaving me alone through all this. It's my family that broke too. It's my dad married to a woman who is trying to teach him how to have a relationship with me. I'm hurting, Mom. I miss you. I want to tell you about Jack and hear about Italy. Please come back for Christmas."

"If you missed me that much you would have told me about him. I don't know what's gotten into you, but you're asking a lot from me. I can't give up everything I have here just so you can finally gush about some boy."

"You know that's not the only reason why I want you to come home."

"I didn't raise a selfish daughter, Roly. This isn't fair."

"What's not fair is the fact that you didn't raise me at all. You gave up on being a mom after Brady died. You didn't see me. I wanted to work on building a relationship, finally, when we had something real to bond over, but you left me. I don't know why I expected anything else. You've always given the bare fucking minimum."

My mom inhaled sharply. And I waited for some kind of defense that justified this. Maybe even some words of comfort. I'd probably be waiting forever at this point. "Cheryl Jane, you have no idea what I went through. To lose Brady and have to put all my effort into you... you weren't sweet and giggly like him. You didn't want cuddles and to help with chores. You just wanted to play and attention and all my energy when it was already going into my grief. Then, there was your father asking so much of me too. I couldn't do it. Now that I'm here, I remember how it feels to breathe. Back home, it was just too much. *I couldn't breathe.*"

I froze. I was too much for my mom.

She waited. Did she want words of comfort from *me*? For understanding? I stayed on the line because it felt like the sick pleasure of pushing on a bruise. A bruise that had been there nearly all my life. More than a bruise, but I had to minimize the pain in my head to deal with it.

She sighed. "I'm sorry I wasn't a better mother. I don't know what else to say."

The first sob escaped me then.

"Cheryl?"

Matty took my phone away. He looked angrier than I'd ever seen him. I didn't even know we were at Jack's until then. I turned and cried into his chest. He smelled the same as he had since we were thirteen after I told him he stunk and he figured out showers. He felt so sturdy and present. He was here. He'd always been here. I told myself my mom's words didn't matter. This was just growing pains. What it meant to be an adult and pick your family. I chose Matty. I always had Matty. It didn't get rid of the pain in this moment, the hurt was too fresh. I was still crying when Jack opened my door and they got me unbuckled. Jack pulled me out of the car and into his arms.

"I'm… sorry. I'll, I'll stop soon." I told him. He just rubbed my back and exchanged hushed words with Matty.

Matty came back to my side and ducked to make eye contact with me resting my head on Jack's shoulder. "I'm going to go grab some comfort food, okay? I'll be right back, you alright with Jack?"

I nodded and let Jack lead me inside. As soon as the door to his apartment closed, I took off my coat. My skin was tight and crawling. There was too much emotion underneath it and I couldn't stand it. "I need to use my unhealthy coping mechanism." My shirt came off.

Jack looked startled by the change in my demeanor. I just focused on him and how good I knew he could make me feel. "What?"

"Your room. Now. Please. I don't know if it's good for me, but I want to stop crying. I want to feel good."

"Roly…"

I met his look. I wiped my cheeks and stepped closer. I caught his lips with my own, deepening the kiss more quickly than usual, reaching down and stroking him on the outside of his jeans. His breath caught and he didn't back away. He tilted his head and met me press for press. The tears stopped and my heart started back up, filling me with life again when my mom left me so empty.

I pulled him into his room and shut the door. We didn't make it to the bed. We didn't even take our clothes off all the way. Jack's pants were still around his ankles when we sank to the floor.

"Thank you," I said, working above him, watching his muscles contract with pleasure as I rocked my hips, rubbing just the perfect spot. "Thank you. I love you. I love this. You feel so good, Jack."

"Shh." He pulled me down to kiss me, hand tight in my hair in a way that made me moan. "I'd do anything for you. Don't thank me."

"Touch me. Like I taught you."

He did as he was told, expertly bringing me closer to release in perfect rhythm with my hips. I reached back and stroked his balls, making him jump, then applied pressure to the skin underneath. I stroked and worked in tandem with him until I was gasping his name and he was making sounds of agreement.

It was quick and dirty and perfect. We were fully clothed and folding his sweaters when Matty came back with a couple of pizza boxes and the disgusting sugar cookies from the grocery store that he knew I loved.

He wiggled his eyebrows at me. "I knew that would help."

"Nothing happened," I said, far too innocently.

"Whatever." Matty laughed. Jack blushed. I kissed his warm cheek and fixed his hair. I let myself forget what my mom said, pushing that constant bruise to its place in the very back of my mind.

***

The days leading up to Christmas were surprisingly busy at the restaurant even with the students on break. Big families who knew they had to look forward to cooking huge meals over the holidays came in and created an hour-long waitlist. I was called in twice and made more money from generous Christmas tips than I had even over graduation weekend.

I was exhausted and ready for the days off by the time I picked my way out of my apartment between Jack's stacked boxes with my suitcase of clothes ready for the five days I planned to spend at my dad and Stacy's house. Jack was waiting for me in the parking lot. I couldn't even dread the time away from Fort Collins. He gave me a long, lingering kiss once I got inside his warm Jeep.

"The roads look good even though it snowed. Traffic might be bad with other people going home for Christmas, though," he said. He rubbed his thumb on the back of my knuckles as he warmed my hand in his.

"Okay. Just be careful. It'll be fine."

He kissed the tip of my nose. "I will. Promise."

Jack paused before turning back to the wheel. He seemed to brace himself before turning to me. "I think I want to be more supportive," he started. My eyebrows furrowed. Did he mean while driving?

"Okay...?"

"I just, I hate seeing you like you were when you and Matty came by. I don't want to push you, but I want to be here for you. I love you and I want to understand everything about you, Roly."

I broke eye contact, looking out the window. This was big. Jack had probably put everything together, but I'd never explicitly told him. This was one of the last secrets between us. It wouldn't be the quick explanation I gave Nate to tell him why my dad and I were the way we were. It would be about me. Why I was messed up in the ways I was. Why Jack had to work so hard for me to let him in and how much he meant to me now that he'd burrowed his way into my being. He'd stuck around and hadn't asked questions until now. Always seeming to know exactly what I needed. I could give him this. He'd earned it.

To my surprise, I was relieved that we'd made it this far. I was almost excited to let the wall down, to fully let him in. Jack meant that much to me.

I wished there wasn't a console between us while we talked

about this. I leaned over it, pressing my face into Jack's shoulder. "On my fifth birthday, I wanted to go to my favorite restaurant. I don't even really remember it, but I made a big deal and we went and I had cake and everything but I guess I didn't want to leave when it was time. I threw a tantrum while my mom was driving us home and she turned around to try and calm me down. I don't really know the details after that. I think another car hit ice and my mom wasn't looking to avoid the crash. They hit the side of the car where my brother was sitting."

Jack's entire body stiffened.

"He died," I whispered. "I didn't understand it. I kept trying to play and be normal after but my parents were grieving so badly, I think I just shrank into myself. None of the kids wanted to play with me when I was so sad. They turned to bullying after a bit. My parents stayed together, but every year their relationship got worse. My mom cheated and my dad pretended he didn't know. My dad worked a lot and wasn't around much. He took a promotion that meant he spent a lot of time traveling to nearby towns. When he was home he slept on the couch until they converted the office into a bedroom. As I got older, I acted out more for attention, but my dad never noticed and my mom would make me feel guilty instead of seen. We fought a lot. She blames me and herself for Brady's death. She blamed my dad for not helping her with the grief. She read a lot to escape and we just… drifted. Brady had kept my family together and happy and without him, it crumpled. Matty became my family and I have a hard time trusting other people who want to make their way in."

"Roly, I—"

"I trust you, Jack. I really love you. There isn't a lot you can say to change anything about my past, but you make every present day better."

Jack shifted so he could look into my eyes. His face was so raw. No one had ever looked at me like he was now. He opened his mouth, but our phones vibrated at the same time. It was Stacy asking if we were close in a group message.

"We should probably go," I whispered.

Jack gave me a long, lingering kiss, saying more than anything he might have voiced.

He let me go to put both hands on the wheel. As he pulled out of the lot, he turned the conversation to lighter topics and asked me how Matty was doing at his sister's house again and then what Andrew's plans were for Christmas. As glad as I was to have finally told Jack about Brady, I was grateful for the subject change.

"Well, Andrew's Jewish so his family doesn't do anything on Christmas specifically. But he's been busy because he and Matty are going to Italy on the twenty-seventh."

"What? Without you?"

"Well, I was invited but I never committed. I was hoping my mom would be back by now and didn't want to give her an excuse to stay in Italy longer. And now I don't think I want to see her. I got a refund on my ticket."

Jack frowned. I could see him wanting to touch me and reached to rest my hand on his thigh instead. "I guess that makes sense," he said, pushing into my touch but never breaking his focus on the road. "I would love to go to Italy one day. Shame your mom spoiled it for you. But that'll be super romantic for the two of them."

I laughed. "Yeah, I'm kind of sad I'm not going, but it'll be nice not having to third wheel for them."

"And I would have missed you too much."

I rolled my eyes. "Shut up."

It was the happiest I'd ever felt in a car. Jack and I sang to my Taylor Swift playlist the rest of the way. He knew most of my favorite songs by heart now. I used to associate Taylor Swift only with good times involving Matty. I worried for a moment that if things ever went poorly with Jack, he might ruin my favorite artist for me. I pushed the thought away. No one could ruin Taylor Swift and Jack and I were good. So good.

We pulled up to Stacy's too soon and I marveled at the feeling of not wanting to get out of a car. "Are you coming inside?" I asked.

"I promised Amelie I'd make dinner with her, but we'll all be over tomorrow for lunch."

We kissed and I pulled back, staring at him for a long moment. He started to look uncomfortable, a blush spreading on his cheeks. "I really love you, Jack."

He looked touched. "I really love you too, Roly."

I forced myself to leave his car. He waited to back out of the drive until I'd opened the front door, then I watched him drive away. The night air was brisk, but Jack's warmth lingered as I went inside.

"Hey, Roly-Poly." My dad got up from the couch and come around to hug me. I was surprised by the ease of his greeting, the way he felt familiar yet bigger. He must be eating well with Stacy. The thought made me sad. How many times had I made my own dinner? What had my dad eaten those nights? I knew it hadn't been my job to take care of him, but I was glad he had someone that did now. Or at least someone who made sure he was taking care of himself.

Stacy was right behind my dad with a hug. Nate gave me an awkward fist bump. I took my little stack of presents to the tree and set them there, stopping to stare for a moment at the full skirt. There were presents for Jack and Amelie, gifts from my dad to me, from Nate to me. I had a stocking and a pair of pajamas underneath that matched the sets beneath Stacy's, Nate's, and my dad's.

Stacy saw me looking at them and laughed. "It's a silly thing I always did with Nate. Matching pajamas we put on Christmas Eve and wore on Christmas morning. It made the cutest pictures. If you don't want to wear yours tomorrow, that's fine."

I laughed and touched the soft flannel outfit. "That is cute."

I used to go to Matty's every year on Christmas Eve to make cookies with him and his sister. I'd bring some home and eat them in bed. My parents always made an effort on Christmas morning. I loved the day and the gifts they splurged on, likely in moments of parental guilt. But half the time the whole day spent together ended in fights and my mom storming out of the house to get a Christmas drink with friends.

This tradition was so simple and pure. Just a mom trying to make the day special. Something picture worthy and dependable. I'd be happy to wear the pajamas.

We spent Christmas Eve wrapping last-minute presents and eating sandwiches with Jack and his family when they came over. Amelie liked me more this time around, sticking to my side. She was fascinated by me in a way she hadn't been over Thanksgiving. She kept bringing up Jack's ex-girlfriend and asking if I knew her.

"Lindsey used to take me to the candy store," she informed me.

Jack, the traitor, left me on my own to deal with the comment, pretending not to hear and fighting a smile. Amelie and I were sitting on the floor in the basement with the origami books she'd brought. I was trying to figure out the cat. Its head was supposed to be able to wobble when I was done.

"Lindsey sounds nice. I'm glad Jack has good taste."

"You know what else tastes good? Candy."

I snorted. Jack's shoulders shook as he fought his laughter.

"Well, I won't be able to take you to the candy store anytime soon, but maybe you'll like what I got you for Christmas."

Jack glanced back at that, his eyes asking the same question Amelie voiced. "You got me a present?"

"Well, yeah! I figured you were going to get me one so..."

Amelie's eyes widened impossibly. She looked at Jack in a panic. He was outright laughing now.

I couldn't hold in my own laugh as I poked her in the shoulder. "I'm teasing, but maybe now you'll know better than to pester me to take you to the candy store."

She looked a little confused but also delighted. "Sorry. Did you actually get me a present?"

"Just something small."

"I'm small so that's okay."

I nodded seriously. "That's what I was thinking."

"You did that wrong." Amelie took the sorry-looking cat head out of my hands and set to work trying to fix it, scooting to sit closer to me as she did. My heart melted a bit. I didn't spend a lot of time with kids. I always made a point to talk to them and tease them at the restaurant and noticed parents tipped more when I did. This was different though. Earning Amelie's trust felt new and amazing. Jack's eyes softened as he watched us. We shared a smile over her head.

"Do you and Jack kiss?" Amelie asked. Jack's eyes snapped back to the TV. Nate came back down from upstairs, arms laden with snacks even though we just ate.

"Ew, Amelie. Don't make her talk about kissing Jack."

Amelie giggled. I suspected she had a bit of a crush on Nate. I leaned into her ear and whispered, "All the time." She squealed and scrambled away as if I had cooties, laughing all the while.

I crawled over to Jack and went up on my knees to kiss his cheek. "See?"

"Nate's right," she cried. "That *is* gross!"

Nate made gagging sounds and Amelie giggled some more. Jack nearly fell over the arm of his recliner when he leaned down to return my kiss, full on the lips. Amelie squealed and ran out of the basement, making us all laugh. A few moments later Jack's dad yelled down the stairs, "Quit scarring your sister. That's our job as embarrassing parents."

"*Daaaaaad.*" Amelie already did a great job sounding like an aggravated preteen.

"Let's go to your room and exchange presents," Jack told me, still bent so our faces were close.

"Disgusting," Nate said.

"I mean real presents. I doubt we could exchange anything else before the parents get suspicious."

"I think we could if we really tried," I said innocently.

They laughed as Jack took my hand. He stopped at the Christmas tree to grab a large red gift from the pile his family brought over and we went upstairs, calling we'd be right back. My dad looked ready to say something, but I tugged Jack to hurry.

I shut my door behind us and kissed Jack soundly, the two of us falling into my bed. Hands roamed and heavy breathing turned to moans. Jack pulled back, "Sorry, as much as I want to, I can't stop thinking about our parents getting mad and that means I'm thinking about our parents right now."

I laughed and reached for my present to him on my night-stand, stomach fluttering as I hoped he'd like it. I probably spent too much money on it and hoped he wouldn't be able to tell. He picked up the red bag he had dropped by the door. We sat cross-legged on the bed facing each other. He was smiling and adorable and I didn't bother fighting the urge to kiss him again. I wished we could stay here, floating and happy, separate from the world.

I handed Jack his present. He was an eager gift unwrapper. It made me laugh to see him tear through the paper. He opened the velvet box and took out the simple silver bracelet inside. "It has music notes on it."

"From Fearless. By T—"

"—Taylor Swift." He swallowed, looking up at me from under his long lashes. "Half of that song is them in the car together."

"And her learning how not to be afraid."

Jack stared at me, eyes brown to green and full of love that made me forget what it felt like to ever be unsure around him. "I don't want you to be afraid."

"You saw me at my worst at the wedding and you still made the first moves. You bought me coffees and asked me out and made the effort. Even after the dress incident and how much Stacy means to you, you wanted to be friends and you gave me a chance. I wouldn't be feeling this happy right now if you hadn't put in the work. I love you for that. You've been so great, Jack." He dropped his eyes. I took his hand. "You don't have to wear it, I know it's a dorky gift, but I just wanted something that shows how I feel."

Still not looking at me, Jack handed me the bracelet and offered his wrist so I could put it on him. Something about the way he wasn't meeting my eyes made my stomach twist.

"I'm sorry, my gift isn't as thoughtful." He handed me the red bag.

I smiled as soon as I saw what was inside. "It's so cute! I love it!"

"I figured Trevor would look good wearing it."

"Oh, he will." It was a simple wicker basket that would fit on his handlebars, complete with a cup holder. I missed my bike then, wishing I could put it on Trevor right that moment. Jack was smiling at me again. Maybe he had just been worried I wouldn't like the present. I climbed into his lap and kissed him. We got a bit further this time before there was a knock on my door. Jack yanked his hands out from under my sweatshirt.

His pop yelled from the other side. "We're going to leave in ten! Get rid of the evidence, Jackie."

Jack groaned. "Nothing is happening, Pop."

"*Suuuure.*" We heard him go back down the stairs.

Jack brushed my hair out of my face. I watched his eyes shift between mine as he stared at me.

"You're so beautiful. I hope you have an amazing Christmas. Call me if you need anything. I'm sorry I only got you a twenty-dollar bike basket."

I laughed. "I love you and my bike basket."

"I love you."

He kissed me soundly one last time. I stayed in my bed as he got up and left. The front door closed soon after and I heard their car pull out of the drive. I smiled at the ceiling, fingers going to my slightly raw lips. I already missed him, but I'd see him soon. I could trust that.

There was a vibration next to me that was unfamiliar. Feeling around, I found Jack's phone under my blanket. It must have fallen out of his pocket while we kissed.

I'm not usually a snoop. I had no desire to look through Jack's things while this heat and trust flooded me, but the new message on the screen gave me pause. Stacy had texted him. *I forgot to give you gas money for driving Roly. I'll give you some cash the next time you're over. I appreciate you bringing her down for us* and a heart emoji.

I stared at the message, confused. Jack never mentioned needing help paying for the gas. I would have been happy to contribute for the rides. In fact, I felt bad now that I hadn't offered. Matty and I usually split the cost but I'd been so concerned with letting Jack drive me for the Thanksgiving then distracted this trip I forgot to contribute. Stacy promising the money was strange, too. I remembered him taking the money from her the other day. And it felt weird she was acting like he was doing her a favor for driving me when I had made the plan to drive with Jack... I was still staring at the message, undoubtedly overthinking it, when my dad called me down for dinner.

Unsure what to make of the text, I tried to force it from my mind. I went downstairs and ate, focusing my attention on Nate and my dad. Every time I looked at Stacy, I had that strange feeling of dread. I wanted to trust what Jack and I had. I didn't want to be afraid. But he hadn't met my eyes after I gave him my gift and told him that. I didn't want to be, but I was afraid. I kept looking at my dad and remembering what he became in those years he tried to make it work with my mom. Loving her and trying to be romantic only to slip away a little more every time she rejected him.

The dread was getting worse the harder I fell for Jack. Was it intuition? Somehow, I knew the answer to that question was in Jack's phone. If I just opened the messages to Stacy, I'd probably find out I was worried over nothing. Maybe he was just embarrassed to ask me for help paying when I didn't offer. Then it was all on me. What was the worst I would find in their messages?

We dressed up in the pajamas and took pictures around the tree, Stacy smiling so wide her cheeks must be hurting. We laughed as we tried to get Ruby to sit and look at the camera and she just stared back at us, tongue lolling and tail thumping. My own smiles felt forced. I kept thinking about the stupid text.

Why couldn't I just forget about it?

Jack texted Nate from his dad's phone to let me know he didn't have his phone and would be by tomorrow to look for it. Nate teased me that Jack just wanted another excuse to see me and had left it on purpose. I laughed and thanked Nate for passing along the message. I didn't mention I'd already found the phone. The churning dread kept me quiet.

I was proud of myself for only staring at the phone that night and not unlocking it. Even in the morning, I got through the gift unwrapping and breakfast without opening the messages. It was such a violation. I didn't want that between us. I loved Jack. I wanted to trust Jack.

I was terrified of Jack.

When I went upstairs to grab my sweater, I stopped and stared at Jack's phone. It was lighting up with Christmas wishes from his friends and relatives. Stacy's message was still unopened at the bottom of the list. I sat on my bed slowly. If I opened it, he'd know. All those texts wouldn't be on the lock screen anymore. But why couldn't I get this feeling out of my stomach? I felt nearly sick at this point.

I swiped on Stacy's message. I'd seen Jack put in his passcode before and teased him because it was so simple. He trusted *me*. I hesitated. I wanted to believe in the warmth his presence stirred in my gut. I had felt it so strongly yesterday. Why couldn't it overshadow the cold dread of this morning? I wanted it to. But...

One. One. One. One.

Stacy's messages opened.

They didn't text often, so it was far too easy to get the gist of their communication for the last few months. Eyes blurring rapidly with tears at what I found, I scrolled to the first messages that mentioned me right after the date of the wedding.

It was bad. It was so bad.

Jack, I know you're looking for a new job. Maybe you could apply at Moonbean? Matty mentioned to me that he and Roly go there a lot.

Why would I apply to a place she likes?

For me. I'd really like an "in." If you two become friends, maybe she and Nate will and then she'll have an easier time accepting me

Stacy that's weird

Please Jack. She's a sweet girl, she had a hard time at the wedding and it started you two off on the wrong foot, but I'd like to know her better. You can tell me what she's like. Just apply and see what happens. I think she could use more friends, it doesn't sound like she has many

I wonder why…

I got the job and she came in today. She seems to be doing fine.

I'll send you some money, buy her a coffee from me. Don't say it's from me though, not yet at least.

That's also weird Stacy

Thanks Jack!

How are things going?

Pretty good. She's not actually that bad.

I told you! Are you still getting the money for the coffees?

Yeah, but you don't need to keep sending it

Nate's coming up to see you this weekend. I'm sending him with some cash so the two of you can go see Roly at work

You're like a third party stalker

What's she like?

She's nice. She doesn't have a lot of friends but the people who work at Moonbean say she's a good customer.

What do you think?

I think she's cute.

You should ask her on a date. Somewhere nice, I'll pay.

That's weird Stacy

Don't you want to?

At this point, not really, but I'll take one for the team and do it for you when the time is right

The messages went on. She asked him if I'd be coming when he came to visit Nate. She told him he should try to hang out with me on Halloween because it was always a fun night. She told him she'd give him money for gas if he brought me up for Thanksgiving…

She'd paid him to befriend me. Paid him to take me on dates. Told him to do all the sweet things that made me fall for him.

She's not actually that bad. I'll take one for the team and do it for you.

The words were so cutting. All my excitement getting to know him. All those jittery moments of butterflies. Every time he comforted me and made an effort to spend more time together… all for Stacy. All for this new family I never asked to be a part of.

Every message broke me. A brand-new bruise I pressed by rereading the texts because I was too sick to stop. I could no longer distinguish what happened between us because of these messages and what was real feeling. How much of what made me fall for Jack was Jack and how much was my stepmom? The question turned my stomach so hard that I thought I might be sick.

I was so stupid. Yesterday, I listed out all the things that had made me fall for Jack. He hadn't met my eyes. He'd kept this from me. I told him all my broken pieces. I opened myself up to him. He got paid to get to know me.

The trust crumpled. I couldn't conjure any warmth from thoughts of him. Jack. My Jack. How much of it was him? Why hadn't he told me?

There was a knocking at my bedroom door. It was slightly ajar and I looked up through tears as Jack came in. The pain was like a physical blow. I could hardly breathe.

"Merry Christmas! Stacy said she's about ready to start the

charcuterie board. Oh good, you found my phone..." he trailed off, seeing my tears.

I stared at him, the messages to Stacy open in my hand.

His eyebrows knotted with concern. He stepped closer and I stood, backing away.

"Roly, what's wrong?"

I handed him the phone. Scrolled up to the most hurtful messages. To the *she's not actually that bad.* The *I wonder why...*

"Shit. Roly, I—"

"I don't want to hear it. I don't want to see you." My voice cracked and I turned away. I went to my bag and pulled out Amelie's small gift before I zipped it closed, struggling as my hands shook. I jerked the strap over my shoulder as I straightened. Jack stood still, shock on his face, grip lose on his phone. I handed him Amelie's present and pushed past him out the door.

"Roly!"

"Don't touch me."

Jack's hand fell to his side, the paper around Amelie's gift crinkling in his fist. "Please," he whispered. "Let me explain. I can make this better."

I glared at him. "What could you possibly say that would be enough?" I meant to finish that sentence. Enough to explain this? Enough to excuse not telling me? But I saw how leaving it at that hit him deep and at that moment, I relished the pain I caused him in return for my own.

He didn't follow as I ran down the stairs. That hurt too. How easily he let me go. I grabbed my dad's keys from the side table.

"Roly, what's wrong?" my dad asked, turning from his football game. He was still wearing the pajamas. He'd been pink-cheeked and smiling all morning. Proud of the gifts he picked and touched by the ones he received. He was so happy here.

I couldn't ruin it for him. *I* wouldn't tell him.

"Ask Stacy and Jack." I ran out into the cold.

FIFTEEN

BY THE TIME I pulled into the garage, my tight grip on the steering wheel was painful. When I pried my fingers off, they were shaking. The roads had been snow-covered and my tears made driving difficult. But there had been few other drivers out and I made it home safely.

Home.

I looked up at the small place. The faded maroon paint and blue-gray trimming and door. My mom had painted it herself, back when she smiled and wore her hair in loose buns. Overalls and sweaters that lost their shape the more I pulled on them. Back when she was brimming with energy and patience.

It was funny how I could remember that version of my mom better than I remembered Brady. I remembered hugs and wrestling matches and her trying gymnastics moves with me. I faintly remembered Brady giggling in the background. My dad wasn't there so much with work, but my child-self had adored my mom. She'd been everything.

And I was too much.

Exhaling shakily, I grabbed my backpack and went inside. It hurt more than I anticipated to see how long the house had been empty. The layer of dust. The lack of shoes kicked off by the door.

My mom had cleaned before she left for Italy. She had purged the place of my dad's belongings. It wasn't the same.

But I knew one place that would be.

I went up the stairs, looking at the family pictures on the wall that hadn't been updated since I was four. It hit me sometimes, how fucked up grief could make a person. We'd stopped even trying to be a family when Brady died. Or my parents did. The only new pictures were impersonal school photos where I barely smiled and me accepting gymnastics medals, looking at the parent who showed up as they took the picture. There weren't any of just the three of us until I graduated high school. Right before they officially separated.

I was probably in more pictures at Matty's house than I was here.

I reached the top of the stairs and made my way down the hall. I paused in front of Brady's door. The bruise was hurting. It was so old and familiar. Its pain comforting compared to the fresh hurt Jack inflicted. I pressed on it harder and went inside.

My brother's room was barely touched. Only the bed gave evidence of the nights my mom had spent in here. There were Brady's drawings on the wall. He loved drawing the four of us and our house, always depicted as bright red by his hand. There was even a drawing of me surrounded by roly-poly bugs. His toy chest was overflowing. I swallowed when I was hit with the memory of the time I came in here a few days after he died and played with his toys. My mom had yelled at me and ordered me to never come in here again. I knew Brady was more important then. That I should have put him first.

But there was the bear he always gave me to play with when we played together. That was what I had been after that day. I picked it up now. I hugged it as I sat on the bed.

Brady's death was such an old pain, but the scars hadn't healed right. They'd become layered. His death had taken my ability to make friends. Children didn't understand sadness like I carried. Maybe if we'd moved by the time I was feeling better,

Matty wouldn't be my only friend today. Maybe if my parents had tried harder to move forward, I would trust people more. I would give more of them a chance. It wouldn't matter when the people I did let in ended up hurting me.

Maybe then my only successful relationship wouldn't have been with a boy who needed to be paid just to talk to me. I had loved him so much for making the first moves. For seeing *me* and trying.

I buried my face in the bear and let myself cry some more. I *knew* that wasn't what people did. I knew I couldn't trust people not to hurt me. That Matty and Andrew were the exceptions. I should have been more careful. I should have been warier. I should have asked Jack about his relationship with Stacy sooner. I should have told him I wanted to come first and we never would have made it this far. Never would have exchanged I love you's and all those hours in each other's arms. He would have just told me she meant too much.

I shouldn't have trusted Stacy. I should have been warier of how badly she wanted to get to know me. I should have kept things light and easy so it didn't hurt so bad now. I didn't even know when she made it past arm's length with me.

I should have protected myself. Taken care of myself like only I knew how to do.

I didn't know how long I sat there, crying into my dead brother's stuffed bear. Eventually, the door cracked open, a weight lowered next to me on the bed, and familiar arms wrapped around me.

"Roly, I'm so sorry. Please tell me what's wrong. I need to hear it from you."

That was my dad for you. Needing me to put in the effort so he'd know how to help me. Making me help myself, yet again.

I was so tired. "It doesn't matter, Dad. I'll get over it. I'll figure it out." Like I did everything else. Like I learned how to grieve Brady's death on my own. Like I learned to accept no one wanted to be my friend. Like I learned how to lean on Matty. As soon as my dad left, I would call Matty. That was the only thing I could imagine helping right now.

My dad cleared his throat. He was stiff next to me, an arm still around my shoulders. He cleared his throat again. "I'm sorry I didn't do a very good job, Roly."

His words echoed my mom's. I almost rolled my eyes. I couldn't comfort him right now if that's what he was searching for.

He went on. "You know, this is the first time I've been in here since he died? I wanted to come up, but your mom made it her space. She needed somewhere private to grieve and I didn't want to intrude on that. I didn't know what to do to help her, or you, or even myself. When none of you came to me, I thought space was the answer. When my own pain hurt, I gave myself distance from that too. My therapist and I have been working on that. On letting myself hurt. It takes someone a lot braver than me to let yourself experience all that pain. Even if she may have lost herself to it, I admired your mother for that. She really, really knew how to love."

My dad laughed a little. He ran his hand over Brady's pillow. "To tell you the truth, I was jealous when Brady was born. Before that, your mom and I were everything to each other. Then suddenly, I was her second favorite. I loved him and I tried to be a good dad to him, but it wasn't until we had you that I felt like I had a person too. Even then, I know I wasn't there enough."

My dad was crying. The sight was shocking enough to stop my own tears. He drew in a breath. "Now, though, I think your mom knew on some level Brady didn't have a lot of time with us. She gave him a lifetime of love in his seven years. She gave him the best little life. I love her for it, but it broke something in her when she had to stop giving her love to him. I can only take comfort in the fact that he got all the love he deserved and I have to hope that one day, she and I will be able to show that to you too. We're a bit behind, I know, but I want to do better. And I thought Stacy was capable of that kind of love. I thought you two would be good for each other. I shouldn't have let her do my job. I should have been there, making sure our families blended. I shouldn't have just expected it to happen. I shouldn't have stepped back yet again while you had to deal with the pain of your family splitting."

I didn't have words for that. For what it meant for him to say that to me. To feel seen by my dad. I turned and pressed my face into my dad's chest. He hugged me tightly. A real, uninhibited hug. The pain lessened enough for me to draw in gulping breaths of air as I sobbed. I hurt over Brady's death, but it had ruined me to lose my parents. To grow invisible and know they were just out of reach, yet nothing I did made them see past Brady to look at me.

But now, my dad was looking at me. He was taking my side in this. He thought Stacy was in the wrong and acknowledged she'd hurt me. He respected my mom and acknowledged that our family was over but it hadn't been all bad. It wasn't just pain. There was love there, even if I had been right in thinking it was warped and unfair and painful.

My dad rubbed my arms and told me he was proud of me. He told me he was sorry. He told me I was beautiful and smart and that he loved me so much that his therapist was working with him on how to feel that too.

We finished Christmas together, watching TV in the living room and ordering takeout from our favorite restaurant. We talked about Brady and my mom. We talked about the moment he knew the marriage was over while I had still been holding on to hope. He told how he and Stacy met, both of us realizing I didn't even know the full story. It was pretty hilarious, involving an exploding ketchup bottle and the awkwardness of meeting after only talking online. He told me what it was like trying to get close to Nate and how watching him and Stacy together he was slowly learning what our relationship had been missing.

I told him about living with Matty and Fort Collins. He smiled when I mentioned riding my bike and we remembered together how he taught me to ride with Brady cheering me on the whole time. He'd been so excited running behind me that he'd tripped and had been the one to go home with a bloody knee while I never once fell off the bike seat.

I told my dad about working at a restaurant and how I wasn't sure I wanted to finish school. He told me he'd help me if I needed it. That I should do what makes me happy and follow my gut because I was so smart.

I told him about Jack and how confused I was.

He sighed and smiled a bit. "The only thing I can say is, if he's worth it, don't give up. Give yourself some time, but don't ignore the issues until it's too late. Talk to him. Make an effort. Work through the pain knowing there could be something beautiful on the other side. It doesn't have to be today, but if you love him, that's something special. If you can forgive him, try. You have to take every moment of love and happiness you can or else you'll just make yourself and the people around you miserable."

I leaned my head on my dad's shoulder and watched the Christmas movie playing. I didn't have the energy to try to even think it through right now. Maybe tomorrow or the next day, I'll be able to separate what Jack and I built from what Stacy influenced and see if it was worth it. For now, I just let myself accept my dad's comfort. I sat with him on the couch and we both felt our pain and acknowledged our love.

I slept in my childhood bed that night. Waking with the sun streaming through my white curtains, I panicked for a moment before realizing where I was. I missed my bed in Fort Collins. I missed Matty on the other side of the wall. I miss Jack's arm holding me close even in sleep.

The events from yesterday caught up to me. I blinked hard and pulled up my covers, glancing around. It was eerie. My room was as unchanged as Brady's since I left. Gymnastics trophies and medals on a shelf. There were still empty places that I had reserved for awards before I quit. I quit when I realized it wasn't what would get me away from my parents and Denver. I was a decent gymnast, but I wasn't great, and it wasn't worth putting up with my teammates. I started working at the diner down the street instead as a line cook.

My dresser had some books and school binders on it. My nightstand sported a dusty mug with a dried-up tea bag in it. Everything was simple and impersonal. Nothing like the room I had made my own in Fort Collins. I could feel the coldness of Brady's room seeping in from next door. I always had.

I hated this room growing up. I hid in the basement or at Matty's house. Had I run here yesterday for comfort or to punish myself? I had listened to my dad yesterday. I took a lot of his words to heart but… I wasn't ready for the feelings I had for Jack. I wasn't made to love like that and that's why I hurt so badly right now. We'd only met months ago. If I could get over what he and Stacy had done and went back to him, he might realize without the incentive he wouldn't want me. I was too much. He knew about Brady, but he hadn't seen the true effect his death had on me, had he? Jack would still leave, only I'd be even further gone for him.

So, I wouldn't call him. I wasn't going to text. I held tight to the ragged edges of my heart and let it break over and over as I thought about his texts to Stacy. I got up for the day.

I wouldn't call him.

My dad lingered with me for a while, but I could tell he was haunted by a night spent on the couch and wanted to go work things out with Stacy. I told him to go, assuring him multiple times I would be fine on my own. I was always fine on my own. Well, maybe not entirely alone. I would call Matty before he and Andrew left for Italy. I had a feeling it would be a long talk. I put it off, not quite ready to examine what happened. I wasn't ready to put it into words. What if what Jack did didn't seem like a big deal to Matty? What if it sounded major and Matty hated Jack even if maybe one day I… no, I wouldn't. Matty could hate Jack. It didn't matter. It was over.

I hated how badly I missed Jack already. I had grown so used to him. Not hearing from him felt like I was missing a limb. It hurt that he hadn't tried to text or call. Not that I would have answered.

I cried in the shower and thought about breakfast, but that would involve leaving the house. I found coffee but after drinking it I only felt more anxious and off-center. I was starting to panic. Matty would be leaving tomorrow. I'd be so alone. I didn't want to do this without him. Now I really couldn't call him. He'd hear it in my voice and cancel his plans with Andrew because I was hurting. I had to just swallow it. I had to figure it out. Maybe ask my dad for a ride back to Fort Collins to avoid Jack and at least be in a place that felt like home.

I was pacing in the living room, biting at a hangnail and fighting tears, when there was a knock at the door. A glance out the window revealed Jack's burnt-orange Jeep parked on the street outside. Ice flooded my veins. My stomach turned so much that I swallowed to keep the coffee down.

I couldn't do this.

Jack knocked again.

I was not ready.

I wanted Matty.

"Roly, I'm just dropping something off. I can leave it here on the step. It's… It's from all of us." I could see in the frosted glass that his head was resting on the door as he talked. "I just know when I'm hurting I want my dads. I know you have a different relationship with your parents, but we got you tickets to go to Italy with Matty and Andrew. Maybe it'll help to be with your mom. Maybe it'll at least help to be with Matty."

I walked toward the door. He was so close.

"I'm so sorry, Roly."

I yanked open the door and he nearly fell into me. He looked awful. Hair untidy and dark circles under his eyes. I'd never seen their color so muted.

I doubted I looked much better.

"Roly." He sounded so desperately pained. When would anyone look at me like this again? It hurt like a thousand paper cuts.

"I don't want to hear it. I can't right now. I just want to feel better for a moment."

His eyebrows knotted as he took me in. Understanding cleared his features. "I really don't think—"

"Then get the fuck out." Since when was I capable of putting that kind of steel in my voice? It made Jack flinch.

Since the wedding, I realized. Since I talked back to Jack. Something about him had always made me braver. I held onto the steel.

He debated on the step, cold air infecting the house.

Finally, he nodded. "For you," he said.

I swallowed how that made me feel and stepped back. He set an envelope on the side table. He toed off his shoes by the door and took off his coat. Then he looked at me, waiting.

And I… faltered. "I don't know what I want. I just want to feel better," I whispered.

He couldn't look at me with that soft expression. I didn't want to see it. Before I could say anything, Jack took change. He grabbed my hand and led me to the couch. He kissed my neck, behind my ear, my temples and cheeks, everywhere but my lips, knowing I didn't want that either. I accepted it all, the tightness in my chest easing for the first time since his phone lit up with a text from Stacy. I focused on the feel of his body. The touch of his skin. His hand worked the string of my sweatpants and he pushed them down, then my underwear. He pushed me back into the couch and knelt between my legs.

He kissed up my thighs. He looked up one last time to make sure what he was doing was okay. Whatever he saw on my face encouraged him. I let my head fall back on the cushions as he grabbed my calves and jerked me closer. Then he went to work. Just like I taught him. Just how I needed.

He licked slow and even up my clit, fingers circling my

entrance until I was wet enough to encourage him to stick first one, then two fingers in. Palm to the ceiling, his fingertips found the perfect spot. I let out a breathy moan. His tongue started moving faster, pressing harder. He sucked at me and kissed and hummed and groaned until my body was languid and my thoughts were finally, beautifully silent.

Not silent. Filled with only Jack.

I'd let it hurt later.

He never said a word. I didn't know if I did. He gave me exactly what I wanted, working diligently and patiently until my hands were in his hair and my legs were shaking. Still, I kept my head back, unable to look at him.

"That's it," he murmured, breaking the silence. "Come for me, Cheryl."

And it was the sound of his voice that did it. With a gasp and a spasm, I came so hard I must have been pulling out his hair. He stayed with me, licking and kissing and soothing me through it.

Even when I finished panting and gasping, we stayed how we were. I stared at the ceiling. His breath warmed me between my legs. I suppose I should have felt exposed with him down there, but I knew the only way I could feel vulnerable right now was if he saw the look on my face. If he could tell how hard I was trying not to cry. How badly I wanted him to stay.

He rested his cheek on the inside of my thigh and I felt his tears on my bare skin then. I heard him sniff. He was holding my ankles tight like he didn't want to let go.

How could he make me feel so incredible and yet so low? I felt dirty for making him do this, to kneel in front of me while he was hurting. But I didn't want him to move.

Exactly why I should make him.

"Goodbye, Jack." I still didn't look down.

He drew in a shuddering breath that broke my heart all over again. He kissed the inside of my thigh and wiped his tears off my leg. I closed my eyes as he stood and went to the door. As he put

on his shoes. The sound of his coat zipper was so loud in the after-
math of what we'd done.

"I hope you go to Italy. I hope it helps. Goodbye, Roly."

The door clicked shut.

I broke.

SIXTEEN

I WALKED SLOWLY up the narrow stone steps. I'd been in Italy now for five days. We'd taken trains from city to city, talking, laughing, drinking until we were too loud to the Italians around us. I think I gained ten pounds, but we couldn't stop eating. I'd seen the Duomo. Verona. The countryside. The peace of this little country. Andrew had planned and taken charge of everything. He shocked Matty and me by speaking fluent Italian. He laughed when he saw our faces and explained his grandparents had immigrated to California and that his family spoke mostly Italian at home still.

"I thought I was the Italian friend," I complained, though we all knew it was mostly in last name only at this point.

It was a strange juxtaposition, the quick pace of our travel and our attempt to take everything in alongside the slow-moving day-to-day life of the people around us. They ate early and went home before nightfall. The streets of Venice last night had mostly been full of tourists. We talked quietly as we walked the rivers. Sometimes about Jack, sometimes about the fight Andrew and Matty had over the phone when they couldn't find each other at the airport. It was all easier to talk about here. It was also easier to ignore. I'd asked Matty and Andrew not to give their opinions on my fight with Jack. I wasn't ready to hear them yet, so they just let me talk.

They did a good job making sure I didn't feel like a third wheel. I made sure to make plans for myself and go on walks often so I didn't ruin the sweet romance they were obviously experiencing here. It had been a good balance of time to think and time to forget. Of happiness and calm.

Jack was right. Italy had helped.

Now it was time to see if he was right about the other thing.

I knocked on the door to the apartment, feeling strangely nervous. I held onto the conversation I had with my dad and remembered his encouraging emails. It was possible for a parent to learn. Possible for me to trust them to do better.

Could my mom though?

She opened the aged wooden door a crack. Her eyes, the same light brown as mine, widened and she threw it open the rest of the way, drawing me in for a hug. Her hair was mine too, strawberry blond and soft against my cheek. "Oh, bug! You look so beautiful." She stepped back, smiling.

I was shocked to see tears in her eyes. She looked younger. Healthier. "So do you."

"Italy is good for everyone, I suppose. Look at you." She put a hand on my cheek and gave me a watery smile.

"Don't cry, Mom."

"I'm trying, bug. I really am. I just missed you so much."

"You did?"

Hurt flashed in her eyes and she sighed.

"I mean, I missed you too, Mom."

"Come in." She stepped aside and gave me a quick tour of the little apartment she was renting. There were plants thriving on her shelves and books all over the place. It surprised me. She never kept a plant alive back home. I picked up a few of the books, smiling at the titles I knew. It made me feel closer to her to see our love of romance books was still shared.

"Sit here. Tell me all about your trip. Will I be seeing Matty at all? I miss him too."

I laughed a little awkwardly, unsure how to deal with my mom's undivided attention. I told her about the trip, about Andrew and Matty and how great they were to travel with. I refrained from mentioning my time alone or why I'd decided to come.

My mom smiled and nodded and asked questions. She promised to show us all the best Venice had to offer before we left the day after tomorrow. Her smiles made me go back to dim memories of her before Brady's death. We warmed to each other and I felt so happy in her presence it was nearly terrifying. Maybe she was right not to come back. Maybe what she needed was to stay away from Brady's cold bedroom and the haunting memories around our house.

Or maybe I was seeing her differently after my conversation with my dad. Looking at how alive she was here, his words made even more sense. She'd given everything to Brady in the short time they'd had together. Could I begrudge my brother that love when she'd been unable to extend it to me after his death? Could I be mad at her after she'd been broken so badly? What had she owed me as a parent? As a human being in deep pain?

There was a dip in the conversation. I shifted in my chair and cleared my throat, willing to make an effort. "How is Marco?"

My mom blushed. Her eyes went to her laptop. She cleared her throat too. It was weird. She looked more embarrassed than anything. Not blushing happily from a new man. Her cheeks were burning red and she still wouldn't meet my eyes. She put a hand on her stomach. *Oh god.* "Mom, are you pregnant?"

She stared at me, blinking, and then burst out laughing when she realized where her hand was. She laughed harder than I'd ever seen her laugh, wiping tears and holding her side. She laughed so hard I had to join in, relief flooding me. She finally started catching her breath, "Roly, God no. I'm not pregnant!" She fell to laughter again and my cheeks hurt from smiling.

She calmed somewhat and wrung her hands. "I'm not pregnant. But… I have a confession."

I raised an eyebrow. "What is it?"

Her pause was killing me. I had to know. Was she engaged? Was she staying here forever? Moving in with him?

"There isn't a Marco. Well, there is, but I'm not dating him."

"What?" I frowned with confusion.

She bit her lip, eyes going back to her laptop, then to me. "I'm, I'm writing him. I've been writing a romance book. I made him up and I've been going to all these different places for inspiration with my setting. It's been so amazing. Such an escape." She laughed, blushing even deeper red beneath her tan. "I might have become too… emersed. It was a silly lie. What am I thinking? Writing a book at my age? It was too embarrassing to admit that while your father's having his second great love, I was on my own making one up. So, I lied and made you think I was moving on too. That both of your parents are finding love after we split up. My love is just for something new, not someone new."

"Mom, that's amazing! Can I read it?"

Her smile was shy and pleased. I barely recognized the woman in front of me. "You really want to?"

"Of course! That's so exciting." I couldn't deny my relief.

"So, you don't hate me?"

"I never hated you. You let me down and I wish you'd been more honest with me, but I talked with Dad and he made me understand some things."

My mom leaned closer. "What did he say?"

Wondering if I should be telling her, I explained what he said about her reaction to Brady's death. She turned to the window for a long time. Her voice was broken when she spoke. "I treated him so horribly. I knew he hadn't loved Brady like I did. It's… so sweet that he thinks that of me. I don't deserve his good opinion at all."

"Why? Why did you cut us out so badly?"

She swallowed. "Writing this book, I've put my main character in my same position. She pushes people away and doesn't know if loving is worth the pain it brings." I drew in a sharp breath. "I think I was also punishing myself. Because I was driving that night. Because I couldn't say no to you when you wanted to go to dinner even though the roads were bad. I loved making you smile and Brady wanted to go too and I should have been firmer. I don't —didn't think I deserved you and your father after that. I was so scared. But I think, for me, my problem has always been about forgiveness. I've had to work on forgiving myself and accepting what people offer. I've made these realizations with my character, but I've still been so scared. Too scared to come home and try to be the heroine I need to be in order to be happy. It's so much easier to pretend I can do this on my own. Be happy on my own."

"Do you think it's worth it? If you could go back in time, would you marry Dad again?"

She twisted the ring on her finger and I realized it was her wedding band. She'd never taken it off. "It's painful to think about those first years together. Because I was so happy. It amazes me how happy I was." She laughed humorlessly. "Maybe I just had all the happiness of a full marriage, like how your father said I loved Brady so much. It hurt to lose that happiness and I wish I could have looked at your father without seeing Brady. I can't say I should have done more or tried harder because I truly don't think my grief would have allowed it, but maybe I could have found help. Maybe I could have been kinder to him. I don't know if I would go back in time if it meant going through that pain again but… if I found someone today who made me feel like that, I think I would chase the feeling."

We fell quiet. I tried not to think about the way it stung that she didn't mention me as a factor in whether or not she'd go back. She would never be the perfect mom, but if I wanted a relationship with her, I just had to accept that. I could only let her be the mom she was capable of being.

"You would fall in love again? Writing and reading about it isn't enough?"

"It's enough. For me now, it's enough. And being here. I'm not going to go looking for anything, but if it fell in my lap, I would embrace it." She looked at me close, expression softening. "Roly, what happened with that boy?"

"I'm trying to decide if it's worth forgiving him for something he did when we first met. I'm hurting so badly over him. I don't know if it's worth going through the pain again if something happens."

"You love him?"

"Yes."

"You miss him?"

I nodded.

"Do you think he'd do it again, whatever it was?"

That question made me cold because I'd seen his face when he realized he hurt me. "No. He wouldn't." Did that mean after all this, I still trusted him?

"Did he make your life better? Did he make it easy to love him?"

I felt a tear spill over. "It was the easiest thing I've ever done."

"Then don't punish yourself for falling. Let yourself be in love, Roly. If he's lucky enough to hold your heart, then maybe he deserves it."

I laughed and sobbed a bit at the same time. "You've been writing too many romance books."

My mom shrugged. "If he doesn't deserve you, by the time you are ready to let him go, it'll be easier. You'll have realized he's not worth it."

"What if he realizes I'm not worth it?" I whispered. The real fear.

"Then he's a fucking idiot."

We laughed together again and my mom reached for me. Our relationship wasn't fixed, but we'd always been able to talk about my lovelife. I knew how to accept this version of my mom's love. Jack *was* right. A hug from her made me feel like a completely different person.

I woke up to Matty and Andrew still chatting beside me. A glance at the screen on the seatback in front of me told me we still had an hour until our layover in New York before the flight to Denver. I stretched.

"Good morning, gorgeous," Matty said. I didn't love the teasing look in his eyes. "I'm glad you stay so hydrated. This is truly an impressive amount of drool on my shoulder."

I wiped my cheek and burst into laughter. He was right. It was impressive. I made a halfhearted attempt to wipe his sleeve, but the damage was done. "I'm sorry."

He shook his head. "I'm just glad you finally got some sleep."

Andrew leaned around him. "How are you feeling about going home?"

"I'm not sure what I feel."

"Do you think you'll talk to Jack?" Matty asked.

"I think I'm ready to hear your opinions on the matter before I decide."

Andrew and Matty shared a look. Matty grabbed my hand and nodded to Andrew to go first.

"You should sit down and talk to him before you decide anything. Maybe he has money problems and was embarrassed so he didn't tell you. He wanted to keep dating and let Stacy pay. That's a different story than she paid him to date you. Either way, I think you guys loved each other enough that he deserves a chance to apologize. You should make your decision based on what he says."

I nodded. It was good advice. I turned to Matty. He squeezed my hand. "I like Jack for you a lot. You were so happy with him and he made a space for you to be brave. I think he and Stacy owe you an apology, but I also think Jack wants to give you one either way. There aren't a lot of guys out there like him and Andrew. Remember what you told me when I was so scared to date Andrew?"

"Suck it up and be happy."

Matty smiled. "Exactly. Look how well that advice turned out for me? Have you ever seen a more beautiful, thoughtful, Italian-speaking man? Jack might not be as great as Andrew, but I think you should give him a chance. Just don't rush yourself. Ultimately, this is your choice. All I'll say is, if you don't want to keep things going with Jack, I expect to see you dating other people. Not just hooks ups. Keep trying."

"Okay." I swallowed and held up my pinky to swear on it. "Either way, I'll keep trying."

Because how many people had come in and out of my life that I never made an effort with? How many people had looked at me pityingly when they heard about my brother and I never forgave their initial reaction to move past that moment? How many of the kids who couldn't deal with my sadness talked to me in class years later but I couldn't forgive them enough to respond?

What would my life be like if I hadn't followed my mother's example so perfectly and shut everyone out? If I hadn't learned the safety of distance from my father?

When I tried to imagine more friends, Matty and Andrew were still the most important people. When I tried to imagine moving away from all the people I never forgave, I thought about Fort Collins.

When I thought about dating, I only saw Jack.

SEVENTEEN

WHEN WE WALKED into our apartment building and started up the stairs to our floor, I felt dead on my feet. I was braced and ready for the pain of seeing all of Jack's boxes stacked around our kitchen and living room area, but so tired I couldn't imagine having a real reaction. Would we still need to help him move in with Nate?

I still didn't know how I wanted to navigate that relationship. Nate had seemed so hopeful, but I hadn't heard from him either. I didn't particularly feel like reaching out. Every memory of him was too drenched in Jack. There was no way he'd want to be in the middle. No way he'd choose me over his best friend.

I froze when I turned the knob on our door. "Um, Matty, did we forget to lock this?"

"No, I gave Lynn a key before we left so she could keep an eye on the place if we needed it."

"I texted her a bit ago and she wanted to meet us here," Andrew said.

Lynn and Priya were inside, smiling widely. The Taylor Swift candle was lit and her music was playing from the speaker over the TV. The apartment seemed strangely empty. Jack's boxes were nowhere in sight and his smell was masked by the artificial scent of the woods.

It shouldn't have made my heart drop.

We ordered pizza and cheesy sticks as we settled in. Matty and Andrew showered first and when it was my turn I stood under the spray for too long thinking about Jack. When I got out, my eyes were only slightly swollen and I reached for my phone, tempted to call. But I hesitated. He still hadn't reached out. He'd come by to give me the tickets, but he'd been willing to drop them off and leave. At this point, I thought I wanted to keep trying, but the fact that he wasn't gave me pause. If I was being honest, I was waiting for him to call first. To have an apology and an explanation like Matty thought he might.

I wanted him to prove he made the effort for me on purpose, not because of Stacy. The fact that he walked away without a text hurt. Maybe he hadn't wanted to hurt me and maybe he wouldn't do it again in the same way, but what if he didn't think it was worth trying again?

It was enough for me to exit his contact information. I texted my mom and dad to let them know we made it home and shut my phone in my room.

"I mean American pizza is alright, but now that we've been to Italy, I'm just having trouble eating it," Matty was saying as obnoxiously as he could, copying those kids who returned from semesters abroad and couldn't talk about anything else.

Andrew nodded in sympathy and murmured in Italian. We spent the next ten minutes convincing Priya and Lynn he had picked the language up super quickly on our trip until Andrew was the first to crack and started laughing.

We settled in for a movie, but I think within ten minutes Lynn and Priya were the only ones awake. It was Lynn's fault though. We were both on the big couch and she started playing with my hair. I think it was a silent show of comfort since she and Priya definitely knew about Jack, having helped move the boxes out, but they hadn't said anything yet. Maybe we'd do some kind of girl's night or trip soon and I could tell them what happened. I fell asleep planning it in my head.

The next morning, I got up late for my opening shift. I biked as quickly as I could and showed up sticky with sweat. Luckily, Priya kept deodorant in her drawer under the register. I ran through the opening side work and Priya showed up for our Thursday lunch shift.

We both still had tables when Maya showed up. I put their orders in quickly and brought Maya's iced tea, nearly running and sliding into the seat next to her.

She turned with an eyebrow lifted. I took a deep breath. "I called the school today. I dropped out."

Her mouth fell open. She had only told me to take a year off. I worried she'd be disappointed or tell me I did the wrong thing, but then she laughed and held out her hand. I shook it, smiling.

"What a brave thing! School will always be there, but your happiness is more important. What are you going to do?"

"I'm thinking about applying for one of the nicer restaurants downtown. In the meantime, I asked for more hours here since I won't have class or homework. If I don't move restaurants, I might ask to train for a manager position to put on my resume. I know I won't make as much, but if I ever want to own a restaurant, I have to learn how to run one."

"That's the goal then? Owning a restaurant?"

My admission made me breathless. "Yes. I think I might save up for culinary school."

I heard one of my tables shaking a cup of ice and rushed off to make a round.

When I came back, Maya was still grinning and Priya was there. "Alright." Maya clapped. "Now that that's settled and you are looking happy with yourself and your goals, what are we going to do about this boy?"

My light mood darkened. I shot Priya a look and she held up her hands. "I just tried to warn her you guys broke up so she didn't mention him."

Maya turned to me, grabbing my hand. " Miss Cheryl. I could tell you liked this boy. Did he mess up so badly you won't trust him again?"

I looked at our clasped hands. Her skin was cool and soft, veins and splotches across the back. "I think it would be hard for him to make the same mistake twice. But he hasn't called."

"What hurts more, what he did or being away from him?"

I took a deep breath. "Worrying that if I did get back together, the next time we break up it'll hurt even worse."

"And the next boy? Or girl, sorry. Does that worry hurt when you think about them and breaking up?"

"I don't know."

"It'll always be a fear. He might not ever mess up again, but he could leave you in other ways. When my Bernie got Alzheimer's, I lost him. But I wouldn't trade a day. We were together for fifty years and you know what all that time taught me?"

"What?"

"We, maybe especially men, always have more to learn. It's the people who listen to us and accept our lessons that we need to keep around. And for us to be deserving of that kind of respect, we have to do the same."

Priya leaned forward. "All I'm saying is, I like Jack."

I fiddled with Maya's discarded brown paper silverware band. "I've been thinking I'll go talk to him. I'm not ready to give him up yet. But what if he's not willing to accept my boundaries when it comes to Stacy? She did a lot for him."

Maya mimicked my tone. Tough love all the way. "But what if you're just coming up with excuses to put off talking to him and overcomplicating things in your head?"

Priya snorted. "There you go, Roly! Time to talk to your man."

And the words didn't fill me with dread. I wished Jack had spoken up first. I wished I could trust him to put me first. I wished I didn't feel like we weren't over when maybe he did.

But it didn't matter. I missed him. I wanted to forgive him. I wanted to try. I had to know if he felt the same.

• • •

That night, I stared at the origami animals on my nightstand and let myself hurt over Jack's absense. I let the feelings flow and reached for a crane. Maybe one day he'd make me new animals. Right now, I had to know what he'd written.

I had to press the bruise.

In little time, I was laughing through my tears. As always, Jack had said the perfect things within these frogs and cats and cranes made of receipt paper.

You have toothpaste on your shirt

Everytime you walk in here it gets brighter

You look cute today

I tried a lavender fog. Not a fan, sorry. Lavender tastes like soap, you weirdo

Amelie wants me to buy her a bike like Trevor after I showed her a picture of you biking

Insert Taylor Swift lyric here about how much I love you

I'm going to try and make a crane, let's see how this goes

You're like a shot of espresso

Did you know I think Moonbean is a weird coffeeshop name? People don't drink coffee at night when the moon is beaning

I love you

You make me really happy

I saw you trip just then… smoooooth

I'm so glad we met. I'm even glad you spilled on Stacy. Your elbow in my stomach was best thing to happen to me

I got up the next day and readied slowly. I put my hair in two braids to wear with my beanie. I did my eyeliner twice when I wasn't happy with it the first time. It was too cold to dress up, but I wore my favorite sweater and cutest snow boots.

Matty was in his room still, the door shut. He'd sent out a text in our chat with Andrew saying he was tired of us. This was just Matty-speak for he was taking a day to himself. He'd probably go to a bookstore somewhere once he was done sleeping in. Then he'd go to lunch by himself. Maybe see a movie. Then he'd come home and curl up in his room to read the new book he bought. I had work so he'd have the night without me in the apartment. Maybe I'd volunteer to close so he'd be asleep by the time I got back.

I loved knowing someone so well I knew what he was doing even when he needed time away from me to recharge. I loved knowing Andrew would probably text me soon to see if I wanted to get lunch or hang out because they've been so careful with me since the breakup.

I hoped by then things would be looking up.

I unlocked Trevor and started my ride to Moonbean, laughing to myself when I thought of Jack's note about the coffeeshop's name. I peddled slowly and carefully. It was a warm day for January and there were patches of slush I had to navigate. I didn't mind biking in the winter. As long as I wore layers it usually wasn't bad. But there were days I was tempted to ask Matty for his car. There were days I wished I didn't clam up with fear at the thought.

I had an appointment next week with my new therapist. Maybe that would be the first thing we worked on.

I was biking slowly to plan what I wanted to say but also, I could admit to myself, because I was afraid. I'd left him so easily and what if he didn't want me back? What if there was too much hurt? What if my words and making him get me off while he was in pain were too cruel?

What if he said no and it wasn't my choice anymore? I liked being in control. Now that I thought I was capable of forgiving him, it would all be on him. My hands were sweating in my mittens.

I forcefully stopped this train of thought. This was just another excuse. Just fear trying to stop me from putting myself out there. Just more worry that I couldn't trust people, which meant I was still struggling to forgive Jack. I needed to let him know what I was thinking so he could make the choice on his own. At that point, it wasn't about me.

I just had to do this. I couldn't keep wondering what would happen.

The conversation wasn't even going to happen today. I was just going to see him in person to ask to talk when he was free. It was too big a moment to happen over text, but it wasn't the big talk yet. Little steps. I could do this.

I pulled to a stop and locked my bike. There were enough clouds in the sky that I could see inside the big windows of the brightly lit coffee shop. I froze, taking off my sunglasses so I could see more clearly.

Emily was back from Italy. She was smiling and happy. The semester had treated her well. I forgot how nice her hair was. It curled beautifully even in the ponytail she had to wear behind the counter. It bounced with every head tilt and movement. Her hair was what first drew me to her. Then her eyes. A unique light brown that was almost gold. A freckle in one iris. I had gotten lost in her eyes, staring at that freckle that was only hers, so many times. I was arrested in her gaze enough that months ago, I considered asking her on a real date. I'd been willing to put myself out there and attempt commitment.

Then there was her kindness. No one smiled as freely as Emily. It was so warm and perfect. I'd seen kids come into the coffee shop and fall under her spell in a second. She was someone who just loved people. Loved being around them. Loved making them feel special.

She'd convinced me she thought I was.

Now, I watched her convince Jack.

My Jack. Who used to watch me warily when we started out. He was giving Emily that genuine, unguarded smile I worked so hard for. He was laughing. When she reached out and touched his arm, he looked down at her hand and his eyes warmed. Her fingers rested right above the bracelet I'd given him.

He was wearing it, but he was under her spell.

I wasn't right for either of them.

Happy, whole, and loving people weren't made for me. I just brought them down. I was sad and too independent and untrusting. Emily would tell Jack about Italy in a way that made him wish he was there. She wouldn't bring up her mom's sadness and the way her mom never mentioned her when talking about the great loves of her life. Emily would offer to drive Jack places. She wouldn't put stress on him about being a college dropout because Emily loved school. Her face lit up when she talked about it. She wanted to be a teacher too.

Emily was enjoying her life. She didn't have things to work on. At least, not on the level I did. It wasn't fair of me to try and drag Jack back in when I hadn't even started the real work. That was next week and it wasn't his job to hold my hand through the process.

Jack smiled and turned away from Emily to go back to making the drink in his hand. I watched him for a moment longer, hating that I couldn't read his face. Then I turned away and got back on my bike, swallowing past my tight throat when I looked at the basket on Trevor's handlebars.

I would miss Jack. But it wouldn't take him long to stop missing me.

"So, you're not going to talk to him?" Priya asked at work that night. I knew I was moving slowly. My smiles were too forced and my tips were suffering for it. Priya had to pick up the pace to cover for me most of the shift.

I shrugged. We were rolling silverware. Everything else finished. The bar side of the restaurant was loud and mostly packed. I almost wished I bartended watching them work and wishing for the distraction. But I couldn't keep up with my tables on this side tonight. I would have done terribly over there.

"Roly, talk to me. You looked so excited yesterday." Priya rarely spoke so gently.

"It's just... when I went to see him at work, I saw him talking to another girl that works there. She's so sweet and was making him laugh and," I pulled in a shuddering breath and dropped my eyes, focusing entirely on the forks, knives, and napkins in front of me, "and they looked so good together. He never really seemed at ease in my presence. I wasn't... I don't think I was good for him. I have so many issues."

Priya rolled three sets in quick succession before she responded. "Didn't we all agree that was his choice?"

"Priya, he hasn't even tried to text me. Maybe that's him making his choice. What if he's realized he's better off without me?"

"Roly, what if you spend the rest of your life wondering if he's better off with you?"

"I don't think I'd wonder that. I know he'd be fine without me. I know he'd be better."

Priya set down her last roll so loudly I jumped. "Stop. Okay? Tell me five reasons you, Roly, make a good girlfriend."

"What?"

"Stop being so hard on yourself. I want to hear the positive before you try to convince me of the negative." Priya stopped rolling entirely and sat back in her seat with her arms crossed and her dark eyes blazing.

I fumbled, but she waited. The clangs from the kitchen, the radio playing, the shouting and base in the bar were familiar and comforting sounds. Priya wasn't going to move until I answered her. "I think—"

"No, only facts. What makes you a good girlfriend for Jack?"

"Um, I was really good at fucking him."

"Good, that's one." She held up a finger.

I relaxed a bit when she accepted that. I wasn't sure if she would. "I was... Priya, isn't the fact that I can't think of anything just more proof of how bad a girlfriend I was?"

"You need to give me four more reasons, Roly."

I thought back, trying to think of the times I made Jack's guard fall. "I made him laugh."

I earned another finger. "Three more."

"I trusted him in ways I don't trust a lot of people." That trust had meant a lot to Jack. It had made him love me more.

"Two more."

I couldn't think of anything. Jack was always there for me when I needed him, yet I'd barely shown him appreciation. I'd barely thanked him for anything. I didn't return the favor. The more I tried to think of why I was a good girlfriend, the more I realized just how bad at it I was. "Priya, I don't think this is working."

"Why should Jack be with you?" She was ruthless. When she saw my tears, she reached for my hand, but she didn't take back the question or lower her other hand with its two fingers up.

"Because I love him?" That was all I had going really. I knew I loved him like I'd never loved anyone else. Maybe I hadn't said it enough or complimented him often or thanked him for all those things he did, but he was wrapped in every fiber of my being. I missed him so much.

"One more, Roly. What did you do that made you different? That made him love you?"

I thought about his nervousness regarding sex. How confident he'd grown in the time we were together. How he'd gotten to his knees for me when I needed it and kissed and licked me exactly right. I thought about his mentions of his ex, how by the end whenever she was mentioned he didn't even blink with pain anymore. He'd known his value. Maybe I'd helped him figure it out. Maybe that meant he knew he was better than me now, but at least I helped him get there. "I convinced him he wasn't boring. That he was a good boyfriend and I wanted him just how he was."

Priya nodded and squeezed my hand. "What are five reasons Jack is right for you?"

I blinked. That was so easy. "He's so patient. He was always excited to see me. He let me be sad around him and was willing to do anything to make me feel better. Really anything. He's so beautiful I could stare at him for hours, especially when he's... never mind. He made me feel so powerful. He loved me. He trusted me. He—"

"I said five reasons." Priya smiled as she cut me off. "Roly, those reasons aren't nothing. For Jack, they might be everything. I guarantee he'd have as many reasons to date you as you have to date him. Even if he just has the five reasons you gave me, those might be exactly why he doesn't want anyone else. Those might even be enough to make him feel like he doesn't deserve you. Talk to him. Please. You guys have something special and it's hurting everyone around you to see it go to waste."

She started rolling again and I followed her lead, letting her words wash over me. I tried to imagine Jack feeling like he didn't deserve me and it was too easy. Too in line with his occasional lack of confidence. He'd accepted money from Stacy to date me. He didn't know I thought that might be forgivable. What if he was too afraid to try and apologize? What if he didn't think he was worth it? And that was the question I knew I needed to be answered. I couldn't live with thinking Jack didn't believe he was good enough for me.

"I'll try again tomorrow. And if I back out again, I'll probably try on Sunday. I'll keep trying."

"Good." Priya smiled.

I went into Moonbean the next morning. I forced a smile when I saw Emily behind the counter.

"Roly! It's been so long! How are you?"

She was happy to see me, but not that nearly breathless excitement I used to get from Jack. I wanted a shouted *"Hey!"*

"I'm good. How was your semester abroad?"

Emily talked about her time in Italy as she put me in for a Lavender Fog and swiped my card. She didn't leave me time to make any comments and I realized this was how our conversations had usually gone. Her talking at me while I smiled and thought it was because she was interested. Maybe she never had been. Maybe I had liked her because there wasn't space for me to say anything wrong in our conversations. Maybe I wanted to take that risk now.

"Thanks, Emily. Um, is Jack working in the back?" I finally got the question in as she handed me my drink.

She looked surprised. "No. Jack is off today. Are you guys friends?"

"Kind of. It was nice seeing you!" I turned and left. I only took a couple sips of my drink. She didn't put enough lavender in it. Had Jack ruined me for other baristas as well as partners?

I put the Hooked Up podcast on in my headphones. I went to an old episode about breakups and how heartbreak had been what it took for Riley to move to New York and rekindle her friendship with Alma. How it had led to great things in her life. She cried as she talked about her ex, but it was a hopeful episode. I needed it now. Even if Jack didn't take me back, I could find happiness and success.

Stopped at the light near my apartment building, I debated turning and going to Jack and Nate's apartment to see if he was there. I was impatient now that my mind was made up. I needed to know if it was time for me to move on and find my happiness like Riley had. But in the end, I didn't feel emotionally ready to face them both at once. I could text or call, but that still didn't feel right. I wanted Jack to see my face, see how badly I wanted it when I asked him for another chance. Maybe that wasn't fair to him either though.

Another day wouldn't hurt us. I could wait until tomorrow morning to try Moonbean again.

When I got home, Matty was in the shower. His phone was ringing on the kitchen counter. I ignored it as I took off my coat and bent to undo my boot laces. Right after it stopped, it rang again. By the time I was out of my wet shoes and crossing to my room, it had finished. His phone pinged with a text. Then another. I couldn't stifle my curiosity and went to flip it over.

Four missed calls from my dad.

And the texts. My world zeroed in on the screen.

Hey Matty! Call me when you get a chance.

Roly is going to need a ride to the hospital there. Nate and Jack were in an accident, but I'll need you to tell her about it face to face so she's not too upset.

I set Matty's phone down carefully, like it was a ticking bomb. I stepped back from the counter. There was a ringing in my ears. I could see Jack smiling. I could see Brady's empty bedroom. I could see my mother crying and crying and crying. My dad begging her to get into the car, we had to go, but she was so scared.

I hated driving. I hated cars and other people on the road and death and the crunch of metal.

I ran for my shoes, blinking past my tears as I laced them on again with shaking fingers. I went so fast, that I gave myself a rope burn. I zipped my coat so quickly I distantly felt the hairs I caught and ripped out. I ran for my bike, jumping down the last stairs of our apartment building.

I wanted to scream at the number of attempts it took my trembling fingers to unlock Trevor. I'd forgotten my mittens on the counter next to Matty's phone, but I couldn't care as I finally freed my bike and took off.

I pedaled harder than I ever had before. I wove through traffic. Horns honked and people shouted out their windows. All I could think about was Jack. Staring at the road when he wanted to look at me. Listening so intently to every word I said. His gentle voice in the morning. The way he moved. The way he laughed. The light in his eyes. This world was so cruel. I knew better than anyone it didn't take much to snuff out the light that was someone like Jack.

It started to snow and was blowing wind, the weather changing in typical Colorado fashion. I ignored it. I pedaled harder. Nate was on the other end of this bike ride too. Quiet and shy, he'd been trying all along to follow my lead. To do what it took for me to let him in. What if I never got the chance? What if I blew it all for nothing?

By the time I reached the hospital, I was sweating inside my coat but my fingers were red and numb. It had taken me too long to get there. I dumped my bike on the lawn by the emergency entrance and ran inside, catching myself on the sliding glass door as my tired legs nearly gave out.

The man working at the desk jumped up and ran around, clearly thinking I was injured. I put up a hand to hold off his concern. "I need to see Jack Matthews!"

I barely heard his response. I accepted the tissue someone handed me but didn't dry my frozen cheeks. It was taking them too long. The ringing in my ears was getting so loud that only sheer force of will kept me from passing out. Kept me forcing in gulps of air. My whole body was trembling from adrenaline and exhaustion and fear. The nurses looked more concerned about me than the patient I was demanding to see.

What if he was already dead? Jack couldn't be dead. Nate couldn't be dead.

Please don't be dead.

They started to walk me toward a room and tried to stop me in a quiet hallway. A voice told me to breathe. I shook my head. This was taking too long. They didn't want to tell me the truth. That they were dead. "Please. Where's Jack?" I was begging.

They gave up when I only kept repeating the question. We went through a doorway. Around a corner.

And I heard his laugh.

EIGHTEEN

THE NURSE almost didn't catch me as I sagged with relief. I straightened as I sucked in a breath and ran. There was Jack, just standing there. Talking as he waited for the vending machine. Holding a dollar. Standing. Smiling.

Alive.

I made some kind of noise that drew his attention. He had a slim bandage on his eyebrow. A bruise on his cheek. I couldn't see any other hurts but as he stepped toward me, eyebrows knotted with concern, he moved just fine.

I threw myself at him and held him as tight as I could. When my legs finally gave out and I lost myself to the tears, it was only Jack supporting me. He held me back as tight as I was holding him, murmuring comforting noises and asking the nurse questions when he realized I was beyond responding for the moment.

When I finally caught my breath, I leaned back only enough to touch his face. "How bad are you hurt?"

"Jesus, Roly, your fingers are icicles."

"Jack, how bad?"

"I'm fine. I'm okay. I told your dad to call Matty first. What happened? Where is he?"

"I saw a text on his phone. I thought…"

"Shh. It's alright. I'm fine, okay? I promise. And Nate is too. They're just checking his wrist now. It might be broken."

I nodded. "Okay. Okay." I stared at him, trembling still.

Jack waited. As patient and caring as ever.

"You're fine? You're really okay?"

"I'm not hurt, Roly." He had the audacity to smirk. "Maybe it's time we stop reading texts on other people's phones?"

And I broke down again, burying my face in his neck. "Jesus, your nose is frozen too." He tilted his head, trapping my face to warm it.

Jack led us to some chairs in a hallway, never once letting go. He sat us down and assured the nurse he could take it from here. He took my hands in his and tried to warm them. I gripped him back. Slowly, my breathing evened out. My head was still light and spinning with relief. He was okay. He was holding me.

"I'm so sorry, Jack. I was going to tell you. I tried on Friday but you were talking to Emily and I wasn't brave enough. Then I tried today and… I could have missed my chance. I'm so sorry. I'm so happy you aren't dead."

Jack snorted but his smile was sad. It made my heart drop. I would have pulled away if I didn't need his constant touch assuring me he was alive and well. He must know that. It's why he wasn't letting me go. It was enough for my eyes to fill again.

Jack let go of my hands to cover my wind burnt cheeks. His thumbs brushed at the tears that fell. "Roly, don't apologize. You didn't do anything wrong. I messed up so bad. I should never have taken that money from Stacy. I wish I was the guy you saw me as. I wish I hadn't been so stupid and that I had been more understanding. I judged you and I'm sorry. I'm sorry."

"You didn't call. I thought you might not care."

Jack looked pained. "I didn't think you'd want to hear from me." He swallowed hard. "I couldn't imagine you giving me another chance. I thought you were better off finding someone more like you. Interesting and brave and—"

"Jack, stop. No one is as good as you." I took a deep breath.

He was okay. I let that sink in and pushed on. "Only… if Stacy hadn't given you the money, would any of this have happened?"

"Roly." Jack let his forehead rest on mine. I must have lost my beanie at some point. "You should have heard Nate teasing me at the rehearsal dinner and wedding. I couldn't stop staring at you." Every cell in my body warmed. Jack pressed on, only sincerity in his hazel eyes. "I think I hated Matty up until the moment your dad said he had a boyfriend. I thought he was your date, and I was so jealous of the way he was making you laugh. After the wedding, I wanted to show Stacy I was on her side, so I acted reluctant to talk to you. You should have felt how my heart skipped when I learned you lived here. I'm surprised they could read my application at Moonbean I filled it out so quickly. The texts were just an act. I was broke and I shouldn't have taken her money, but it was the push I needed to get the guts to talk to you. I wanted to but I was nervous. I didn't think you'd be interested when I was such a dick about the spill. I know I don't deserve you, but—"

"Shut up." I took in a full breath, lighter than I'd felt since Christmas. Because I believed him. I trusted him, even after everything. "Of course you deserve me, Jack. Just let me buy my own freaking coffees from now on. I only want you. I want you so bad that I forgive you and will trust you if you promise not to do anything like that again."

"I promise. I swear I'll never hurt you and next time if I do, I'll make it right." He pulled in a deep breath, thumbs still brushing my cheeks. He was so alive. I loved him. "You can really forgive me?" he asked.

I hoped it didn't hurt him when I grabbed his neck and crushed his lips to mine. He expertly gentled my frantic kiss until I drew in a shuddering breath against his lips. Calm finally came then. Jack moved to kiss away my tears. "I'm right here, Roly. I'm not going anywhere."

"We're getting you a bike."

"I don't know if now is a good time to tell you I really don't think that's safer."

"Cars are cursed. Bikes are good for the planet."

Jack laughed softly against my lips and kissed me again. He kissed me until I was melting, that familiar swirl of heat rising in my core. Only Jack could undo me so quickly and thoroughly.

"Ew," Nate said, walking toward us with his arm in a sling. Jack kept an arm around me as he pulled back, smiling and unguarded. "I guess I was just taking one for the team, huh? Wrecking my car so you'd get back together."

I winced a bit at the expression, the same one Jack used in his texts to Stacy. That hurt might take a while to dull still. Jack tightened his grip on me. "Anything is worth more time with Roly," he said.

I had to smile.

***

Stacy was struggling. Jack told me she'd been an emotional mess when Nate moved out. Now she was running around their small apartment cleaning and constantly checking Nate was okay. It was nice to see, even if I wasn't entirely sure how I felt about her. My dad stood off to the side, faintly amused. We exchanged a look. Between his mother and mine, neither of us knew how to deal with Stacy's flurry of worried maternal activity.

Jack took it all in a stride, jumping up more often than not to help her even when she shoed him away or turned her nurturing attention to the bruises on his face. Eventually, she sat him down on the couch next to Nate and looked over them both staring up at her. "Good. Stay still and rest."

As I knew it would, Stacy's attention turned on me. "Can we talk, Roly?"

Right now, the open spot next to Jack on the couch was much more appealing, but I nodded and we went into Nate's room.

Stacy wrung her hands and I realized not all her frantic worry had been about Nate's injuries. "I owe you an apology."

I nodded because she did.

"I'm sorry," she said simply. "You're smart and I'm sure you know why I did what I did with Jack. I know it wasn't the right way to go about things and all my reasonings when I started have since crumbled. I don't know really what else to say except I hope you understand my intentions and my hopes that we can start over. I truly am sorry."

I could see it in her eyes that she was. "Stacy, I have two parents. They might not be perfect, but I don't want another one. Your marriage to my dad didn't mean anything regarding a relationship with me. If we start over, it'll be slow, and I hope you go into it with the understanding that the most you should expect is friendship."

Stacy nodded, blinking away tears. "I would love to be your friend, Roly."

"Okay." I turned for the door, more than ready to take my place next to Jack.

"You should know," Stacy's voice stopped me before I could turn the knob, "since Halloween I've been finding extra fives and tens in my purse. I couldn't figure out where they were coming from until I saw Nate's Venmo history. Jack has been sending the money to him and Nate's been putting the cash in my bag. Jack probably didn't want to hurt my feelings by giving it back, but he did. He paid it all back, even before you knew about it."

"Thanks for telling me." I smiled and went back into the living room, letting my dad ruffle my hair as I passed him and he went to go check on his wife. Stacy let him in, stepping into his arms as he reached back to close the door. He winked over his shoulder at me.

"Roly will just have to be the deciding vote, then," Nate was saying. He and Jack turned to me in unison on the couch. "A comedy or a horror film?"

"I think I had had enough adrenaline for one day." I sat down next to Jack and held him close.

His eyes softened and his nose dipped to brush mine. "Romcom it is."

They started the movie and I whispered in Jack's ear. "I hear you paid Stacy back."

He blushed and laughed a bit. "Well, actually you did. I mostly used those tens you gave me for tip."

I laughed and shifted us so I was in Jack's lap. I couldn't say why it being my money made everything better, but it did. When Stacy and my dad came out of Nate's room, Nate moved to his recliner and Jack lifted me and settled me back on his lap on his own. Of course, they had brought the ugly chairs up here from Stacy's basement. Somehow, even though I was in an apartment I'd never seen before with my dad's arm around Stacy and Nate staring at us all looking relieved, I felt right at home.

"NO."

"Yes."

"He didn't."

"My *white* couches, Riley!"

"Why would a guy want white couches? What single guy has white furniture in his apartment?"

"He insisted he'd been the one to pay for them, so they belonged to him!"

"Did he?"

"Well, maybe, but I picked them out!"

I laughed along with Riley and Alma and I finished locking the door of Blue Cravings behind me. Despite the restaurant's name, nothing on the menu was blue. But the food was delicious and the cheapest thing on the menu was the artichoke dip appetizer which cost fifteen dollars. I was calm and relaxed, my feet hurting but I smelled like garlic and red wine, not beer. I stepped onto the busy sidewalk and tipped my head back to take in the lights crisscrossed above, lighting up the night.

It had taken me two weeks of training to learn the proper etiquette for an establishment like Blue Cravings. A whole month until I was able to tell Matty and Jack I could drive myself to work. Three months later, my mom had come in and told me it was her new favorite restaurant and it almost compared to Italy. Now, I was six months in, driving myself to work on the cold days and riding Trevor whenever I could because I missed him. I was in the running to be head server once Hillary left. I knew exactly who I wanted to recommend to fill my shoes and Priya was asking me for updates daily. We missed working together, even though we hung out nearly every weekend with Lynn, Nate, Andrew, Matty, and Jack. Our squad, she insisted on calling us.

After Maya's funeral, we'd started hanging out more. The older woman had left us her collection of CSU t-shirts. We wore them all the time and laughed about the things she used to tell us and how much of a gossip she'd been. My last conversation with her was when I got this job. She'd been so happy for me. She'd asked if they served good tea here for when she visited.

Her loss had been a blow, but her family had come up to me and Priya at the funeral and told us how much she enjoyed spending time with us. They all called me Cheryl and cried when they hugged me. I cried too and held them back. Grief was a familiar feeling for all of us and we shared it well despite having just met.

Riley and Alma were still chatting in the headphone I was wearing, debating how big of a red flag it would be to go to a guy's house and find all white furniture. "My first thought would definitely be that he had a girlfriend," Alma laughed.

A voice spoke out to my right, familiar enough that I didn't even startle. I pulled out my headphone, already smiling.

"Hey, gorgeous, wanna ride?" Jack stepped into the streetlight and wiggled his eyebrows.

I looked him up and down, pretending not to be impressed. "Sorry, I'm taken."

"Damn, he must be super hot to land a girl like you."

"Oh, he is."

Jack grinned and stepped closer. "Is he funny?"

"He has his moments."

"Does he keep you guessing?"

"He knows better."

Jack laughed at that. He reached for my waist and I danced out of reach. "I told you! Taken!"

"I don't see a ring on that finger," Jack said. We both froze, breaking character and laughing nervously.

Jack shook his head and reached for me again.

"At least take a girl to dinner first," I muttered, letting him wrap his arms around me.

"One second, I just need to call Stacy real quick and borrow some mo—"

I cut Jack off with a kiss and broke it quickly, smiling. "Are you thinking about parents right now, Jack?"

"Well, we are in public. I have to remain semi-decent."

"Let's not be."

"I can arrange that. If your boyfriend won't mind."

"He'll never know," I murmured. I fell back into character, this time it was more sexy than silly. Jack's eyes darkened.

He leaned in, lips in my hair. "Fuck me like it's our first time, Cheryl."

I drew in a shaky breath, heat instantly pooling in my core. "I rode my bike. Go to my place and be ready in my chair."

Jack kissed me hard, but I didn't have to tell him twice. I laughed at how quickly he ran to his car.

"Drive careful!"

"I always do. See you soon."

He ducked in but I shouted as he was closing his door. "I love you!"

He opened it just as quickly, popping his head out. "I love you!"

People were smiling and laughing at our exchange. I grinned and ran to Trevor, excited enough as I jumped on and started peddling that I was almost sure I could beat Jack to Matty and my apartment. I hurried inside and Andrew and Matty smirked knowingly from the couch. I tried to make myself seem casual as I took off my coat. Our latest Taylor Swift candle was supposed to smell like champagne. Its slightly fruity scent filled the room and made me feel perfectly at home. We'd signed the lease for another year while Andrew got his master's and Matty worked his internship. None of us were in a hurry to leave Fort Collins and I fell more in love with the city every day.

I opened the door to my room. Jack was there, flipping through the romance novel I'd left on the chair he now occupied. He was entirely naked, entirely hard, and grinning up at me. His voice was low and excited when he spoke, carefully dropping my book off to the side. "Hurry, we don't want your boyfriend to catch us."

I locked the door and crossed the room, unbuttoning my white shirt, loving how Jack's eyes followed the movement. Enraptured. "Alright, but you have to stay quiet in case he comes home. Hands on the armrest, Jack."

He whimpered and did as I said. I melted.

I loved him so much. This thing between us never got old and never dimmed. We fought sometimes, but we could never stay mad long. He'd held me as long as I needed when Maya died, never once shying from my pain. My mom liked him. My dad liked him. Stacy and Jack's dads and Amelie liked me. Our life here was steady and simple.

It was easy loving Jack, but never, ever boring.

ABOUT THE AUTHOR

KC Fletcher graduated from the University of Wyoming where she studied English and Creative Writing. She is working on a self-publishing career under two pennames, KC Fletcher for her adult books and Kelly Cole for her younger audience. KC is most active on Instagram (@kellycolebooks) and enjoys sharing her latest and favorite reads. She lives in Wyoming with her two crested geckos and her dog, Maya. She spends most of her time writing and playing seemingly endless hours of fetch (not with the geckos).

Visit her website at www.kellycolebooks.com for more information.